THE WOMAN WHO KNEW
WHAT SHE WANTED

T0272918

The Woman Who Knew What She Wanted

THAMES RIVER PRESS
An imprint of Wimbledon Publishing Company Limited (WPC)
Another imprint of WPC is Anthem Press (www.anthempress.com)
First published in the United Kingdom in 2013 by
THAMES RIVER PRESS
75–76 Blackfriars Road
London SE1 8HA

www.thamesriverpress.com

The moral rights of the author have been asserted in accordance
with the Copyright, Designs and Patents Act 1988.

All the characters and events described in this novel are imaginary
and any similarity with real people or events is purely coincidental.

A CIP record for this book is available from the British Library.

ISBN 978-0-85728-345-0

Cover design by Sylwia Palka

This title is also available as an eBook

THE WOMAN WHO KNEW WHAT SHE WANTED

William Coles

THAMES RIVER PRESS

Dave Cameron's Schooldays

"A superbly crafted memoir."
—*Daily Express*

"Try *Dave Cameron's Schooldays* for jolly fictional japes. It helps to explain the real Dave's determination to whip us into shape."
—*Edwina Currie, The Times*

"A piece of glorious effrontery… takes an honourable place amid the ranks of lampoons."
—*The Herald*

"A fast moving and playful spoof. The details are so slick and telling that they could almost have you fooled."
—*Henry Sutton, Mirror*

"A cracking read… Perfectly paced and brilliantly written, Coles draws you in, leaving a childish smile on your face."
—*News of the World*

Mr Two-Bomb

"Compellingly vivid, the most sustained description of apocalypse since Robert Harris's Pompeii."
—*Financial Times*

For my great mate Mark Pilbrow,
a pig-farmer's son – much like myself

ACKNOWLEDGEMENTS

Like Kim, I was also a waiter at the splendid Knoll House Hotel in 1988. I went back there recently and it was like stepping into this most fabulous time warp. Children are still not allowed into the dining room at suppertime, and *incredibly* still not a single television to be found in the bedrooms! So as it is, even in this ultra high-tech twenty-first century, families are still being forced to read books and play games, and even, on occasion, actually talk with each other in the evening. Long may it continue! The sights at the Knoll House are also just as breathtaking as they were twenty-five years ago: the Agglestone is still there, the pirate ship and the beach huts and the Dancing Ledges, they're all still there – and I don't doubt that they'll still be there even a hundred years from now.

My thanks to the artist Jono Freemantle who provided me with all those lovely details about what it is to be a painter; and to Rudi Schultz, that dry old sea-stick, who conjured with pictures of beds and beach-huts. And my thanks, as ever, to Margot, my wife, who sometimes wonders, I know, just what is fact and what is fiction in these love stories I write. Perhaps one day I will go through these novels and underline the events that have actually happened to me in black. Those that are based on hearsay will be underlined in green; and those that have sprung from nothing more than my most lurid imaginings will be underscored in brilliant scarlet.

Perhaps.

CHAPTER 1

Is it my nature only to appreciate what I have long after it has left me? When I'm in a long-term relationship, locked tight with a lover, it is so easy to take things for granted: to dwell on the irritations; to lose sight of everything that was once good and kind and decent; to forget the things that I first fell in love with. Instead, my lover's looks, her laughter, her enthusiasms, they all become submerged by a dead weight of the mundane and the routine.

Always, always, I want more. For a few weeks, a month, I can be content. But then, even if I were dating Helen of Troy, I would start to wonder. What if…

My eyes wander and the daydreams begin. Would *her* lips taste any the sweeter? Could I? Should I? Would she?

But there was one woman…

Yes, there was one woman, who kept things so fresh and so chilli-hot that there was never even a moment for complacency.

Of course, it ended – as all stand-out love affairs must. But when I look back on my time with Cally, I am nothing but grateful. Even the little sting in the tail, for that also I eventually – eventually – came to thank her.

I know little about women. But what little I do know is largely down to Cally. She taught me what is classy, what is cool; what is seemly, what is gross. Above all, she taught me that in a relationship the correct route across a square is by three sides. That is, in all dealings – whether with a lover, a wife or a mistress – it is very rarely wise to boldly state your needs. Rather, a man must learn to be canny. When he has a goal in mind, an aim, a yearning, he must travel towards it obliquely.

I can still remember Cally as she told me this one universal truth. It took me a couple of minutes to digest. I pondered it, repeating what she said. She just chuckled, poking at the fire with a piece of driftwood. 'You haven't got a clue, have you, Kim?' she laughed. 'One day when I'm nothing more than a memory, you'll realise this is wisdom speaking.'

'Wisdom?' I jeered. 'And what wisdom, pray, is she speaking out of?'

'You are a disgusting little puppy,' she said, 'and like all disgusting little puppies, you are going to have to be taught the error of your ways.'

I remember her hands tugging at my belt.

'Again?' I'd asked.

'If you know what's good for you – which, come to think of it, you probably don't.'

Even now twenty years later, the memory of it brings a smile to my face. With some of my other lost loves, I can barely even remember what happened from one year to the next. But with Cally, I can recall actual conversations; I can remember the exact way that she would raise a wry eyebrow, thereby issuing a bedroom command that could not be ignored. Above all else, I can remember her laugh. The deep, throaty, joyous laugh of a woman who was proud to vent her more noisome emotions and who didn't give a damn who heard her.

But if there is one lesson from Cally etched into my memory, it is that each and every day was to be grabbed by the throat.

Of course, I'd heard that much before – who hasn't? *Carpe diem*! Seize the day! Go for it! Get it while it's hot! Or, as my grandfather, a farmer, liked to say, 'This ain't no rehearsal.'

And that's what Cally did – and that's what she gave me. The knowledge that this life: it's the only shot we've got.

As we get older, and as we pass the grim, grey mantle of destiny onto the next generation, there is a tendency to accept the ordinary. There comes a belief that, actually, 'middle of the road' isn't too bad.

But not Cally – she fought, raged, against the very thought. Anything for her, anything at all, to avoid getting stuck in that warm, wide rut that can come with middle age.

And I guess, I suppose, that was one of the reasons why she took up with me as a lover.

I was young, just twenty-three years old, and eager to taste life's smorgasbord. And Cally… she was eager too – only to a factor of ten.

What I still find truly remarkable is that many women her age seem to content themselves with life in a rut. But for Cally, every day it was where's the fun? Where's the action? What's the maximum amount of excitement that can be extracted from my next twenty-four hours on this earth?

Not bad. Not bad at all for a woman who, at forty-four years old, was more than two decades my senior.

But then Cally was, of course, a woman who knew what she wanted.

And most of the time, she got it.

CHAPTER 2

There were consequences to the pair of us trying to extract the maximum amount from each and every moment – some hair-raising, some illegal and some downright dangerous. During my time with Cally, I lost at least three of my nine lives. Each time was different, varying in degrees of spontaneity, foolhardiness and drunkenness.

But to give you just a taster of what could happen when I was with Cally, I will tell you about our little party on Midsummer's Eve. It was indicative of the sheer weirdness that could occur when Cally was in charge.

It had been a late night at the hotel, diners dawdling over their coffees and their brandies as they contemplated the dusky skyline. Meanwhile, I and the other waiters and waitresses had to smile pleasantly and amenably, as if there was nothing we enjoyed more of an evening than hanging around in the dining room of the Knoll House Hotel.

I have not been there in a long time, but back then the Knoll House was an old-style family hotel on that glorious strip of England that is Studland, Dorset. This piece of coastline is famous for many reasons, not least its nudist beach, as well as Old Harry, a spectacular chalk arch that's been carved from the coast. But my romantic heart will for ever associate Studland with the smugglers and the corsairs who would run brandy casks, skeins of silk and fine Virginian tobacco to the wild caves that surround the Dancing Ledges.

The hotel was a throwback. There were no televisions in any of the guests' rooms. Instead guests had to indulge in such old-fashioned pursuits as card games and drinking and – think of it! – conversation.

Children were welcome – it was, after all, a traditional family hotel – but they also had to know their place. The children had a separate dining room, awash with minders who were all absolute sticklers for good manners and hearty eating.

The main dining room, spacious, unchanged since Enid Blyton used to take her table in the corner, was the adults' safe haven. Children were banned at night-time and had to amuse themselves in their bedrooms while an army of nannies paraded the hotel corridors. Guests would dress up for dinner and would be personally welcomed into the dining room by the hotel's avuncular proprietor.

Although I can remember everything about Cally, my memory of the hotel itself is a little rusty. But as I recall, there were about twenty or thirty serving staff, young men and women marking time in Dorset as they decided what next to do with their lives. We weren't paid much, but we did get free lodging and we had the boon of each other's company.

The dining room had well over seventy tables, with each waiter and waitress catering for about twenty guests. But come the end of the dinner, it did not matter if your every table had been cleared and set for breakfast – we waiting staff could only leave after the very last diner had quit the dining room. What did it matter that we had parties planned; pints to be supped in the Bankes Arms; and red-hot lovers waiting for us on the Dancing Ledges with a great bonfire fanned by the sea breeze?

My guests had all long gone, so I was fooling around by the puddings at the central station. These puddings were the stuff of legend. The guests could come up and have as much as they wanted; some would skimp on their main courses to come back for seconds and even thirds of these extraordinary puddings, each accompanied by not just ice cream but whipped cream and thick pouring cream.

Oliver, a tall, angular German who spoke impeccable English, had also already laid up his tables for breakfast and was gazing at the puddings. They filled an entire table.

'I think,' said Oliver, 'that I will start with the crème brûlée with some fruit salad and some whipped cream. Then, because I will still be hungry, I will try the trifle, but this time with the pouring cream. And after I have finished that, and because I think I will still be hungry, I will have a large slice of the chocolate gateau.' Like a dog at the butcher's window, he stared soulfully at the puddings. He had a pronounced Adam's apple. It jumped up and down as he swallowed.

'A good selection, my friend,' I said. 'But I'm going to start with the trifle. With whipped cream and pouring cream. Then the crème caramel. And to finish, not one, not two, but three brandy snaps.'

The brandy snaps were my favourite. I've no idea, even now, how brandy snaps are made, but they were like brittle brown cylinders of spun sugar and filled with the thickest whipped cream. Another waiter, Roland, had once filched a brandy snap from right underneath the chef's nose, and we had shared it with Janeen on the staff's star-lit patio: at first brittle but then melting on your tongue, delicious with the cool cream.

Roland sidled over. He had one table of golfers still nursing their double Armagnacs. 'I'll have the cheese,' he said. 'The Roquefort. Best thing ever to come out of France. And if I take their dregs, there might even be a glass of red for me.'

'No, no,' said Oliver. 'The cheese must come after the pudding—'

'The French say before.'

'The French!'

And so, as we waited for those four inconsiderate golfers to quit the dining room and go to the bar, we bickered and salivated, constructing mythical feasts that could never be eaten. For although the guests could have their fill, the staff were never allowed a morsel. They were the perfect Tantalus. Every night we would see them, glistening, evermore enticing; and every night, come the end of the evening, they'd be wheeled out of sight to be stored in the hotel's cavernous fridges.

Janeen sidled up. She'd been outside having a cigarette. She was blonde and quite sexy, and once upon a time I'd fancied her, but all those feelings of ardour had evaporated like the morning mist. This had yet to become mutual. There was still a husk of lust in her heart for me.

'Coming to the pub, Kim?' she asked.

'Not tonight, thanks.'

'You and your mystery lover!' she said. 'You reek of it!' She clutched at one of my wrists and made a play of sniffing at my tunic. 'Who is she?'

I smiled as I disengaged. 'My muse.'

'Who's that when she's at home?'

I was about to lie my reply when one of the golfers suddenly realised that we waiters were still hanging on their departure. He hustled his drunken friends from the room and five of us descended on the table. The table was cleared and re-laid in less than one minute.

We were about to leave when the pastry chef, Michael, fat and happy, called us over. 'There's a last slice of gateau if you'd like it.'

I'd never tasted this gateau before. It was the hotel's signature piece: four thick layers of moist chocolate cake, mortared together with whipped cream and topped off with grated milk chocolate. We stood in a circle. Forks were shared out and each of us was allowed one single perfect mouthful. We grinned, looking at each other as the chocolate lingered on our palates. Michael glowed with pleasure. Such a small thing. But as with everything in life, and women in particular, we only appreciate a thing if there has been much struggle in acquiring it.

Cally, I knew, was already waiting for me, so I waved my goodnights and darted back to the staff quarters. These were a cluster of breeze block cells, containing little more than a bed and a basin and built-in wardrobe. On cold wet spring mornings, the very walls would weep in sympathy. We were tucked away at the back of the hotel, with a view that comprised either fir trees or more of the hotel's rudimentary staff quarters.

What did I care? It was a clear summer's night and my lover awaited me. I took a moment to hang up my white tunic, a Nehru jacket with blue collar and piping, brass buttons down the front and my name tag on the breast pocket. My black trousers went onto a separate hanger and my black lace-ups were kicked beside the bed. I tugged on jeans and a T-shirt and an old Yankees baseball jacket. I didn't take my wallet – I wouldn't be needing it where I was going. Did I bother to lock the door? Of course not: I had nothing worth stealing.

I walked back up the hill to Cally's car. It was an absolute beauty, a sky-blue Mercedes sports car with the top already down. That afternoon, I'd left Cally painting by the sea and had driven back to the Knoll House. That first time behind the wheel, I hadn't really opened her up as there had been too much traffic and too many blind spots. But now that it was night and the roads were clear, I thirsted for speed.

I eased out of the hotel drive and for a short while pottered along, revelling in the sea breeze and the star-bright night. I'd never driven an open-top at night. It was thrilling, the wind whipping through my hair and slicing at my cheeks as Van Halen pounded out over the stereo.

I stamped the pedal to the floor, the gears throbbed and the engine roared. I took a too-tight bend on the wrong side of the road and almost went straight into the trees. The car bounced off the kerb and I screeched to a stop. Heart pounding, I checked my bearings and put the car in gear. Much more sedately, almost sheepishly, I continued on my way, tooling through Swanage and out along the coast. Driving at night to be with a new lover: is there anything more exciting?

For along with everything else, there was also the prospect of our imminent lovemaking. I knew, for a certainty, that we'd be making love that night. But when? Immediately? Would I kiss her languorously and then without a word start to unbutton buttons, pop rivets and unzip zips, before soundlessly we made love beneath the cliff face? Or would there be a kiss and a tip of tongue before we sat cosily by the fire and exchanged our daily morsels, all the while anticipating the lovemaking that was to come? And then the caresses and fondles would become ever more urgent until the conversation was abandoned.

I parked up and started to walk through the fields to the coast and to the Dancing Ledges. Perhaps it's just the memories talking, but I still find the name so evocative. They say the Dancing Ledges are named from the waves that used to dance over the rock flats at high tide. But for myself, I like to imagine the smugglers capering in the firelight by the side of the sea.

I was wondering what Cally would have brought to drink that night. She was quite wealthy, I knew that, and I think we could have drunk champagne every night if that's what she'd wanted. But sometimes it would be a bottle of chianti, sometimes Sancerre, or ice-cold kummel. Once, she had even obtained a bottle of absinthe, green, sickly, wickedly potent.

Long before I reached the cliff, I could see the smoke swirling on a fierce wind and hear the waves booming onto the rocks below. The sea was running high and fast, with white tops rolling in as they pounded themselves into frothing surf on the black granite. The rocks gleamed in the moonlight.

I stood at the cliff edge. The fire was twenty, maybe thirty yards out, right on the very edge of the Dancing Ledges. The larger waves seemed to be all but crashing onto the fire itself, though it would be a while yet before the high tide began its shimmering dance over the ledges. Closer to the cliff face was the pool. The ledges had been cut out by quarrymen and, while they were at it, they had also carved themselves a swimming pool. It was rippling, rectangular, and the high tides cleansed and replenished it. At night, when the Dancing Ledges were a flat grey slab, the pool seemed to turn into a wide black window.

Cally was squatting down by a rock with her back to the fire – my secret girlfriend. During those early days, we were the only two people who knew about our relationship. It wasn't that I was embarrassed or ashamed of Cally. I loved her. I just didn't feel the need to have to explain this love to anyone.

I suppose before I met Cally, I also might have curled my lip at the thought of a young man with a much older woman. If you haven't experienced it yourself, then doubtless it seems perverse, unnatural – even taboo. It's fine enough, these days, for an older, richer man to take up with a woman half his age. But when it's the other way round, a mature woman and her – how I hate the phrase – 'toy boy' lover, then people tend to be much more suspicious about motives. She, the older woman, is seen as disgustingly depraved – while the younger man is little more than a pampered sponger, on a par with a gigolo, being paid to deliver the goods in the bedroom.

Well, I've been there. Not that I expect you to understand – at least not right now – but perhaps one day you will have a better idea of how a young man can fall heels over head for an older woman. I could just trot out some trite cliché about age just being a number; or age just being a state of mind. Or I could quote Mark Twain and tell you that age is an issue of mind over matter – and if you don't mind, it doesn't matter. But the truth is this: I have met men and women in their twenties who have already acquired the fusty dullness of middle age. Cally, on the other hand, was that rare breed, like a teenager to her core, hungering for adventure.

What does it matter? It went in, and it went out – and it worked.

Even before I had started to scramble down to the ledges, Cally had spotted me. She had this uncanny radar for me, which told her instantly when I was at hand. She looked up and she waved.

I climbed down and stalked over to the fire. She was drawing on the rock with a stick of charcoal. I don't know how long she had been drawing, but the picture stretched a full three yards across the rock, a herd of wild horses thundering across the heath. It was very fine, similar to the 30,000-year-old cave paintings at Lascaux in France. I liked it all the more for the fact that within a few hours it would have been washed clean by the sea. Its temporality only added to its power.

Cally was a professional artist. Even when she didn't have a canvas in front of her, she was always doodling on whatever came to hand – paper napkins, receipts, books and fliers and even, yes, million-year-old rocks on the Dorset coast.

'How was the car?' she asked. With three quick flicks she etched out a perfect horse's mane.

'I'm going to get myself an open-top.'

'Borrow mine any time you like,' she said. 'Seriously.'

'Thank you.' I stooped to kiss her, a kiss on the cheek and then a kiss full on the lips as my arm curled around her shoulders. In a moment the horses were abandoned.

'Let me look at you,' she said, arms round my waist as she kissed me again. 'Let me feast my eyes on you.' We sat there by the fire, the flames thundering in the wind, and gazed at each other. And what I saw was a woman who was in the very prime of her life – she was five foot two, exactly a foot shorter than me, with a mane of chestnut hair, slightly spattered with the afternoon's paint. Around her mouth and eyes, delightful teasing lines which were permanently on the verge of creasing into a laugh.

'We're very close to the edge,' I said.

'Just how I like it.'

'And what are we drinking tonight?'

'Brandy,' she said. 'Brandy for heroes. Brandy for lovers.'

As usual she had a thick waterproof rug and her fabulous wicker basket. Inside it were two apples, some Emmenthal and some biscuits and an old horn-handled Laguiole lock knife. The bottle of Cognac probably cost more than I earned in a fortnight. She had already opened it and I could taste the brandy on her breath.

We drank from two exquisite brandy balloons made of cut glass and so big that just one could have held the entire bottle. Cally loved beautiful things – not that she was materialistic, but there were certain occasions when nothing but the best would do. Her wine glasses, her tea cups and her crockery were, without exception, gorgeous both to the eye and to the touch; her favourite bed was a vast queen-sized playpen that she had shipped over all the way from the forests of Malaysia.

She topped up her own glass, poured me a tot and, like druids studying some ancient runes, we swirled the brandy, watching the amber ride through the glass rainbow before inhaling it deep into our lungs.

There was a slight indent in the ledges, about the size of a single bed, perfect for lying in, and we nestled against the rock. We sat shoulder to shoulder on the rug as the fire blazed into the night. She must have taken some time gathering all the driftwood, for the fire was three, four feet high, the flames licking over the rock as the sparks were blown by the breeze. Beneath us the thundering charge of the waves was followed by the boom as they smacked into the base of the ledges and then the rumbling suck of the wash back. It was invigorating, the occasional wet flicks of the waves and the contrast of the heat of the fire on our faces.

Cally put her glass down and looked up.

'The stars are bright tonight,' she said. As I looked up, before I'd even said a word, she whipped her cashmere scarf round my neck and held it tight as if she was on the verge of choking me.

I looked at her quizzically. I did not know what she was doing, but I knew she had her reasons – and that in her own time she would make them known to me.

She laughed and then just as quickly released me before rewarding me with a kiss.

'You know the Thuggee in India?' she said.

'The bandits?'

'They would travel in twos and threes and little by little they would join up with the huge caravans that travelled across India. It could take weeks before the whole band had been assembled.'

'And then?'

'And then, when the time was ripe and the Thuggee were sitting around the fires with the rest of their fellow travellers, the leader would look up into the night sky and he'd say—'

'The stars are bright tonight.'

'Yes – and that was the cue for the massacre. The rumals would fly and the knuckles would crack and in under a minute every man and woman would have been strangled to death. The children though, they were sometimes left to live to become Thugs in their own right.'

'How sad,' I said. It was difficult not to picture such a scene at that very fire where we were seated. 'So for thousands of travellers, those words, "the stars are bright tonight", would have been the last words that they ever heard.'

'Not a bad way to die.' She retrieved her glass. 'There you'd be, gazing up to the heavens and dwelling on the great infinity of all that's out there, weighing it up against the complete insignificance of your own life – and then suddenly, a noose round your neck and it's over. It would have been very quick. Better than cancer. Better than dying in a hospice. Anything but a hospice.'

'So what if it was cloudy?' I asked.

'History does not relate,' she said, before adding matter-of-factly: 'Let's make love.'

I kissed her with abandon, my tongue roiling against her teeth. 'Where and when do you want me?'

'I want you now and I think… I think I want you just here, right on the edge of the ledge,' she said.

Her hips and bosom swayed seductively from side to side. She had a rhythm all of her own. She danced by the side of the fire, accompanied only by the hissing wind and the thrum of the sea.

'And how shall I please my master?' She tied up her top like some Oriental dancer, so that I could see her belly. 'Would you like to undress me – or would you like to watch?'

'Strip,' I commanded. 'I want you to strip.'

She smiled at me, arch, wicked, as she pulled off her cashmere jumper. Riding boots and tight white riding britches soon followed. Now she stood before me, right on the edge of the ledge, in bright silhouette against the night, wearing only panties and a silk bra, luminous white in the darkness.

'You're liking this, aren't you?' she said, one hand on her hip as, like a lingerie model, she cocked her knee.

'Mmm.'

She smiled again before unclipping her bra. It fell at her feet and then she hitched her thumbs around the top of her knickers and in one graceful movement had pulled them off.

Naked, Cally stood before me, buxom, curvy, ample. She had hips and a tummy and robust legs and large full breasts, each the size of a honeydew melon.

She was one of the most beautiful women I have ever laid eyes on.

Not for Cally the faddy diets and the soul-destroying quest for the body beautiful. She ate and drank as she pleased and be damned to coltish legs and gamine figures – and, for that matter, to hell with formal exercise and sweating in Lycra in Stygian gyms. What she had, above all else, was something that some women only seem to acquire with age: a ring of steel confidence that proclaimed to the world, 'So I could lose a few pounds here, and I could be a little tauter there – but actually, I'm pretty damn gorgeous just as I am.'

It only took me another ten years to work it out for myself. That what we are attracted to in the opposite sex is not looks or wealth or power. Rather, what we desire is the confidence that can come with these boons. We are parasites for confidence – we love it and we leech off it, in the hope that some of this intangible magic will somehow be sprinkled onto our own shallow lonely lives.

This is especially so with a person's looks. If you feel gorgeous, if you know for a fact that you have the body beautiful, then you won't be swayed by pictures of supermodels or trite advice on how to slim for the summer – because you know that you've got it and you're so smoking hot that you can play the field until the day you die. Not that you'd necessarily want to; but in your heart, you know that anyone, anyone at all, is just there for the taking.

Cally sashayed along the edge of the ledges. Occasionally the waves would lick upwards, sending trickles of seawater over her legs and chest. All the while, I watched and I marvelled, aquiver with desire, knowing this spectacular woman was mine for the taking; yet knowing also that I wanted this moment to go on for ever. As so often in my life, anticipation is often even more heady than the actual event.

She came to a standstill just a few feet from me, stretching upwards, her full breasts almost defying gravity. Her feet were planted on the lip of the ledges. She was side on to the fire, and her skin had this glowing corona, like the moon's dark face as it eclipses the sun. Even now I wonder if she knew what she was doing – or whether, as ever, she was just pushing things to the limit. There was hunger and there was lust and love, and all salted with this spice of danger.

'Are you happy?' she asked.

'I am quite deliriously happy,' I said.

'Would you be happier if we were making love? You could be touching me?'

'Everything comes to he who waits,' I said. 'Are you happy?'

'I don't think it's going to get any better.'

She jumped, *entrechat*, her feet crossing back and forth in the air; she had been a dancer, but had given it up for her horses.

'Do you have to do that?' I said. 'It's making me nervous.'

Another waved crashed into the side of ledges and the water fountained up, cascading over her back. She laughed out loud.

'The question is,' she said, her teeth beaming white in the darkness as another wave boomed; by now she was completely soaked, her wet skin gleamed in the firelight, 'if this is as good as it gets, and if we're never going to be any happier, then why don't we just end it all now? Why don't you join me?'

It was an interesting question. There were once two French newly-weds who hit upon the exact same argument. Knowing that they could never, ever be any happier, and that their lives had each reached a mutual peak, the groom had shot his bride and then blown his own brains out.

I found the whole idea repellent. Who knows how it's all going to turn out? The one thing I did know was that we are not gamblers who should quit while we're ahead. Instead, we are like hogs in the field. We must suck up, devour every ounce of happiness that comes our way – and if we find one delicious truffle, we don't stop; we keep on snuffling until we find another.

'Have you got a death wish?' I said. 'Come and make love to me.'

'You're right,' she laughed. 'And you're so young too. How thoughtless of me. You still have your whole life ahead of you and I—'

Her words were abruptly cut off, as she disappeared in a thundering haze of water and spume. I jumped up and my glass shattered on the rock. The fire hissed as the seawater licked at its edges.

I stared out into the darkness, squatting on the lip of the ledge. Cally was a way off, her head seal-slick as she bobbed in the water. She was lit up quite clearly by the flames.

'Are you okay?' I called.

'Fine!' She waved at me.

Her head rose quite steeply in the water and much, much too late I realised that the wave that had taken her over the edge was a mere ripple compared to the monster that was coming in.

I threw myself flat onto the rock, head tucked tight into my arms. The wave broke over me, hard and full. The water surged deep over the Dancing Ledges and an instant later I was sucked over the edge and into the dark, choppy sea. The fire was dowsed and our only light was from the half-moon.

'You're all right?' Cally called. She pulled towards me.

'I think so,' I said. 'What about all your things – your basket, your rug?'

'Forget that,' she shouted. We were lifted up on the swell as another wave banged into the ledges. 'You're not cold are you?'

'No.'

'We could swim round the coast. Better to stay here.' She was utterly calm as she swam, not remotely concerned as the black waves crashed all about us. It was the very oddest sensation as we bobbed in the darkness in that wild sea. The waves seemed absolutely mountainous as they pounded the ledges.

'And then what?'

'We glide in on a big wave.' She had to shout to be heard over the sea's roar. 'Scramble up the path. Then we'll be home free!'

'It sounds so simple,' I called, and even though we were swimming for our lives, she still laughed at me.

'It will be,' she said. 'Don't worry. By the way, I love you. Very much.'

'I hope you're still saying that tomorrow.'

I hauled off my Yankees jacket, an old gift from an old girlfriend. It drifted and sank. We trod water in the heaving swell.

Cally shouted away to keep my spirits up – though for herself, I don't think she could have cared one jot that we were in such danger.

Cally looked over her shoulder, caught sight of a huge wave scything towards us. 'This is it!' she called.

We went in like body-surfers, hands outstretched in front of our heads. The wave swept us in clean over the ledges. I lifted my head out of the water and caught sight of the cliff-face looming high above us. We were going much too fast. I tried to turn so that my feet took the brunt of the impact. The wave smacked into the cliff, jarring the side of my body. It stunned me. I was on the verge of being sucked back out to sea when a strong arm caught me about the waist. She held me tight as the water boiled over the ledges.

'Quickly,' said Cally. 'Now!'

I staggered to my feet. The water seethed about my waist. Cally, agile as ever, was already out of the water. She hauled me upwards. I was still dazed, but even as the next wave crashed onto my legs, I was scrabbling up over the rock, my hands clawing and clinging to wherever they could find a purchase.

I didn't fully regain my senses until we had reached the top of the cliff. I threw myself on the grass, coughing up seawater and bile. Cally lay beside me. She was holding my hand. For a while there was silence as we stared up at the stars, and then she started to chuckle. And that's what I remember most about the night: not our adventure on the ledges, not the kissing, not the swim, but Cally's laugh. More than any other sound, that laugh captured the sheer rapture of what it is to be alive. What a tonic it was.

'That was lovely,' she turned onto her side, still chuckling, her belly rippling with giggles as she held me tight. 'Thank you. Are you okay?'

I think I was in shock, though I hid it. 'I'm pretty well. How are you?'

'I feel so randy,' she said.

'Now you tell me!'

'Come on!' she said, hauling me to my feet. 'Let's get to the car and get the heater on. You still have the keys?'

I patted my pockets. Amazingly, they jangled against my side.

She kissed me hard, wet, on the mouth. 'I think that might have been quite close,' she said.

'Please don't ever do that again.'

'Come on,' she said, already leading the way back through the field. 'I want to make love.'

And so we did, in the passenger seat of the Merc and with the heater going full blast. Is there anything to touch the ecstasy of a condemned man who's been given a last-minute stay of execution?

CHAPTER 3

So how came I to be languishing in Dorset in 1988 while the rest of my peers were busy-bee drones in the City, working their way up the corporate ladders, with dreams of fast cars and mortgages? Why wasn't I apprenticed to some trade where I could learn about litigation or tax or copy-writing or brokerage or any of the other respectable London jobs that pay by the million?

The answer is simple: I had no idea what it was that I wanted to do. It is the curse of modern times that the bright young things can do whatever they want, live wherever they want, sleep with whomsoever they want – just so long as you go for it, you too can have it all. If you have that dream, that vision, there's never been a better time in history to seize your destiny. If, on the other hand, you're a dabbler, a dilettante, there's lots of things that you might like to try; and lots of things that you might be reasonably good at. But in this era of specialisation, there is little room left for the dabblers who drift like honeybees from one flower to the next.

After nigh on fifteen years of school and university, I had a clutch of qualifications but no star on which to hitch them. So instead I'd been travelling for nearly two years and had become embroiled in yet another disastrous love affair. I don't know why it is, but in affairs of the heart, I'm a magnet for the cataclysmic. Not for me the girlfriend who drifts into my life and who slowly ebbs out; rather, they tend to end things in the most spectacular fashion. If I were to sum up all my great affairs of the heart, the word that would most generally fit the bill is 'Disaster'. But of course they end disastrously. After touching Himalayan peaks of happiness, where is there to go but down? So after university I had yet again been scalded by love, and as a result took off travelling.

After nearly two years in Asia, I returned home to London. It was not long before my father started asking just when it was that I would fulfil my destiny.

'Why don't you just try something – anything?' he'd said. 'It doesn't have to be for the rest of your life. Anything at all. Damn it – you might even like it!'

I'd had a shot at becoming a croupier. Dreams of wearing a sharp suit and a snappy bowtie as I riffled through the chips and smiled at women who dripped in diamonds. I'd lasted a week; done for by my lousy maths.

A career in copy writing: failed at the first hurdle. A career in selling insurance and cashing in on all my blueblood acquaintances; I walked out of the interview. A career as a Lloyds underwriter, such a grand title for such tedium. A career as a trader, screaming and haggling in the pit with the other hyenas.

'I've got some friends in the fashion industry,' said my stepmother, Edie. She had been a model once and was still holding on to her beauty.

My father was reading the *Telegraph*, puffing away on one of his high-tar cigarettes. He had been a no-nonsense general and certainly would not have put up with any of this nonsense from his subalterns. How he had mellowed. There was slight flicker of the eyebrows, as if to say, 'God help us!'

'Lots of lovely girls,' Edie continued, sipping on her bitter espresso. 'You might like fashion – really.'

My father gazed out of the kitchen window. 'Oh look,' he said. 'There's a young pig flying over the top of the eucalyptus.'

'Have you ever thought about writing about your travels?' Edie said. 'Travel writing's becoming very popular.'

'My God!' He stubbed out his cigarette. 'Now there's a whole herd of the buggers doing a fly-past!'

Edie gave him a wan smile. 'If you're not going to be helpful, darling…'

'I'm going to do the crossword.'

He left and soon after, Edie squawked, 'Is that the time?' and followed him.

With nothing better to do, I started to clean the kitchen. What to do, what to do? I was the boy of destiny, but where to go to follow my nebulous star? Like every other stripling, I suppose I dreamed of women and money and expensive holidays and, above all else, impressing my peers and my friends, so that they were incapable of doing anything else but falling to their knees in the most abject adulation.

I flicked through some photo albums. Pictures of my mother, long dead now, and my father when he'd once known what joy it was to be alive. Pictures of military parades that I'd attended, tapping my feet to the drummers' beat; first days of term; old tree-houses; stately homes; and then, in a small cluster of pictures from a holiday from the distant past, the Knoll House Hotel.

I smiled. I must have been about six years old and it was one of the last holidays that I'd ever had with my mother. I hadn't thought about it in years. But I remembered it. I remembered a playground and a pirate's ship. I remembered shrimps from the rock pools that had been boiled up in an old paint can. And a day on the beach when we'd rented one of the huts, my mother smiling and my father laughing as we had tea in the snug as the rain thrummed on the rooftop. A little pitch-and-putt golf course, as I hacked in the heather with cut-down clubs. And, bizarrely, I remember a vast ski jump that had been pitched beside the swimming pool – built not for the guests but for the proprietor's daughter so that she could follow her ski-jumping dreams. I wondered if she ever made it to the Olympics.

It was odd that I hadn't thought about the Knoll House before. Looking back, it might have been one of the happiest holidays of my life.

On a whim, and because all my friends were at work that morning, I called up directory enquiries, found the hotel's number, and in under a minute was being put through to Anthony, the hotel's manager.

21

He sounded jolly; we hit it off immediately. It was March. By coincidence, the hotel was just about to open for the Easter break. It had been closed for three or four months during the winter and Anthony had just returned from his UK recruitment tour. Over the phone I must have somehow conveyed that precise mix of friendliness, punctiliousness and subservience that are required of a good waiter. Anthony hired me on the spot. Could I come down the next day? I could have kissed him I was so happy. In one bound, Kim was free!

Sure, up until five minutes earlier, I had never once considered a career in the catering industry. But in a matter of moments, I was already smitten – I'd be out of London; I'd be away from my parents. Life on a hotel campus with waiters and waitresses and a regular routine. I might be marking time, marching but not moving forward, but at least I would be on the move.

'You're going *where*?' Edie was horrified.

My father seemed rather pleased. 'The Knoll House,' he meditated the next day. 'I haven't been there in years.'

He wanted to drive me down that morning and if I had been more perceptive I would have let him. Young men may like to fly solo, but they forget that there is a special pleasure for parents to put themselves out for their children. Instead he gave me a lift to Waterloo Station. He was on his way to the Stock Exchange. He never much talked about his work – or perhaps I just never asked him about it. He was wearing a suit with a dark tie, his jacket slung on the back seat.

We took his personal Mini, rather than the family Mercedes, which meant that he could smoke. He loved that brown Mini. We had gone down a little cul-de-sac near to where we lived in Chelsea. It was a quiet street and the road was sealed off with a number of bollards. He drove straight at the bollards at about thirty miles per hour. Just when it seemed that a crash was inevitable, he flicked the steering wheel. With two wheels on the pavement and two wheels in the gutter, we flew through the bollards. The Mini bounced back onto the road. He was laughing so hard he started to choke.

He nudged me in the ribs. 'Thought the old man had lost his marbles?'

'You'd have had a fit if I drove like that!'

'Once – probably.' He puffed at his cigarette before flicking the stub out of the window. 'I discovered that road a month ago. I'm not even sure it's a shortcut. It's probably a long cut. You should have seen the expression on Edie's face when I first took her there. "We're going to crash!"' he cried, in a high-pitch squeal, laughing. 'She was as white as a ghost.'

He laughed again, lighting up another cigarette with one-hand as he double D-clutched down to second.

'I don't know,' he said. 'I think it might have been better if I hadn't gone straight into the army. Should have seen some of the world. Lot of stuffed shirts in the army.'

It was a part of my father that, for a long time, I had never known existed. For so long he had been this humourless army officer, but since a severe accident that I'd had at school, it was as if he'd given up trying to train me like some well-tended vine, for ever pruning and shaping and nurturing with fertiliser. He had come to accept that there was much joy to be had from watching me grow, even if the end product might not be what he'd first envisaged.

'So what happened to you?' I asked.

'I don't know. There was a time when the army was the most important thing in the world to me. And then things happen… You get a better sense of what's important.'

'There was a time when you wanted me to join up.'

'What an imbecile!' he said. I was not sure if he was referring to himself or the biker on the Ducati. 'You'll like the Knoll House,' he said. 'I'll come and visit you when you've settled in. There's a pub just the near hotel, the Bankes Arms. Full of dark crannies. Used to go there with your mother.'

We tore into Waterloo station and parked in the taxi rank. 'Do you need any money?' he asked, stretching to the back seat for his wallet.

He peeled off some crisp red £50 notes. 'Here's a couple of hundred. Send us a postcard some time.'

I stretched over to give him an awkward hug and made to kiss him on the side of the cheek. There was a time, a few years earlier, when he would have shrunk from such overtures, but he had learned to accept these indignities from his eldest son.

On the pavement, I waved. He gave me a formal salute. It was rather nice, actually. Of all the extraordinary things that can happen between father and son, I enjoyed his company.

I caught the train down to Poole, which carved through genteel, staid Wiltshire. I was aware that a new chapter in my life was beginning; aware I had no inkling as to what might be on the next page. Perhaps not adventure, but certainly something different.

I wondered if there might yet be love on the horizon. It had been a long time since I had kissed a woman. Some men are capable of bouncing back after a bad break-up. They don't even bother to lick their wounds before immersing themselves straight back into the hostile element. But I was still tired, punch-drunk and the wounds still raw and tender; if you have ever been in love, then you will know how it is. Not that I'd been foreswearing on women for all time, not by any means. I had been having a time out.

So I did wonder about love. I did wonder if in the Knoll House there might be the one. But would it be the slow burn that only comes with time, months and months before you realise that the jewel that you've been searching for is right in front of your very nose? Or would it be the *coup de foudre*, the lightning bolt that left me prone and smitten in under a minute?

In my naïve way, I hoped that it would be the latter. When lightning strikes, it's so quick that it seems to blot out all else. You're rendered so helpless that you lose your appetite and, when in her presence, are hardly capable of speech.

I caught the bus through Sandy Banks. Even in 1988, Sandy Banks was one of Britain's most costly pieces of real estate. But I preferred the dirty, functional ferry, in splendid contrast to the manicured lawns and the spit-polished yachts. For pedestrians, the fare was fifty pence. The wind hissed off the waves bringing with it a spit of rain. I sat outside on one of the summer benches. The clear cold felt like balm, icing at my cheeks and frosting my hair. A young boy stood at the back of the ferry tossing bread to the gulls. The birds swooped and whirled and never once missed and every time they snatched up the bread, the boy would laugh. Standing on sentry-duty by his side was the boy's father, looking ever more miserable as the cold rain sliced through his jumper. He was only a little older than myself; what a trooper to have committed so young – to have found his soul mate and to have decided that she was the one. I wished him well, as I do all my fellow travellers in this crazy journey of love and lust where nothing is certain, except the cataclysmic crash that will come at the end of it all. Still – better by far to be travelling, disasters and all, than to be sitting there remote and loveless on the island shore, gloating with self-satisfied smugness at the sight of the little ships that are foundering in the sea.

It was only a short ferry ride and on the other side of the estuary: Studland, home of long-remembered holidays. I wondered if I would ever be able to recapture that first careless rapture.

I had planned on walking to the hotel and was strapping my rucksack to my back when a green Volvo estate pulled over to the side of the road. The front side window eased down. It was a woman, blonde, a pleasant smile. She was only a little older than me.

'Like a lift?' she said.

I was about to tell her that I'd be fine. But instead I found myself saying, 'Thanks.'

The car belonged to the family of the boy with the bread and the cold, wet man. I heaved my Bergen into the boot and joined the boy in the back.

'Where you heading?' asked the man. The heater in the car was going full blast. It was wonderful after the wet wind on the ferry.

'The Knoll House,' I said.

'One of the staff?'

'I'm one of the new waiters.'

'We sometimes go there for dinner,' said the woman. 'We'll have to look out for you. My sister would like you.'

'Would she?' I asked. 'Is she anything like you?'

'My sister would definitely like you,' she laughed. 'What's your name?'

I was formally introduced to Mark and Julienne and little James.

'Do you know about the Knoll House's puddings?' said Mark.

'No. They any good?'

'They're the main reason we go.' The boy laughed and the woman smiled and the man patted her knee, and I glimpsed an instance of the small pleasures that are to be had from marriage. They are not like the adventures of being a single man; there is none of the electric heat that comes with waiting for your lover at the airport; there is no thrill of the chase, nor that exquisite ecstasy that comes with the taste of new love. But there are compensations: a child's smile; a cup of tea in the morning; a peck on the cheek as you go to work; and a warm meal, perhaps, when you return. Forgive me, for I know full well that this is just me, perverse to a fault. It would not matter if I were the Bachelor-King or if I were married to the most beautiful woman that has ever walked this earth. Whatever I've got, I will always want what he's having.

They dropped me at the bus stop by the hotel and they all waved me off as I shouldered my rucksack. 'Good luck!' said the man.

'Don't forget about that sister!' I called after them.

I gave them an affectionate wave that ended in a sloppy army salute.

I looked up at the hotel. Perhaps there was a prick of memory, but I didn't recognise the place. It was solid, white, comfortably robust and it stood at the top of a hill with sweeping views out over the forest and down to that grey wash of sea. The building seemed to be pre-war, purpose built as the perfect family hotel.

The drive curled round the hotel and as I walked up I finally saw something I recognised, without a doubt, from my childhood. The pirate ship was still sailing serene in the playground, with its black sides, its ropes and its wheel on the poop deck. I'd once climbed up to the crow's nest, my mother screaming at me to be careful as my father quietly urged me upwards.

I knew my way to the reception. As I went in, shards of memory continued to spike into the light. A swirling carpet, wooden panels and stained glass windows. It wasn't flash, like some five-star London hotel, but homely and pleasant, the sort of hotel where you would be quite comfortable coming in straight from the beach in your flip-flops and your sandy shorts.

The young receptionist was laughing away with a vigorous man in his forties: the ever-smiling Vicki and my new boss, Anthony. He, too, almost always smiled, save for the very last time I saw him. Now he stood, as he always stood, in his dark suit, positively rubbing his hands with glee at the prospect of whatever the day would bring. It did not matter if the old couple were complaining about their room not being ready, or the young family belly-aching about the pet dog, for Anthony took everything in his most majestic stride. Vicki was also lovely. Too lovely for me. In my perversity, I find that a woman can almost be too lovely and too kind for me to fall in love with them. With the sweet I must always have the sour.

Anthony broke off from his joshing to turn to me. 'And you must be… don't tell me…' He paused, trying for a moment to recognise my face before realising that we had never met. 'You must be Kim!'

'Hello Anthony.'

He came out of the reception, clapped me on the shoulder and shook my hand. 'Welcome to the team!' he said. 'You've been here before, you say?'

'When I was six.'

'It hasn't changed a bit,' he said. 'They've probably even still got the same TV in the communal telly room—'

'Probably showing the same TV programmes,' I added.

'Ooh!' he said delightedly. 'Oh, very good. I like that! My dear Vicki, we have a fly one here. I shall deploy him with all of our tricksiest customers.'

I shrugged and smiled and Vicki smiled at me. Freckles and a lovely blonde bob, and altogether way, way too good for the likes of me.

She was wearing the front-of-house's grey skirt and white blouse and elegant black court shoes.

'Have you had lunch?' asked Anthony.

'I have, thank you.'

'Vicki will show you your room, then. It's not much, I can tell you – in fact, if it were a cell in Belmarsh, it would probably be infringing the prisoners' rights.'

'It'll be fine,' I said. 'I've just been in Asia for a couple of years. The rats would wander through the dorms at night.'

'Well, I haven't heard of any rats here,' said Anthony. 'At least not of the rodent variety.'

He winked at me and we all laughed. I already felt like I was a part of the Knoll House family. Tea was being served in a couple of hours, and until then Anthony encouraged me to explore the hotel, make myself at home. The Knoll House would be opening in a couple of days' time, the Thursday before Easter.

Vicki took me out to the staff quarters. I held the umbrella and enjoyed the feeling of her arm nudging against mine. We walked out past the hotel's new extension, past the playground, and onto a tarmacked path that meandered through the firs to the staff quarters. They were behind a little hillock and shielded by more firs: a long strip of breeze block.

'How long have you worked here?' I asked Vicki.

'I came a year ago,' she said. 'I was a waitress but they moved me to the front of house.'

'You were wasted in the dining room.'

She giggled charmingly. 'These rooms aren't great. But we have a lot of fun. I met my boyfriend here last year. He's a barman now.'

'I bet a lot of the staff start dating each other.'

Again, another smile. 'Most do. Some of them even get married.'

'I bet he'll soon have that ring on your finger.'

'Maybe – who knows.'

She gave me a key and I opened the door to room number eighteen. It was warm and fuggy with a single bare light-bulb hanging from the ceiling. A bar-heater was on in the corner and with the window closed, the condensation was dribbling dark on the breeze block walls.

I scanned the room, taking in the grey-tiled floor, the built-in bed, the basin and the tiny wardrobe. On the bed was a pillow, white sheets and – of course – a grey blanket.

'Perfect,' I said.

'I'm sure you won't be spending much time here,' she said. 'Loo and showers are in the wash-house round the corner.'

'Perfect.'

'If you want more blankets, just ask.' She hovered at the door. 'See you at tea.'

I unpacked my rucksack and hung up my two pairs of black trousers. I placed my shirts, jumpers and the rest of my clothes in the two drawers. I had three books, including *War and Peace* – a book that I not so much wanted to read as thought that I ought to read. I had bizarrely thought that there would be plenty of time for reading at the Knoll House, but as it was I did not read a single word of *War and Peace* while I was there, nor have I since.

I switched off the heater, opened the window, and tried to bounce on the mattress. It was as hard as a Judo mat. It would be some weeks before I ever had a good night's sleep there.

I walked back to the hotel through the rain, gave a wave to Vicki at the reception and started to explore. On the coastal side of the hotel, there were bars and lounges, and set aside from the main hotel was the crèche and the children's dining room. The communal TV room seemed like it was out of some bizarre time warp. It was the only television in the entire hotel, and was surrounded by perhaps thirty or forty beige-coloured armchairs; the only time I have ever seen anything like it was when I used to visit my grandmother in her retirement home. Only the most desperate telly-addicts could stomach the room.

Up the main staircase, I found something else I remembered from my childhood. A chair, a Chippendale-style armchair, with wooden armrests and a padded green seat. But it was a chair for a giant, the seat fully four feet off the ground. I sat on it, my feet swinging easily above the ground. How many thousands of guests must have done the same thing before me? Or, perhaps more pertinently, how many of them, I wondered, ever had the nerve to make love on that monstrous old antique?

Upstairs, an army of maids was already giving the hotel its spring-clean. I checked out a couple of the sea-view rooms. They were the most expensive rooms in the hotel. I was surprised at how low-key it all was. They were the sort of rooms you might find in a friend's holiday home by the sea. Each room had just a couple of twin beds, a desk and armchair and an unfussy bathroom. In place of a television there was a radio on the bedside table. I still marvel at the incredible chutzpah of the hotel's managers, so wilfully denying their guests one of the most basic staples of modern life.

Hands in my pockets, I ambled through the warren of bedrooms, eager for the next excitement. The hotel smelled clean and aired and fizzed with expectation. To everyone I smiled. They all said hello. It seemed as if by joining the staff I had been elected into this most exclusive and affable club.

There were many more rooms on the top floor – scores of rooms, I do not know how many. As I walked along the corridor, I could hear a man's voice. He was a Londoner. 'Come out tonight,' he said. 'See the lads.'

A woman replied. Her English was good, but accented; perhaps Scandinavian. 'You're so classy, Darren.'

The irony was lost on him. 'So you'll come?'

I padded quietly along the corridor.

'I don't think so,' she said.

'You'll like it.'

'Yeah.' It is difficult to express all the different meanings that she managed to convey in this single word, but I think the chief of them was mocking humour.

I walked past the room. The door was of course open. Darren was slouching against the door frame, his hand cupped over the top of the door. He looked very cool in blue jeans, white T-shirt and a tight-fitting grey V-neck. He had cropped black hair spiked with gel. He wore baseball boots with the laces undone.

Beyond Darren, I had a glimpse of the woman. Her name, I later learned, was Annette. She was the prettiest of all the housemaids and was making up one of the beds. She was in the maid's uniform, a blue gingham dress to the knees. I saw cheekbones and a mass of honey blonde hair.

Darren scowled at me. I winked.

Over the years, the carefully timed wink has become a part of my very fibre. It has such a wealth of meanings. I use it as a greeting; and as a riposte; as a flirtation; and it can also be a goodbye. It is that wonderful weapon that every child should have learned by the age of seven. My father used to deploy the wink at all times. I remember how he would be entertaining important army grandees, but would still, when he caught my eye, have time to give me a little sly wink, as if to say, 'It's all one big fat joke, isn't it?' He had quickly taught me to wink – properly – with either eye. It would take me some years to learn how to use it judiciously. At one stage, I would even wink at teachers after I'd recited the answer to some question. Senior citizens also did not care much for a wink, perceiving it – correctly – as a sign of puppish disrespect.

But girls... Girls can, on the appropriate occasion, be charmed by a wink. It has an edge. I remember a summer party when I was a teenager. I'd just left school and was standing out in the garden with a group of students. I don't know what we were talking about, but for a second my eyes wandered. I caught the eye of a girl. She had shoulder-length black hair. I had never seen her before. It was only for the briefest of moments. On instinct I winked at her. She blushed and laughed. But I know she liked it. She told me so herself.

Winking has many uses, but it should be remembered that a wink can also be an incendiary. When I winked – cheekily, breezily – at Darren, I was in fact giving him a little dig in the ribs, as if to say, 'Bit of a fall you've taken there.'

Then I gave him my most disarming smile before continuing to stroll on down the corridor. I could feel his eyes burning into my back.

At teatime, I wandered over to the dining room. There was a screened off section, tucked away in the corner, where the staff had their meals. I could hear a number of them already gathered for tea. I felt no urgency to join them and instead went over to the broad bank of windows that looked out to the sea. I tried to recall whether I'd been in the room before, but nothing seemed to prick me. Rain was spitting at the windows, as I stared out at the grey swirl of the ocean.

'It is not really swimming weather, is it?'

I turned. I liked the sound of his voice. It was very precise English, with the slightest hint of a German accent. 'Spot of rain isn't going to put you off, is it?' I said.

He smiled at me. 'No, it is not going to put me off. But you, on the other hand; you are obviously a fair-weather swimmer.'

'Me?' I laughed. 'I love swimming in the rain.'

'Especially when it is cold.'

'And a biting wind. You can't beat it.' I said. 'So shall we have a dip after tea?'

'I think it would be… how do you say in England? …churlish not to.'

He sounded like the very image of some of the bluff army cadets that I had known at university. I laughed and thrust out my hand. 'I'm Kim.'

'Oliver,' he said. 'Oliver Braun.' We shook hands. I looked him in the eye and I liked what I saw. Oliver was an eccentric string bean, a good hand taller than myself, with silver-rimmed glasses and tufty hair that had to be flattened down with gel. Instead of jeans, he was looking preternaturally middle-aged in grey slacks, white shirt and – of all things – a green cardigan. But on Oliver, somehow it all worked. He had large white hairless hands and an Adam's apple that was permanently jiggling in his neck. He was also, without doubt, one of the most spectacularly clumsy people that I have ever met.

'I think we're going to like it here,' I said.

'Shall we eat?'

As he turned to head towards the staff dining area, he caught one of his feet in the legs of a chair. He swayed for a moment, arms paddling in the air before crashing to floor. The twisting chair sent the entire table thundering onto its side. Another two chairs were upended in the carnage. The noise was stupendous. At least one of the chairs had been smashed to kindling.

I helped Oliver up. It was like watching a newborn foal get to its feet. 'Are you all right?' I asked.

He flicked at his trousers and adjusted his cardigan. He pulled out a pristine white handkerchief and mopped at the cut on his hand. 'It's nothing, thank you, Kim,' he said.

A small crowd of waiters and waitresses had come over. They gawked, fascinated, but said nothing. Anthony had also come down from the reception. He cocked his head to the side and scratched at his neck.

'Not fighting already?' he said. 'You haven't even had a drink yet!'

'I am sorry, sir,' said Oliver. 'It was my fault. I tripped and… the table went over.' He looked at the debris. 'And some chairs too.'

The staff goggled at this strange, exotic creature in their midst. Anthony glanced at them. 'Nothing to see, folks – just another accident in the dining room. Happens all the time, as you'll soon see. Just get back to your dinner.'

As they drifted off, Oliver again apologised. 'I am very sorry, sir – please deduct the repairs from my salary.'

'Tush!' said Anthony. 'Give me a hand setting this table back. The handymen will fix it all up in no time.'

We righted the table and the two broken chairs were taken away from the dining room. Anthony returned with a dustpan and brush and swept up the shards of wood and varnish that were on the carpet. It was strange to be standing there in the dining room as the manager grovelled on the floor cleaning up after our accident.

He looked up at Oliver. 'I'm going to have to watch you,' he said. 'You're going to be a terror when we've got real food and real customers!'

'Yes, sir.'

'Don't call me sir – I'm Anthony.'

'Yes, Anthony.'

'To start off with, just take things slow,' he said. 'It might seem easy. But becoming a good waiter takes time.' He stood up, dustpan and brush in his hand. 'Particularly with someone like you!' He laughed. 'Look at those feet of yours!'

For the first time, I looked at Oliver's feet. They were huge and encased in the most vile, spatulate brown leather lace-ups.

We went over to have our tea and as we joined the rest of the staff, there was a definite lull in the conversation. We could have just grabbed our spaghetti and quietly taken a seat, but after everything that had happened, that seemed tame.

'Hi,' I said to the twenty or so staff.

Some smiled. Two of the nicer waiters waved. Darren nudged his neighbour, Janeen. 'That's the Winker,' he said.

He meant to be heard and I heard him. But know this about me: I have never been one to refuse a dare.

'And you must be the Wanker.' I grinned at Darren as I spooned up some bolognese.

He gawked at me. 'Are you calling me a wanker?' he demanded.

'Well if the cap fits…' I followed Oliver over to a table in the corner. Some of the staff giggled. They looked from me to Darren and back again.

'Who the hell are you with your la-di-da accent anyway?'

I winked at him, goading him. 'I'm the Winker,' I said. 'But to my friends, I'm Kim.'

Darren chewed his spaghetti, wondering how next to insult me. I thought that he was going to start swearing. But instead, Oliver stepped in. 'We are going swimming after tea,' he said, a seraphic smile on his face. 'I have a bottle of Armagnac. Would anyone like to join us?'

The rain hammered at the windows. You could hear it drumming against the glass.

A young guy, plump with blonde foppish hair, raised his hand; that was Roland. 'I'm in.'

Janeen, sitting next to Darren, piped up. 'I'll come,' she said, before adding, 'Come on! It'll be fun!'

As icebreakers go, it doesn't get much better.

CHAPTER 4

Anthony watched in bemusement as we trooped out of the hotel. Janeen had dug up some towels.

'Where are you going?'

'We're off for a swim,' I said.

'All of you?' said Anthony. 'In this?'

'We have this!' Oliver flourished his bottle.

'You're going to need a hell of a lot more than Armagnac if you're going swimming!' said Anthony. 'You must be mad!'

'That's why we work here!' I said.

Anthony gaped before hurrying from the dining room. 'Wait one second!' he called.

We looked at each other. Some nervous; some pumping themselves up; some staring at the monsoon outside. Janeen was cajoling Darren, but he and a handful of others were still refusing to come. I wasn't sure whether it was the prospect of swimming in the icy Channel, or whether it was falling in with something that I had suggested.

Anthony returned with the drinks trolley. He handed over two bottles of brandy, a bottle of Armagnac, some Baileys and some Courvoisier.

'Wish I could be joining you,' he said. 'Somebody's got to hold the fort.'

One by one, we ducked out into the rain. Janeen and another waitress crossed the road and the rest of the bedraggled crew followed behind. No one had an umbrella. We were soaked before we'd even walked two hundred yards. We could not have been any wetter if we had been in the sea itself. It was strangely liberating. Gradually an air of chattering hilarity swept through our motley band of bathers.

'Looks like we have started something,' Oliver said.

'It's going to be a daily event,' I said. 'Before breakfast?'

'Please not before breakfast,' Roland said.

'After dinner?' Oliver said.

'After the pub?' Roland said.

'We'll be keeping the lifeboat men busy.'

We followed a wet path down through the woods to the beach. It was muddy and parts of the path had been turned into a torrenting stream. Oliver slipped, taking out Roland as he careened down the hill. The pair thumped into a silver birch. Roland swore and we laughed. There was this realisation that we were on an adventure. We were all soaked, our clothes drenched, but no one gave a damn. It was a magical half hour.

After the wet woods, the path meandered through dunes of spiky grey-green marram grass. The rain looked like it was easing off and we could even see a glimpse of sunshine fighting through the clouds. The wind was still crisp. At the top of the last hillock, we paused for a moment before linking hands and tearing onto the beach. A girl fell, taking Oliver with her in a giggling heap. The rest of us were all suddenly ripping off our clothes, as if possessed by this delirious frenzy, stamping out of our wet trousers and hauling the clinging shirts from our backs.

Was it drink? Had they slipped something into our food? Or was it just this ecstatic release that you can sometimes share with a stranger?

There was a pause when it came to pants and bras. Were we really going to strip off in front of these people we didn't know? In front of these people that we'd be working with day and night for the rest of the year? Was that really such a good idea?

Oliver pulled the stopper of the Armagnac with his teeth and took an almighty swallow before passing the bottle on. Janeen, teeth chattering, gulped some brandy. I can remember Michelle and Tracy, eyes wide at all this heaving white flesh, as they sipped from a bottle of Baileys.

Oliver had opened the other bottle of brandy. He must have poured a quarter of the bottle down his throat without once pausing for breath.

'Let us do it!' he said, and with that, he hauled off his blue boxers. We watched goggle-eyed as he raced naked to the sea.

I am not one to flaunt my nakedness. This was not the sort of thing that I ever did. I had been skinny-dipping with lovers, paddling in warm seas on star-lit nights. But I'd never been skinny-dipping on a frozen English beach with a group of strangers.

Janeen passed me a brandy bottle. I swallowed. It was rough, like drinking liquid fire and I could feel the liquor razoring the back of my throat. The second shot was easier and suddenly I could feel heat and madness pumping through my veins. I shrieked to the skies, hauled down my boxers, and in an instant I was also tearing towards the sea.

I hit the water at a flat-out sprint. It was electric cold, jagging at my skin. Arms, legs windmilling through the ice-cold water, I swam at the horizon. I was a wild thing, in a thrashing frenzy to ward off the cold. I watched as the rest of the crew raced into the water, screaming with excitement and with not a stitch of clothing on any of them. It was an extraordinary sight. Young women with swinging breasts and flailing hair, young men with white pasty, padded stomachs.

Oliver, still with his glasses on, swam over to me. It was still cold, but now at least bearable. 'It is a good start, yes?' he said.

'It's the perfect start.'

'I do not think I have ever managed to get twelve young women to take all their clothes off before.' He sniffed and then added, 'At least not as quickly as this.'

'Hark at you!' I exclaimed. 'I thought you Germans were doing this all the time.'

'On the contrary,' he said. 'It is you little Englanders who are so obsessed with nudity. On the one hand, you are quite terrified of it. Yet in your dark hearts, you cannot get enough of it.'

'You were the first in, though,' I said.

'Otherwise you would all still be, uh…' He paused, searching for the right word, 'You would all still be standing on the beach, quite terrified at your own indecision!'

We had started to swim back when we saw the horsewoman. She was galloping through the surf on a magnificent piebald bullet, the sea and the sand thundering all about her. Almost directly behind her, the sun was setting low on the horizon. She had her head low, almost touching the horse's mane. She was so focused on her horse and the sea and the ground ahead of her, that she did not immediately see us. A couple of the girls, wraith white, were shuffling out of the sea.

The horsewoman eased to a walk, before bringing her horse to a halt in the thin surf. She looked at the girls. She looked at the swimmers' slick black heads out in the sea. And then she clapped her thighs and roared with laughter.

She had pulled up just near to where Oliver and I were walking up the beach.

There was no point in trying to hide my nakedness, so with a touch of a swagger I looked her in the eye. She looked the part, skin-tight white riding britches, a trim beige jacket and brown leather riding boots. The boots reached up to her knees; age and polish had given them a patina of rich chestnut. In fact, now that I think of it, the woman's clothing was absolutely faultless. Everything was of the very best. She was spattered by sand and sea. I could not tell her age. She was lovely.

She started to clap.

I gave her an elegant, practised bow, my hands sweeping out to the side, as if I were on the stage at Covent Garden.

'I wish I could join you,' she said. Her voice was a deep, confident purr, so seductive. It was the voice of a woman in her prime. I guessed she was in her forties.

'Don't worry,' I replied, one hand resting casually on my hip. 'It's going to become a regular feature.'

She smiled, open, friendly. 'And will you be taking many of your Knoll House guests with you?'

'I certainly hope so,' I said.

'Well…' I could feel her eyes raking me from head to toe. 'I better come up and see you then.'

I watched in silence as she cantered off through the surf and into the distance.

On the beach, the others were trying to get dressed, but with wet clothes and not enough towels, it was difficult. The euphoria had passed and, like Adam and Eve, we were all suddenly aware of our own nakedness. The girls hid behind towels as they struggled with their trousers, and the guys turned their shirts into makeshift loincloths, tying them tight about their waists.

I hobbled from one foot to the other as I pulled on my boxers. Only Oliver had no mind for clothes, standing there in his glorious nakedness, the seawater still glittering on his glasses as he drank Armagnac. Michelle and Tracy goggled at him before Tracy rolled her eyes, their own mad swim of five minutes earlier now all but forgotten.

I remembered the four crisp fifties that my father had given to me – was it really only that morning? 'The first round is on me!' I said. Easy come, easy go.

'And the next round,' said Oliver. 'That will be on me!'

It was like a shot in the arm. The team was rejuvenated.

We went back to the hotel. The shower in a Spartan breeze block outhouse was skin-tinglingly hot, thawing me from the outside in.

I tossed my wet clothes into one of the hotel's washing machines and joined the rest of the bathers as we walked to the pub. The Bankes Arms was about a mile away and it was nearly dark by the time we arrived. It was a traditional country pub, with black beams and comfortable chairs. A cluster of oddments decked about the room: animals that had been badly stuffed and Toby jugs and jolly bric-a-brac statues, a cupboard full of games and a wall of books. A fire was blazing hot in the hearth. I liked it as soon as I walked in.

The publican, Michael, was barrel-chested, with a lustrous black moustache and a florid red face. He wore a shirt and tie, with a white apron and clips at his elbows.

He carefully inspected a fifty pound note.

'You don't mind, do you?' he said, holding a note up to the light. 'It's not that I don't trust you—'

'It's just the company I keep.'

'We don't see many of these.' He meticulously scrutinised the next note, checking not just the middle strip but also the watermarks. 'Leastways not from the likes of the Knoll House staff.'

'Maybe I'm different.'

'There's no doubt about that, young man!'

I asked for a Guinness and offered Michael a drink. He had a pint of the local bitter and would sip from it occasionally as he delivered the drinks to the rest of the staff. Individually, they all came up to thank me; some introduced themselves, some not. I was touched.

Janeen came over. She was voluptuous, poured into tight blue jeans and with a clinging V-neck T-shirt. She had full lips that were thick with scarlet lipstick. She came straight up to me and, without a word, kissed me full on the mouth.

'Cheers,' she said. 'I like your style.'

'And I like yours,' I said. I leaned over and kissed her straight back. She smelt of perfume and salt and vinegar crisps.

She let out a rich peel of laughter. She was always laughing. 'Does that mean you're my boyfriend now?'

'I don't know.' I took a first sip of Guinness, my eyes never once leaving hers. 'What would your other boyfriends say?'

Tracy and Michelle were watching, bemused and enthralled at what was being acted out in front of them.

'I *do* like your style,' she said. She was drinking a pint of lager top. When she sipped, an erotic trace of white foam stayed on her top lip. The glass was red with her lipstick.

She was from London, she told me, and, like Darren had worked at the Knoll House the previous year. They'd dated for a while, but apparently things worked better between them when they were just friends.

Like me, Janeen had no idea what it was that she wanted to do with her life. She told me about the unusual spelling of her name. 'My dad was such an idiot!' she said. 'They'd decided on my name, so he went off to the register office to register my birth. He doesn't have a clue how to spell Janine, so he just spells it like how he thinks it ought to be spelt: J-A-N-E-E-N. What a wally!'

She grabbed my hand. 'You're all right,' she said. 'Let's go to the snug.'

'The snug?'

'Yeah, we're gonna snog in the snug.'

'I'll bet you've never used that line before.'

Still holding my hand, she led the way to the back of the pub.

'Are you any good?' I asked.

'Me?' she crowed. 'I'm the best you've ever had!'

'And I've had a few.'

She turned and raised a suggestive eyebrow.

'I bet you have, you dirty beast.'

The snug was the smallest snug that I had ever been into. There was just enough room for a small curved banquette and a round wooden table. There were two candles on the table and it reeked of cigarette smoke.

A young couple were already on the banquette. I recognised them from the beach.

''Ere!' Janeen said. 'Richard, Anna, get your skinny arses out of here! We need this snug more than you do.'

It was all very good natured. 'Anything for the king of the skinny-dippers,' Richard said. He was slight, with a central parting and a thick unruly mop of hair. He shook my hand as he walked out of the snug. 'Don't do anything I wouldn't do.'

Janeen cackled. 'So everything's up for grabs, right?'

Anna smiled as she stepped out of the snug. She had a lovely smile, but I rarely heard her speak. Of all the staff, Anna was the shyest.

Janeen and I squeezed past the table and onto the leather banquette. The walls were dark, all but black in the candlelight. Janeen's thigh was pressed tight to mine. She clapped her hand on my knee.

'The snug,' she said.

'And the snog?'

There was no build up, no elusive pecking as her lips roamed round mine, no gentle glide from kisses to open-mouthed abandon.

She kissed me hard on the mouth, her tongue immediately wet between my lips. I don't know what perfume she wore, but if I were to smell it now, it would be immediately underpinned with the tang of crisps and the smell of smoke and beer.

Janeen was all over me, her hands quickly working their way under my shirt, bludgeoning me with her open red lips. It was surprisingly unerotic. It might perhaps have been many men's ultimate fantasy, to be ravaged by this houri within moments of meeting her. But as we kissed, I found that I was strangely dispassionate, not so much aroused as curious as to what would happen next. How far would she go? How far would I go? Would she want to sleep with me that very night – and if so, would I go through with it? Did I even want to sleep with her? I didn't know.

I had had my eyes closed, concentrating on the texture of Janeen's lips against my own. I opened them. Janeen's eyes were already open. Inches apart, we stared at each other. She broke off and drank more lager.

She ruffled my hair. 'I am the best, aren't I?'

I said the only thing that could be said, 'You are the best.'

'You know what I figure?' she said. 'We could have pussyfooted around. But at the end of it all, I fancy you, you fancy me, so why not just get on with it?'

'A good philosophy,' I said. 'So does that mean we're going to bed later too?'

'You *are* a dirty beast.' Another wet kiss. 'I don't normally sleep with guys I've only just met. But seeing as you asked so nicely…'

'You'll make an exception for me?'

'God, I love kissing you.' She straddled me, her knees on the banquette and her blonde hair hanging in a light curtain about our cheeks.

'You don't like kissing me. You just like kissing,' I said.

'I can like both, can't I?'

'Course you can.' I slipped my hands under her T-shirt and my fingers roamed about her back. 'So along with being an A-grade kisser, are you also an A-grade lover?'

She smiled at me, wicked, taunting. 'What do you think, my dirty, dirty, little beast?'

'Well…' I let the word drag out. 'You're not a virgin. At least, I don't think you are.'

'Dirty,' she said, kissing me again. 'So very, very dirty.'

'I'm not dirty,' I said. 'I'm just cheeky.'

I think I was enjoying the banter more than the actual kissing. Was it possible that I would be able to laugh her into bed with me? I was thinking about it very clinically. It's not that I wanted to have sex with Janeen, but I didn't not want it either. I was curious. I had never once come close to sleeping with a woman that I'd only just met. So, from that point of view at least, I was up for it. It was something new and fresh and untried and therefore, almost by definition, had to be experienced.

I idly looked over Janeen's shoulder. Darren was staring at us. He was drinking a pint of lager and just standing there watching us. I had not seen him since we'd left him at the hotel to go swimming.

'Don't look now,' I whispered in Janeen's ear. 'Darren's watching the floor show.'

She turned round and gave him the finger. 'Haven't you got anything better to do than watch us snog?'

He glowered, drank more lager and walked off.

'Bless,' Janeen said. 'He can be really sweet.'

'Just jealous,' I said. 'I bet once upon a time, it was him who you were snogging in the snug.'

'Right where you're sitting now,' she said. 'Though snogging was only the half of it.'

'Anyway, moving swiftly on.'

'Yes, what were we talking about?

'We were talking about your virginity,' I said. 'Did you really offer it up to me tonight?'

'Please don't be gentle with me.'

It was my turn to laugh. Normally, I'm the one with the rapier repartee, but Janeen could more than hold her own.

Oliver poked his head into the snug. 'At last I have found you!' he said. 'May I have the pleasure of buying you lost lovers something to drink?'

'You certainly can,' Janeen said. She wanted another lager top.

'A lager top?' he said. 'What is the top?'

'Lime cordial,' she said. 'Though blackcurrant's all right.'

'I will try it.' He shambled off to get the drinks.

We went back to kissing. Suddenly there was a terrific crash from the bar, followed immediately by the sound of shattering glass. Everything was still.

Janeen broke off and looked at me quizzically.

'Sounds like it'll be another few minutes before we get our drinks,' I said.

'You think that was Oliver?'

'Who else was it going to be?'

'What's he going to be like as a waiter?' she asked.

'It'll be interesting to watch.'

Janeen attacked my mouth again. The problem with this full-on kissing, and nothing but tongues and wet lips, is that it all becomes rather mechanical. You have an awareness of this shared intimacy, but after a while your mind starts to wander.

I remember thinking, Do I really want to make love with Janeen tonight? I was sure that she would be energetic, and doubtless depraved. I was not at all sure if it was what I wanted. One thing was beyond doubt: it was definitely a very bad move. Taking a new colleague off to bed on the very first day of work? It was nothing but the most feckless recklessness. But on the other hand, Janeen was sexy and up for it, and I was bitterly single and had been for many months, and to boil all my ambivalence down into just four little words. Why the hell not?

Oliver delivered our drinks. He was wearing another cardigan, yellow this time. It was wet and stained all down the front.

'Coming to join us?' said Janeen.

'Yes please.'

With Janeen now perched on my lap, legs to the side, there was just enough room for Oliver to sit next to us on the banquette. A candle toppled over as he squeezed past the table. I righted it.

I was pleased to see him. Kissing Janeen had been quite exciting, but in short order it had become monotonous.

'How you doing?' Janeen asked Oliver, stretching over and ruffling his hair.

He smiled good naturedly, as one might do towards the friendly overtures of a toddler.

'I love your glasses,' said Janeen. 'Can I try them?'

She put them on. 'God they're thick!' she said. 'I can't see a thing! You're as blind as a bat!'

Oliver continued to smile. 'They suit you, Janeen,' he said. 'They make you look very sophisticated.'

Janeen, struck a pose, her index finger light against her cheekbone. 'Like this?'

'Just like my old professor,' said Oliver.

'*Just* like her?' I asked.

'It was a man, actually, well over seventy years old, but the similarity with Janeen is quite striking.'

Janeen took off Oliver's glasses and started to play with them, swinging them between her fingers.

'So tell us, Oliver,' I said. 'What brings you to the Knoll House?'

'What do you think?' he said.

'It's obvious,' I said. 'You're the owner's love child, conceived during a week of passionate madness when he was stationed in Berlin. And now finally, after all these years apart, he wants to get to know his only son. Your mother has been in two minds about it for some time. Of course, she wants what's best for you and is eager for you to get to know your father, your real father. But she still worries about you. How will it be, you coming to Britain like this? Perhaps you will develop a passion for warm beer and pies. And she worries about herself too. Should she come over? Should she visit? What will it be like when, finally, she comes face to face with her one true love?'

Oliver tugged at his lower lip. 'How did you know?'

'It was when I saw you with the owner this afternoon, and the way that he shook you by the hand. As he turned away, there were tears in his eyes. I saw him wipe them away with his fingers.'

Oliver sighed as he steepled his fingers. 'It has not been easy for me, but with friends like you, Kim, and you, Janeen, I believe that this whole experience will be bearable.' He stretched out his long, angular arms and held our hands. 'Thank you, my friends.'

Janeen stared at Oliver, looked at me, and then stared at Oliver again. 'Do you two know each other?' she said.

'We're brothers,' Oliver said. 'Twins separated at birth. I was brought up in Berlin, while Kim was taken back to Britain to be raised by his father's older sister. She was a spinster who lived on the outskirts of London. So although we have never met before, we have an affinity. Instinctively we know what the other is thinking.'

'You're pulling my leg!' she said.

Oliver and I looked sombrely at each other, before breaking into a rich peel of laughter. We chinked our glasses. 'Cheers!'

'So what the hell are you doing here?' I asked.

'My father runs hotels,' he said. 'I wanted to learn about them in somewhere that was far, far away from home. And a good opportunity to improve my English.'

'Your English is already perfect,' I said.

'No, not yet,' he said. 'Though perhaps if I had an English girlfriend.'

'We'll soon sort you out,' said Janeen. 'Specially if you keep on buying drinks for all the staff.'

We joined the rest of the staff at the bar and continued drinking till late. Janeen stood next to me, thigh to thigh and with her arm proprietarily around my waist. I looked at her through fresh eyes. She was quite pretty, brazen and brash and so totally different from anyone else that I had ever dated. Now that the frenetic kissing had stopped, I was enjoying the warmth of her leg pressed to mine. I made up my mind. I was going to go for it. I fancied her. I fancied spending the night with her. What did I have to lose?

In life, I find that I tend to be thrown into one of two situations. The first is like a glacier; there is a grinding momentum to events. It doesn't matter what you do or what you say, nothing can change the slow inevitability of it all, and at times, it seems that the only thing that can end this inexorable grind is death itself. A marriage, a career, children, mortgages – these are the train tracks of our lives which can only be changed through the most incredible force of will. And as we get older, life on the train tracks becomes ever more enticing, and so depressingly difficult to leave.

In the other kind of situation, everything can turn on a sixpence. It does not happen so often now that I am married and middle aged. But there was a time, once, in my youth when but for a misplaced word or a single false step, things would have turned out quite, quite differently.

I never did sleep with Janeen.

As it happens, it all hung on just a few silly little words that happened to burble out of her good-natured mouth.

She'd just been off to the toilets with one of her girlfriends. They came back giggling. The rest of the staff were getting ready to leave. Janeen had a packet of vending machine condoms. She waved them above her head. 'Look who's pulled tonight!' she said.

A cheer went up around the pub. Roland wolf-whistled and the Knoll House staff glanced at me, thinking I know not what.

I do not embarrass easily, but I blushed. Janeen came over to me and, as if picking up her prize from the tombola stall, she slipped her arm through mine and kissed me. Her red lipstick stayed on my cheek. I had been sold to Janeen and she had made her mark on me.

Oliver was inscrutable. 'Would you first like a nightcap?'

I was drunk and on the very verge of taking Janeen back to bed. But from all the madness of the storm, it was like I had glimpsed the gleam of a lighthouse in the night. All at once, I could see the shattered ships that had already smashed themselves to pieces on the rocks.

I looked at Oliver and then I looked at Janeen who now, in the bright light of the bar seemed blowsy compared to that succubus in the snug.

'I'd love one,' I said.

I loosed Janeen's hand from my arm and kissed her on the cheek. 'Thanks for a fun evening.'

'But it's not over yet!' she said.

'I'm all in tonight,' I said. 'But another time…'

'There's never going to be another time.'

'Well.' I stroked her cheek. 'It's been fun anyway.'

We walked back in clusters, Janeen with Darren, while I padded along beside Oliver. The road was not lit and we were enveloped by tendrils of moist mist.

'About that drink,' I said.

'Yes, I must get some more Armagnac,' he said. 'And some more brandy too. I'm afraid it's all been drunk.'

'So there never was any nightcap?'

'No,' he said. 'It was the best I could think of at the time.'

I looked at him, face forwards, striding stolidly into the darkness. Realisation dawned. Sleeping with Janeen on the first day that I'd met her would have been bad, a disaster. It would have been like opening all the stopcocks on board ship just as I was setting sail out to sea.

'Thanks,' I said.

'You are welcome,' he said. For a while we walked in silence. I liked the sound of the gravel underneath our boots. 'She is very pretty.'

'She'll have lots of boyfriends.'

'If that is the case, you are better to set yourself apart.'

'Untouchable. An iceberg.'

'I am told that women are most attracted to what it is they cannot have.'

I snorted. 'Just like the rest of us then.'

I wondered if it was part of our hard wiring. From our earliest years, we hear our mothers say that we can't have something –

whether it's a chocolate or a toy – and from that moment it becomes an obsession. From mere mild curiosity, we suddenly long for this forbidden fruit more than anything else in the world. I find this business of desire all so unfathomable. What is it that makes me swoon one moment and feel entirely indifferent the next? They call it chemistry, but even now, after I have fallen in love many times over, I still have no inkling what it is that creates this elusive alchemy.

CHAPTER 5

Anthony gave each of the knives a polish with his napkin and placed them side by side on the table. He examined the two forks and the spoon before also positioning them on the table. A white napkin was folded and placed onto a side plate. He held the wine glass up to the light and that was also inspected before being placed on the table.

We watched, committing all these little details to memory. For the first time we were in our hotel uniforms, black trousers and white tunics. Some of the waiters felt embarrassed at having to wear this label of servitude. But after a lifetime of school uniform, it was like slipping back into a pair of comfortable old slippers. I liked the tunic and I liked the name tag. I had admired myself in the bathroom mirror. It was a good cut and I looked sleek.

The faces of the waiters and waitresses were a perfect study. Some, like Oliver, were devouring every detail. The old hands, like Janeen and Darren, were standing at the back. I noticed how his hand strayed to her bottom. She moved it away, but smiled all the same. I was lurking somewhere in the middle, feigning interest, as I quietly sized up the women. Michelle was sweet; Tracy was pretty; Janeen was almost sexy. I can't really put my finger on it, but her looks and her hair had this synthetic quality, appealing from afar, but up close it left me cold. I was relieved that I had not slept with her. There were some other women I liked. But no one left me weak at the knees.

'We got that?' asked Anthony. 'The cutlery and the glassware has to be spotless. If it isn't, you don't just dump it back in the cutlery box. You go and clean it!'

As one, we nodded. At lunchtime, we were going to be given our first dry run. A number of locals, friends of the management, had been invited over for a cheap lunch. It was considered to be a safer way of introducing us to fine dining rather than inflicting us straight onto the paying customers.

We were allocated our stations. I was given a number of tables in the corner of the room, set by the windows. Even at a glance, I could see that they were the best tables in the house, with views out over the coast. The best table of all was directly in the corner. With your back to the wall, you looked out at the entire dining room, while out of the windows you had a commanding view of the gardens and the sea.

'This is Enid Blyton's table,' Anthony said. 'She was a regular here with her husband. He was a keen golfer.'

'Who sits here now then?' I asked.

'Wait and see,' he said. 'But let us just say people with high expectations. Such clientele as may be looking for that little bit more.'

'The awkward squad?'

'It'll be your job to make sure they stay happy. Be polite, but not servile. Smile, but without being unctuous. Chat charmingly, but without being overfamiliar. Engage with the clientele, but know when to shut up. And flirt with the girls if you must, but do please, Kim, kindly refrain from sleeping with them.'

'At least in the hotel.'

'And also out of it.' He adjusted some of the cutlery that I had already laid out. 'Leave enough room for the side plates.'

'We set the vegetables in a bowl in the middle and let them help themselves,' he continued. 'You can try silver service if you like, but practice by yourself first of all.'

By chance, his eyes happened to rest on Oliver, who was diligently laying up some of the window tables next to mine. He was placing the cutlery with the most fervent concentration, peering at each knife, each fork, before placing them very precisely onto the table.

Anthony shook his head. 'He means well, that boy,' he said. 'But I'm not sure the dining room is for him.'

'He's eager,' I said.

'I know that!' said Anthony. 'Perhaps if we gave him a trolley…
there might be less chance of him doing himself a mischief.'

'Or the customers.'

Oliver gave the table one last critical survey, before spotting a
smudge on one of the side plates. He snatched up the plate and
polished it with a dishcloth from his belt. His cuff flicked one of the
glasses. It bounced off a chair and fell to the floor, but miraculously
did not smash.

Anthony winced as he walked away. He called out over his
shoulder. 'Oliver! Well done! Good job! You've got it!'

We had an hour to ourselves before lunch. I went out to the
playground and sat on one of the swings. Very gently, I started to
swing. My feet scuffed in the play bark. I wondered if my mother had
ever pushed me on that swing when I was younger.

I wondered if I was going to enjoy working at the hotel.

'Can I join you?'

'Of course,' I said, without turning round. It was one of the maids
and when I looked at her, I saw that it was the pretty blonde woman
who had been chatted up by Darren the previous day.

'Hi,' she said. 'I'm Annette.'

'Kim,' I said. 'Enjoying Studland?'

'It beats Sweden.'

'I've never been to Sweden. I've always wanted to go.'

'And I've always wanted to leave.' We were both swinging in
tandem. She was like a carefree young girl. 'Why do you want to go
to Sweden?'

'The women are so beautiful.' I caught her eye, and there was just
enough edge on my voice for it to glide from the cheesy to the ironic.

Annette laughed. She was beautiful. What a gorgeous moment,
swinging in the spring sun with that beautiful Swede by my side.

'Why did you want to leave Sweden?' I asked.

'The men,' she said. 'So ugly.'

'I'll bet they are.'

'And over in England…'

'The men aren't much better,' I said.

'You said it!'

We both laughed. Although her English was perfect, Annette had that delicious hurdy-gurdy accent that can only come from Scandinavia.

'Tough break,' I said. 'You come all the way over to England searching for fit guys, and all you find is—'

'That I have jumped straight out of the frying pan into the furnace,' she said.

'Why aren't you working in the dining room?' I said.

'All the jobs had gone,' she said. 'But I like it with the maids.'

'Don't have to mix with the men.'

'So ugly!'

'Particularly that guy who was asking you to the pub yesterday.'

'Yes!' she said. 'He was bad!' She looked at me meaningfully. 'But there are many men here who are much worse!'

I laughed. I was so happy, swinging with her in the sun. I looked at her bare legs, and the way her dress clung to her thighs.

An open-top Mercedes sports car, sky blue, was cruising past the playground. There were two women inside. The driver had brown hair and sunglasses, while her companion was a blonde with a red beret.

'Must be coming up to lunchtime,' I said.

Annette waved as I wandered out of the playground. By chance I happened to leave just as the two women were getting out of their car. They were both about forty and chic. The driver, a brunette, was the more understated in a suede skirt and a light top. She had a warm, open face. She was laughing. Her blonde passenger was wearing a tight black skirt and a ruffled blouse in shocking pink. They were on the forecourt when Anthony bustled outside to greet them. He kissed them both before leading them in. His hand was cupped very lightly on the brunette's back.

In the dining room, there was an anticipatory hum as we waited for the first guests. Black shoes gleamed with new polish. Trousers were pressed, tunics pristine. I rubbed my hands together. They were wet with sweat. Oliver was standing by the windows looking out to the sea, his hands behind his back. His Adam's apple bobbled in his throat.

'I have never done this before,' he said. 'My father would not allow it.'

'You're going to be fantastic,' I said.

'I am very clumsy. I smash things.'

'You'll be fine. They'll think it's all part of the show.'

The first diners were coming into the room. Anthony escorted them to their tables. A young family from Swanage was given a table by the windows. The children were on best behaviour.

I gave them a minute to settle and then went over with some menus. I smiled, cheery, effusive. 'Welcome to the Knoll House Hotel,' I said. It was perhaps a little formal, but I stuck with that opening line for the rest of my time there.

I fetched them bread and a jug of water, and milk for the children and a bottle of Sancerre for the parents. I poured the wine, giving the bottle a twist to stop the drips. The man tasted it. 'Lovely,' he said. I filled the two glasses.

Anthony had been watching me from the central station. 'Very nicely done, Kim,' he said. 'Let me introduce you to some diners. I would like you to look after them.'

They were the two women who I'd seen earlier in the sky-blue Mercedes. They were already sitting at Enid Blyton's table. The brunette was sitting with her back to the wall. She had a light smile as we walked over; she was interested in everything and everyone.

'Ladies, this is Kim. He'll be looking after you today. Kim, this is Greta.' The woman with the blonde hair shook my hand. She had a tight, bird-like face, quite angular. 'Hi Kim,' she said.

'And this' – was there a beat just then, or is it my imagination? – 'is Cally.'

Cally smiled at me. She looked playful, fun. Up close, I would have said she was in her late thirties. No rings on her fingers. She was wreathed in a halo of confidence.

'Hi Greta, hi Cally,' I said. We all looked at each other. I wasn't quite sure if it was a social situation or whether I should be getting on with my job. 'Can I get you the wine list?'

'We'll have a bottle of the house champagne,' Cally said. She was English, not country, but she was not City either; she could glide easily between the two. 'Thank you, Kim.'

I walked away with Anthony. He was pleased and laid a hand on my shoulder. I could hear Greta laughing behind us. I couldn't put my finger on it, but there was something quite brazen about her. The other woman, Cally, was the kinder of the two.

I filled a wine cooler with ice and took it out to the table with two champagne flutes. The champagne was in the fridge. I took the bottle and proffered it to the ladies. 'Thank you,' Cally said.

They watched in silence as I peeled back the foil. I unscrewed the cork wire and, very gently, eased off the cork. It hissed as it popped and a trace of white vapour flickered around the neck. I caught a whiff of the champagne. I would have liked to have had a glass myself.

'You've done this before,' Greta said.

'Many times.' Since it was house champagne, I didn't offer them a taste. I poured an inch of champagne into each glass. When the fizz ebbed, I topped up the glasses.

'So do you have a girlfriend?' Greta said. A smile was playing on her lips as she stared at me.

'I don't have a girlfriend,' I said, looking at her steadily. 'Do you have a boyfriend?'

'No, I don't,' she said. 'Are you offering?'

'Are you asking?'

I don't think Greta had expected such a lively interchange. I glanced for a moment at Cally. She wanted nothing to do with this little game. She sipped her champagne and stared out of the window.

'You're probably way too young for me,' Greta said. 'But champagne does make me very randy.'

Again I looked at Cally. She seemed quite serene, oblivious to her friend's banter. She did not look at me.

The two women each had a crab salad. I offered them bread rolls but they did not want any. The dining room was fast filling up. There was no time for any more easy banter.

I remember it being like an endless conveyor belt of little tasks, constantly juggling from one thing to the next. I had about seven tables in all and would scurry from one to the next trying to keep my charges happy: the young family wanted more bread for the boy; the old couple by the window were still waiting for their starters; another family needed their plates cleared before they descended on the pudding table; and in the corner of my eye, I glimpsed Greta waving the empty bottle of champagne above her head.

When I took over the second bottle of champagne, Greta had disappeared to the restrooms. Cally was sitting very easily at the table, her chin upon her hand, watching me in silence.

'What are you doing here?' she said.

'I don't know,' I said. 'I'm marking time.'

'All your university friends are working in London.' I noticed her fingers for the first time. They were strong, powerful hands and flecked with paint. For a moment her hand strayed to her mouth before she touched her neck.

'They are working in London,' I said.

'But you don't want to go because you don't know what to do.'

I laughed as I worked at the cork. 'I didn't know you knew my stepmother.'

'You're different from the other waiters here.'

I suddenly realised why her fingers were flecked with paint. 'So what's it like being the local artist?'

She smiled easily and looked down at her hands. 'Very good,' she said. 'You're going to do well.'

The cork popped and I made to fill her glass. 'Not for me, thank you,' she said. 'Drinking at lunch always kills the afternoon.'

Looking back, I wonder if, even at that very early stage, there was a frisson between us. I think I liked her. I wanted to impress her. And I definitely found her beautiful; age, as I have already said, is irrelevant to beauty. If you've got it, you've got it. But there was also an awareness that Cally was unattainable. She was out of my league.

I could sense that my other guests were all clamouring for my attention. But I wanted to talk to Cally.

'What will you be doing this afternoon?' I said.

'Just painting,' she said. 'At teatime I'll go for a ride.'

'What do you paint?' I leaned over the table and filled her glass with water.

'Animals,' she said. 'Humans. Anything that moves. If you want a still life, take a photo.'

'And the paintings sell well?'

'They do, as it happens.' She smiled her secret smile. 'One day I'll paint you.'

'I don't think I'd be a very good model.'

'I think you'd be perfect.'

Greta bustled up to the table. 'More champagne!' she said. She had put on fresh scarlet lipstick and, I think, more mascara. 'I'd love some.'

I poured her a glass. She nearly drank it in one. Her lipstick stuck to the glass.

'Will you join us in a glass, Kim?' she said.

'I don't think Anthony would approve of me drinking on the job.'

'Go on, be a devil.'

Cally was again looking out of the window. 'Ease up, Greta,' she said. 'It's his first day.'

'Yes, you're right,' Greta said. 'Always too eager. Always have been, always will.' She took the champagne from the ice bucket and poured herself another glass. She was already drunk.

'Could we have two espressos, please?' Cally said.

'I want to come back here,' Greta said. 'Can we come back here soon?'

There was no more time to talk. Cally paid the bill in cash and left a huge tip, though the money wouldn't be going to me. All tips were pooled. Greta was clutching onto Cally's arm as they walked out. They had left half a bottle of champagne. As they went out, Cally caught my eye and gave me a little wave. I raised a hand and smiled.

My other diners gradually drifted away. I marvelled at how small children would not touch a thing and then would suddenly come alive when they saw the puddings, pounding through mound upon mound of cream and chocolate. I was down to my last couple, an elderly pair, who were stolidly working their way through a vast lunch. The man had a large piece of Dover sole and was eating it in the daintiest mouthfuls. I watched him for a while. After every mouthful, he would meticulously place his knife and fork on the plate, and would either say something to his wife, or would sip some water or some wine; it was like watching a soldier ant chew its way through a fig leaf. There was a certain fascination in watching the whole laborious process.

Oliver was floundering. All his six tables were still seated. He was at a table of a family of five and was only just clearing away their starter plates. I winced as I saw him try to clear one of the plates at the table. A piece of potato flicked onto one of the children's laps.

'Can I give you a hand?' I asked.

'Please.' He looked hot and harassed.

'I'll get stuck in.'

I left him to his family of five and started working the other tables.

'How are we doing?' I asked a middle-aged couple. 'Are you all right for drinks?'

'We've been waiting for our main course for the past forty minutes,' the man said. I knew the type very well – tweedy jacket and bright yellow cords, set off by a check shirt and a regimental tie. It was staple fare for ex-army officers. I would have put him down as a major.

'I'll see how they're getting on,' I said.

The man barely grunted a thank you when I returned with their two steak and kidney pies. He muttered to his wife, 'About time.'

A more polite waiter might have left it at that. I've never been very good at being polite.

'I'm very sorry,' I said. 'Were you not aware that the hotel has only just opened today, and that this is the first meal that we've served this year? Were you not warned that many of the staff are virgins, and you, I'm afraid, are the guinea pigs.' I decided to take a shot in the dark. I'd seen the way that he'd tucked his napkin into his collar. He *had* to be a major. 'Though I understand, *Major*, that it is rather good value.'

The man goggled at me. He had already picked up his knife and fork. A large piece of meat and pie was already hanging on his fork, poised a few inches from his toad-like lips.

'Was I talking to you?' he asked.

'If not, then my apologies, Major,' I said. 'If there's anything more that you should require, just give me a wave and I shall scurry over.'

I'd nearly over-cooked it.

The major looked at me with pouchy wine-soaked eyes. He didn't know what to make of it. His wife was concentrating on her pie, like a little chicken pecking at corn on the ground. Her hair was big and blonde and immaculately coiffed, freshly blow-dried that morning.

I thought at first that the man was going to put his fork down and attempt to berate me. The forkful of pie hung there and then greed won out and he stuffed the fork into his mouth.

'Bon appétit!' I said.

I cleared away some plates from another family's table. The rest of the dining room was almost empty. Oliver was ponderously returning into the dining room with another batch of main meals. Very sensibly he had decided only to carry two plates at a time; the more efficient waiters were like a circus act and could carry plates and bowls all the way up their arms.

I was fetching some water for another of Oliver's couples when I heard a small detonation going on at the central station. It was Anthony.

'What are you doing here?' He was speaking to Darren and Janeen and a few other waiters. His voice was tight and clipped. 'Can't you see that Oliver needs a hand?'

'We thought he needed the practice,' Darren said.

'Don't be ridiculous. You've been here for over a year; Oliver's only just started. Both of you should know better.'

Anthony clapped me on the shoulder. 'Good stuff.'

Oliver's tables were suddenly inundated with waiters. Oliver was still chugging away, but now it seemed as if there were two waiters to every guest. Plates were whisked away as soon as the last scrap had been eaten.

There was one table, however, which I was keen to keep for myself.

'And how was your Cake and Sidney pie?' I asked the major.

He removed the linen napkin from his collar and patted at his lips.

'What did you say?' he asked.

I beamed at him. 'How was your pie?' I asked. 'Was it nice and tasty?'

He was not at all sure how to deal with this bouncing irreverence. He continued to pat at his lips, wondering what he could say to put me in my place. I squared my shoulders, leaning back slightly, hands behind my back. Give me your best shot.

'Take these plates away,' he said.

'Of course,' I said. 'That would be my absolute pleasure. Will you try some pudding?' The woman was staring at me. Had anyone ever tweaked her husband's tail like this before? 'I hear the sweets are…' I paused and glanced at the woman, winking at her, 'absolutely yummy.'

The man looked at me. I could practically see the steam venting from his ears, but what could he do? Call over the manager and complain about my language when, to all intents and purposes, I had been nothing other than a model of cheesy deportment.

He threw his napkin on the table. 'Come on,' he said to his wife, stalking off to the pudding table. She smiled at me nervously, as if uncertain what to make of this bizarre creature who had come to torment her husband.

Later, I presented the couple with their bill. I think that after three courses, plus two bottles of wine, plus coffee and mints, the entire meal came to around £15. It was an absolute steal.

The man left a tenner and a fiver on the table. No tip.

I beamed at the major as he tugged his Burberry scarf tight around his neck. 'No tip for naughty Kim?'

He stood there by the table, still adjusting his scarf. 'Once upon a time, I'd have had you thrashed.'

'I thought "once upon a time" was only for fairy tales, Major.'

The major's wife stared at me. 'You are naughty,' she said. Did I detect a hint of a smile?

The major put on his hat, a brown trilby. 'He is an impertinent young jackanapes.'

'I wish you joy of the day, Major.' I gave him my most beatific smile. 'I do so hope that you'll be able to come back soon.'

I watched the pair as they tramped out of the dining room. The major's wife was trying to take his arm, but he was having none of it.

They were almost the last guests to leave. Anthony sidled up to me.

'What was all that about?' he asked.

'What was all what about?' I gazed at Anthony with innocent eyes.

'You haven't already started upsetting the natives?'

'Me?' I said. 'On my first day in the hotel?'

'Oh God,' he said. A tone of amused resignation. 'They're regulars in here, you know. They come in every Thursday.'

'After madam has had her blow-dry in Swanage?'

'That's right,' Anthony said.

'And who are they?'

'Major Steven Loveridge,' he said, 'formerly of the Blues and Royals, and his long-suffering wife, Jemma.'

'So he is a major!' I was delighted. 'It would be a very great pleasure if, in future, I could wait at their table.'

'You?' Anthony said.

'Thank you,' I said.

Not a bad afternoon's work for my first day at the Knoll House; but the major was, of course, only the hors d'oeuvres.

CHAPTER 6

I spent the afternoon serving cold potatoes and cold vegetables to Oliver.

He sat at Enid Blyton's table with a starched white napkin on his lap. In front of him was a pot of Earl Grey with china cup and saucer, two slices of lemon, four slices of white bread, some butter and a pot of strawberry jam. He was always a very fastidious eater and I remember in particular the way that he would spread his butter so that every last square millimetre of bread had been equally covered. Only then would he put on the jam. It was his own pot of jam and expensive. The bread would then be quartered and he would eat it without a single crumb falling onto his lap; this fine dining was in such odd contrast to his general cack-handedness.

'Would sir like some potatoes?' I asked.

Oliver looked up from his bread and jam. 'Yes, I would, thank you, Kim,' he said. 'I would like that crisp little one on top and then that big cold potato right at the bottom.'

'Coming right up.'

I manoeuvred the fork and spoon like a pair of pincers and deftly scooped the small potato onto Oliver's plate. The large potato was more difficult. The technique of silver service is similar to using two rather unwieldy chopsticks. For a moment I thought I had the potato, but then it flicked onto the floor.

Oliver continued to sip his tea. 'I think it is much easier than you are making it look,' he said.

I retrieved the potato and returned it to the bowl. 'Would you like to have a go?'

'Not for me, no,' said Oliver. 'I like putting the vegetables on the table. And the guests, they like to help themselves.'

'Some do; some don't,' I said. 'But if any of our classier guests want Kim's silver service, then I'll be able to provide it.'

Oliver looked at his watch. It was past five. 'You have already given it an hour,' he said. 'And so far you have had eight potatoes on the carpet, as well as the entire bowl of carrots—'

'I'm lucky to have you to practise on.'

'Who was that girl you were talking to in the playground before lunch?'

'What big eyes you have.' I was trying to pick up baby carrots one at a time with the fork and spoon. It had never occurred to me that silver service would be quite so difficult.

'Who was she?'

'Her name's Annette. She's from Sweden.'

'Annette!' he said with satisfaction. 'I like that name. She is very pretty. She is exactly the sort of girl that I would like to date.'

'Don't want to crush your hopes, Oliver, but she said she only came to Britain because she's fed up with dating ugly men.'

'No,' Oliver said. He screwed the top tight onto the jam pot. 'A beautiful woman like that is not interested in a man's looks. She will be attracted to a man's character, to his soul.'

'I hope so.' Another potato tumbled to the floor. The problem came in exerting just the right amount of pressure. Too soft, and the potato would just drop to the floor; too much, and it would ping across the table. It required not just dexterity but very soft hands. As it turned out, it would take me another fortnight to master silver service. It has stood me in good stead ever since; women do like to see the occasional display of proficiency in a man.

Just like the previous night, we all had an early supper of pasta. At seven, Anthony was giving us our final pep talk before we were unleashed onto real paying punters. He had us huddled in the middle of the dining room. We watched longingly as the sous-chefs wheeled out the puddings.

'We're a team,' Anthony said. He was in full dinner jacket and bowtie, quite the captain of the ship. 'That means that we share all the tips, that we start in the dining room together and that we leave it together. So if you can see that another waiter is under pressure, then you go over and give them a hand, rather than just standing here gossiping with each other.' He gave a theatrical roll of his eyes, gazing at each of us in turn. 'And if it's you who's under pressure, then ask for some help. That's what you do when you're on a team.' By chance, he happened to be looking at Oliver.

'So go to, my friends; let's have some fun.'

The waiters and waitresses started to disperse. 'Oh Kim,' said Anthony. He crooked a finger towards me. 'A word in your shell-like?'

Hand on my shoulder, he led me off to a quiet corner of the dining room. I wondered if the major had already issued a formal complaint.

'How are you enjoying yourself, Kim?' he asked.

'Very much, thank you.'

'Now, tonight,' he said. 'A little bit of a star will be joining us for the weekend. He is a ladies' man. I am hoping you will be able to handle him.'

'I'll do my best,' I said. 'Who is he?'

'He is a rock star.' And then he told me the name. Of course, I knew all about Ed McKenny. He was a household name. I even liked a couple of his songs. He had been married at least twice and had several children.

'Okay.' I can't say I was overly impressed. Perhaps intrigued at the prospect of waiting on a rock star for three or four days, but awestruck? Absolutely not.

'Now I want you to treat him just like any other guest in the hotel,' Anthony said.

'Fine.'

'Except… be careful.'

'Be careful?'

'Exactly. Be careful.'

'Okay, I'll be careful.' I had no idea what Anthony was alluding to, but I supposed that he was trying to tell me that Ed McKenny was, like most rock stars, as mad as a hatter.

'Great,' Anthony said, rubbing his hands together. 'By the way, watch McKenny with the waitresses. Don't let them anywhere near him. Oliver can work on his table. You can work on his table. But nobody else goes near him.'

'Why's that?'

'Because I know what he's like.'

'Okay,' I said. 'Just me working on the table, and Oliver if we want a bowl of boiled potatoes thrown into his lap.'

'You've got it.'

The rest of the staff stared at me as I joined them in the middle of the dining room. 'What was all that about?' Darren said.

'Nothing,' I said. 'He said my waiting skills had been exemplary.'

'So what did he say?' Tracy asked.

'Told me to stop flirting with all the waitresses. I said I just couldn't resist myself.'

Michelle looked at me. 'Did he really say that?'

Darren rolled his eyes. And the first of our proper paying guests came into the dining room.

There was a nice edge to that evening. The guests were excited at coming down to the Knoll House for the first day of their Easter break and the staff were eager to be put through their paces. That first night, there was a lot of champagne being drunk.

I'd had about four of my tables in and was pouring out some house red when I sensed this frisson go round the room. There was a lull in the general hubbub. I noticed my guests' gaze drift towards the entrance of the dining room. I knew immediately that my rock star had arrived. I finished pouring the wine and left the bottle on the table.

Anthony was escorting Ed McKenny to his table. The star was with three other people and his every move was being covertly watched by at least half the room.

Anthony drifted towards me as he went off to welcome the next batch of guests. 'Go to, Kim.'

I gathered up four menus and went over to the Enid Blyton table. 'Good evening,' I said. 'Welcome to the Knoll House Hotel.' I gave them a warm smile and looked at them all in turn. There were two teenagers, a boy and a girl, who I guessed were McKenny's children. They were quite trendily dressed and the girl was pretty. She was about eighteen and she smiled at me. There was also a toned young woman with a blonde bob, in her twenties. She wore a very short skirt and was dressed for a holiday in Barbados rather than a chilly Easter break in Dorset; she was gorgeous and moody and she took the menu without looking up. I looked at McKenny. It was the first time that I had ever seen a rock star up close. He was in his late forties, taller than I expected and quite trim. I remembered that in his time he'd been a martial arts fighter; he would periodically beat up any members of the paparazzi who had vexed him. McKenny had spent a lot of time on his hair, a thick thatch of black, which had been teased and tweaked until it looked as if he had been dragged through a hedge backwards. His face was lined, craggy – ravaged from too many drugs and drink and women and whatever other ways that McKenny had found to abuse his body. He was wearing yellow sunglasses. He looked at my name tag.

'Hi Kim,' he said. 'You're going to be looking after us?'

'Certainly am, sir.'

He pulled out an expensive black leather wallet from his jacket and opened it. He proffered two £50 notes to me. 'That's for taking good care of us,' he said.

I smiled. 'There's really no need,' I said. 'I'll look after you just fine, even without the tip.'

'No, take the money.' Again, he thrust the notes at me.

'Give it to the boss, if you like,' I said.

'It's for you.'

'It's fine, honestly.'

I was aware that we were going through a little power play. I did not want to immediately put myself in the position of being one of McKenny's lackeys.

He took back the notes and stuffed them into his pocket. 'Do you know who I am?'

'I do, Mr McKenny.'

'Call me Ed, then.'

'I'll call you Ed, then. Can I get you anything to drink?'

'I want a bottle of vintage Krug, if you've got it.'

'We certainly had it,' I said. 'We may have had a run on the vintage Krug tonight. If we don't have any, I'll see what I can rustle up.'

McKenny took off his odd little glasses and looked at me. Sizing me up.

'See what you can rustle up.'

The other staff, particularly the waitresses, were agog to know what Mr McKenny had said to me. 'He's so gorgeous,' Janeen said.

'I wish I was waiting on his table,' Tracy said.

'You wouldn't like him up close,' I said. 'Horribly lined. And he's wearing yellow sunglasses.'

'That's because he's a rock star,' Tracy said, moony-eyed as she gazed over into the corner. 'Rock stars can get away with any colour sunglasses they like.'

'Even at night.'

'I think he's got sensitive eyes,' Tracy said. 'I used to have his poster up on my bedroom wall. They're lovely hazel eyes. I used to kiss him on the lips before I went to sleep.'

'I don't want to spoil your fantasy, Tracy,' I said. 'But I'm not sure Ed has aged that well.'

'He's so sexy,' Michelle said.

Unlike the waitresses, the waiters were more circumspect. McKenny had what the rest of them all wanted: fame and glory and millions of pounds in the bank, as well as a sultry, brooding beauty of a girlfriend.

I'd found McKenny his bottle of vintage Krug and poured it without mishap. The next time we chatted was when I was clearing away their main courses. Like Oliver, I had decided to take away two plates at a time, rather than go through the messiness of stacking at the table. McKenny had hardly touched his fish; I don't think he'd even had a mouthful.

'Was everything all right?' I asked.

McKenny flicked his hand dismissively.

'What sort of music do you listen to?' he asked.

I stood there by the table with a plate in each hand. It was an unusual way to be holding a conversation. 'I like Beethoven. I like Mozart. But most of all, I like Bach.'

'Good old Johann Sebastian,' he said.

'Do you listen to much classical music?'

The reaction of the three other diners was interesting. McKenny's children were intrigued at how their dad was having a perfectly normal conversation with, of all things, a waiter. His lover looked at me for the first time – she really was extraordinarily beautiful – before staring out of the window. Her hands were exquisitely manicured and she wore a ring with a ruby that was the size of a hazelnut. How bored she seemed. What a waste: all that beauty, but no energy and not a spark of life to be seen. I wondered what they did for fun outside the bedroom.

'I do listen to classical music,' McKenny said.

I smiled. 'Wasn't one of your tunes based on a Beethoven sonata?'

'That's right.' He laughed. 'Didn't have to pay the bugger a penny in royalties!'

'Must be the way forward,' I said. 'If the tunes still hold up after two hundred years, then they're bound to be pretty catchy.'

McKenny poured himself another glass of Krug. They were already on their third bottle. I noticed that he ignored his lover's empty glass.

'Okay,' he said. 'Favourite tune of all time. Give me your top three.'

'Well-Tempered Clavier,' I said promptly. 'First book. Prelude Number 17.'

'I don't know that one,' he said. 'How does it go?'

I sang a little bit of the tune. McKenny's daughter smirked at her brother and then looked back at me. She was cute. I liked her.

McKenny nodded. 'There must have been a woman involved.'

'There's always a woman involved.'

'And your two other tunes?'

It was the first time that evening that I had seen McKenny animated. It was like watching an old snake slither from out of its rocky lair and slowly come to life as it basked in the morning sun.

'Mozart concerto for two pianos, Kirkel Number 448.'

'Kirkel 448? Remember that, Katie.' He nodded at his daughter. 'Another woman?'

'Yes,' I said. 'And for my last choice… Beethoven's Pastoral.'

'You didn't pick that just because you liked it?'

'No,' I said. 'It was my mother's favourite.'

'Ah,' he said, discerning the great shadow in my life. He added with surprising delicacy, 'Mums, God bless 'em.'

'Will you try any of the puddings?' I asked.

'The kids will,' said McKenny. 'I don't like sweet stuff any more. As I get older, I like my food sour and bitter and pungent.'

I could not resist myself. 'But you, however, stay as sweet as you always were.'

He laughed, genuinely laughed, and his son and daughter laughed with him. The girlfriend tapped her fingers on the rim of her side plate. She was still looking out of the window. I could see her reflection in the glass; she was looking at me. Did I detect a hint of a smile?

'I wish I had more people like you around me,' said McKenny. 'I could do with a court jester.'

'Give me a grand a day and I'm all yours.'

'I just might,' he mused. As I looked at him, I though how ghastly it must be to be a genuine superstar, forever gawked at by strangers and surrounded by sycophants telling you just exactly what it is that they think you want to hear.

'You couldn't get me a double espresso?' he said.

'Of course.'

The woman by the window turned to me. It was the first time that she'd looked at me. Thick mascara on the bluest eyes that I had ever seen. I don't think I can recall ever seeing such beauty up close before. Her skin was absolutely flawless. She was only three or four years older than me, but so out of my league that she might have been on another planet. Oddly enough, that was distinctly to my advantage. Normally I am tongue-tied when I am in the presence of great beauty. My thoughts are scrambled and my tongue is rendered into a piece of flopping gristle so that I am not even capable of uttering the few inanities that I do wish to say. But this woman was so unattainable that I wasn't even remotely cowed.

'Can I have an americano, please?' she said.

I had already placed her accent. She was from Texas.

'And an americano for the American,' I said.

There was a momentary intake of breath. 'You're good,' McKenny said.

'You're not so bad yourself, Ed.'

I went to get the coffees.

It was to be the start of an intense and candid relationship that I was to develop over the Easter weekend with McKenny. It was the first time that I had ever been on quasi-casually intimate speaking terms with a superstar. Who knows what, if anything, McKenny got out of it. Perhaps some wit and spark that was not to be found in the rest of his pampered life.

The next day was Good Friday and I was abruptly made aware of one of the more unpleasant aspects of working at the Knoll House: the early starts. How I hate early starts. I'd been out drinking again with Roland and Oliver, and had rolled into bed at twelve thirty.

I had to be up at six, and be shaven, scrubbed and fed by seven, which was when the dining room opened for breakfast. Oliver was bright eyed, bushy tailed – he had a phenomenal capacity for drink – but most of the waiters were looking rough at the edges. In all my time at the Knoll House, we never once learned to pace ourselves, but instead, night after night, would be out on the tiles till midnight. That is the true optimism of youth.

McKenny was one of the first people into the room. He was wearing drainpipe jeans and a tight white T-shirt. His hair, as the previous night, was all over the place.

He knew the drill and helped himself to some apple juice. When I went over to his table, he was reading an array of tabloid papers.

'Morning, Kim,' he said. 'How we doing?'

'Good morning, Ed,' I said. 'I'm fine.'

'What do you think of my girlfriend, then?'

'She doesn't say very much.'

He sipped his apple juice. 'No, Liz doesn't say very much.'

'Quite pretty though.'

'Not much fun.'

'Does Liz make you laugh?'

At this, McKenny really did laugh. It started off softly, just a little chuckle, and then he was laughing so hard that he had to put his juice down.

'Now that is a good question,' he said. 'Does Liz make me laugh? I'm not sure.'

'Oh well,' I said. 'I'm sure she has other qualities.'

McKenny was still mulling over my question. 'Has she ever made me laugh?' he said. 'You know, I don't think she has.'

'What a sorry state of affairs.'

'Not once, though, actually, there was the time she tripped over the cat and ended up covered in a jug of Bloody Mary. She was sitting there on the floor, with these bits of celery and lemon in her hair and a load of ice cubes in her lap. She hated it. Now that, that was funny.'

'Definitely one for the video camera.'

McKenny drummed at his lower lip. 'But has she ever made me laugh genuinely? Through something she's said?' He looked at me and gave a shake of his head. 'I don't think so.'

'Well,' I tried to sound emollient, 'a sense of humour is probably over-rated.'

'But…' He clapped his hand to his forehead. 'What the hell am I…' He trailed off. 'What am I doing with this woman?'

I shrugged, aware that it was probably best to keep my mouth shut. 'Get you some coffee?'

'Please.'

There was more banter that night. I had a very unusual role for a waiter. When I went to McKenny's table, they seemed to come alive.

I don't know whether the children were cowed or whether Liz was bored by her older lover, but the conversation only ever seemed to spark up when I was lingering there. At the end of the meal, McKenny tried to get me to sit down and join them for a brandy, but I was having none of it. Apart from anything else, I was still waiting at three other tables.

I got drunk that night and I got drunk the next night, same as I did every night at the Knoll House, and now we come to the crux, the moment upon which my whole story turns – and without it, who knows how it would all have turned out.

Easter Day, 1988, is a date I will never forget till the day I die.

Still fighting off my hangover, I was going through the motions in the dining room at breakfast. Once again, McKenny was alone and one of the first into the room. He was clutching onto the day's tabloids. It was his third breakfast in the hotel.

'Morning, Kim,' he said. 'You're looking rough. Have a good one last night?'

'I had an excellent one, thank you,' I said. 'Coffee?'

'Please,' he said. 'So where do you young spunks go drinking?'

'The local pub, the Bankes Arms.'

'Do you now?' he said. 'I might join you there.'

'It's not classy, you know.'

'I don't want classy. I've had it with classy. I want gritty. I want real.'

'What will Liz will make of it?'

'Yes.' He drummed out a tattoo on the table with his index fingers; it was actually quite impressive. I didn't know he could drum.

'I'll get that coffee.'

McKenny had two coffees and two slices of toast and though he seemed absorbed by his papers, he was forever breaking off and would stare sightlessly into his empty glass of apple juice. He beckoned me over.

'Kim,' he said. 'Me and Liz. What do you think?'

'You're a very handsome couple.'

'You ought to be a diplomat.'

'Probably got more chance of being a rock star.'

'Any idiot can be a rock star. You just need a large slice of luck.'

'True.' I picked up his empty plate and his glass. 'But you did ride your luck.'

'And look where it's got me.'

'I can think of worse places to be, and worse people to be with.'

He rolled his eyes. 'You don't know the half of it.'

McKenny waved as he left the dining room. My colleagues were suitably awed. 'I wonder what he's like in bed,' Janeen said.

'Dream on,' Darren said. 'Have you seen his girlfriend?'

'She's pretty enough,' Janeen said. 'But I know how to please a man.'

'Don't you just.' Darren lightly cupped Janeen's waist.

'How many lovers has he had?' Tracy asked.

I remembered what Casanova had once replied when asked the same question. 'Mille Deuce,' I said.

'What's that then?' said Tracy.

'Two thousand.'

'Two *thousand*?' Roland said.

'He might have doubled up on a few of them.'

'Lucky bastard,' Roland said.

'I'd still have him,' Janeen said. She was looking at the French polish on her fingernails. It was at least a week old and was well chipped. 'I've never had a star.'

'And when he's done, he could sing you one of his songs,' Darren said.

'Better than lighting up on a fag and blowing smoke in my face.' She glanced meaningfully at Darren.

I always used to enjoy the morning lull after breakfast. We'd have a coffee and read the papers and idle away our time sitting in the staff section of the dining room. In those first weeks, I was quite content to mooch around the hotel grounds, wander through the woods and revel in my new-found freedom. Of course, I still had to do my duty in the dining room, but outside those hours, I was free to do as I pleased, and not a soul to tell me otherwise.

That morning I'd been walking on the beach. It was blustery, the wind licking at the white caps. Two hardy swimmers had braced the sea, but most of the families were snug in their seaside huts. I loved those huts, and one in particular. They were much the same size as a large garden shed, though much more substantial, with walls and windows that were built to withstand the worst of the winter storms. The huts reflected the owners' vast array of tastes, some painted grey, and some pillar-box red, with the outside walls sometimes festooned with rocks and shells and flags and seaweed. The interiors were equally quirky. Some had beds, and sofas and tables and some had even converted the roof space into a mezzanine with just enough room for a low-slung bed. There'd also be a small gas cylinder for brewing up tea and toasting muffins. As I wandered along the beach, head down into the gale, hands thrust deep into my pockets, it looked like very heaven to be sitting in a deckchair on the porch of one of these little shanties, with the wind blowing hard, and the kettle bubbling merrily on the hob.

I found a shell. It was two halves of a beautiful scallop shell and the pearly insides gleamed in the grey light of that Easter Day morning. I put it into my pocket as a keepsake. I find the sea is a great leveller. It puts your life into focus, for as you look out at these waves that will roll on for all time and listen to the ever-same sound of the sea, you come to appreciate just how brief is that fleeting snap of time that we have on this earth. You realise that you shouldn't be wasting a moment of it.

I wanted a girlfriend. I wanted kisses and affection and drowsy sex in the afternoon. I wanted to love. I wanted to be held by a beautiful woman who would tell me, over and over again, that she loved me. I wanted little jokes and stupid names; I wanted to wake up with a beauty by my side and to have her look me in the eyes and tell me she loved me; more than anything, I wanted to be walking along that windy beach, holding the hand of my lover as we stared out to the sea and dreamed our impossible dreams.

I was aware that a song was hissing in the background of my brain and when I tuned in, I realised it was Freddie Mercury singing

'Find Me Someone to Love'. I wondered where I might find my love. Among the staff? The clientele? The local folk of Swanage and Studland with their seaside homes and their prying eyes?

I'd just put on my white tunic for the lunchtime session. The lunches were generally much more relaxed than the dinners, because most of the guests were on half-board and preferred to take a packed lunch and eat *al fresco*.

I was walking towards the staff entrance when I saw Liz, McKenny's girlfriend, sitting on a bench outside the hotel. She was wearing a black fur coat and was smoking a cigarette. By her side were two small quilted Chanel bags.

I very nearly continued on my way, but I realised that she was leaving and that I would not be seeing her again, so I went over. The smell of her cigarette smoke was mixed with the scent of her perfume and the salt tang of the sea.

For a while, we sat there. I wasn't looking at her. I was looking up towards the children's playground.

'I'm sorry you're leaving,' I said.

'Yes.' She took another drag on her cigarette. She was still wearing her ruby ring. She did not have any make-up on and she looked younger than when I'd seen her in the dining room.

'Are you going back to Texas?'

'I don't know,' she said. 'It won't take long to pack up in London, and then…' She trailed off. 'I don't know.'

'Well, I'm sorry,' I said. It all sounded rather lame.

Liz flicked the stub of her cigarette onto the ground and stubbed it out with her stiletto. 'Ed likes you, doesn't he?' she said.

I shrugged. 'I slightly amuse him.'

'It's strange, this whole love thing, isn't it?' she said. Liz stretched out her arms, interlocking her fingers. She held the stretch for a moment and then plunged her arms between her knees. 'One moment you know everything about each other. You know all the little intimacies. You know about the pets and the neighbours and the friends and the enemies. Then it's over. Suddenly everything stops.'

'You're much too young and much too pretty to be with a guy like Ed,' I said.

She looked at me and for the first time she smiled. What a gorgeous smile. I wish I'd told her that.

'I'm dirt poor,' she said. 'I want money. There's only one way I'm going to get it.'

'Do you love these guys?'

'You got a better reason for falling in love, Kim?'

She had a point.

'No,' I admitted. 'I don't have a better reason for falling in love. Though if you're looking for money, that's going to put me right out of the picture.'

I had never before tried such an impish line with such a beautiful stranger. I could not recommend it more. For great beauties are used to having men in their thrall. It is almost as if they expect their male acquaintances to be fawning and tongue-tied, so that when they're confronted by a piece of cheekiness, they find it oddly refreshing. Liz looked at me out of the side of her eyes and lit up another cigarette.

'I guess it does,' she said with a smile. 'But if you were rich…' She paused, the smoke trailing from her nostrils, 'then I'd be all over you.'

I laughed. 'I'll bear you in mind when I've made my fortune.'

'At least I can smoke again,' she said. 'Ed always hated smoking. Typical. He used to be on sixty a day. Now he has a fit if a cigarette comes within fifty yards of him.'

A blacked out limo pulled up outside the front of the hotel. Liz stood up. 'I guess that's me,' she said.

I picked up her two bags and placed them on the back seat.

'Goodbye,' I said. I happened to put my hand into my trouser pocket and my fingers touched upon the shell that I'd found on the beach. I pulled it out. It looked good. The mother of pearl winked in the sunshine. 'Have this,' I said. 'A little souvenir.'

I felt her fingers touch the palm of my hand as she took the shell. She tossed it lightly in the air and snapped the scallop shell down its spine.

'One for me,' she said, giving me the other half, 'and one for you.'

'What a memento,' I said. 'Thank you.'

'Goodbye, Kim.' She gave me a peck on the cheek. I liked the feel of her lips on my skin. They were soft and moist; made to be kissed. 'Better get that fortune soon.'

She got into the car very elegantly, her knees locked together throughout. 'You'll have been snapped up long before I earn my fortune,' I said, closing the door on her.

As the car slid away from the hotel, she smiled and waved her half of the scallop shell at me. I stared after it wondering, wondering, what would happen if I did earn that fortune and if I ever did make that call.

Dinner that night was gruelling. The hotel was full, the dining room packed; it didn't matter how much we gave the guests, they always seemed to be yammering for more. Oliver was as predictably slow as ever – painstakingly slow, but at least he didn't smash anything. Roland and I were helping out with at least half of his tables.

It was the first time that I had a run in with the kitchen staff. I did not really know any of the cooks or the sous-chefs, but since we were all in it together, I had spent the previous three days doing my best to be amicable.

That night, everything in the kitchen was running at full tilt. The waiters, at least in the dining room, were endeavouring to look serene and in control. We were like swans, gliding effortlessly over a millpond while beneath the water our little feet were paddling like fury. But in the kitchens, hot and dripping with sweat, there was this edgy, febrile atmosphere where everyone seemed to be on the very edge of explosive madness.

The head chef, Monty, was unflappable; I never once saw him lose his cool. But under him were several lieutenants, of whom one, Giles, had taken a very strong and immediate dislike to me. I neither know nor care what it was that I had done to offend him. He had blubbery, pasty skin and rank mousy hair that would tuft out from underneath his chef's cap and lay slick against his forehead. He always looked hot and bothered and the sweat would dribble down his cheeks and onto his chin.

The drill was that we waiters had to enter the kitchens through the entrance door and then queue up at the pass until our guests' meals were ready to be served. The pass was a high metal counter, heated to keep the plates warm. On the one side were the chefs sweating away in their hot hell, and on the other were the spruce waitresses and waiters, chattier, chirpier and usually much younger.

Before each plate went out into the dining room, it was usually given a quick once-over by Monty, who would check that it was presentable and that the rim of the plate was clean.

That night, I would guess that there were well over two hundred covers. There certainly wasn't time for any badinage with Ed McKenny. In the kitchens, the pace was manic, just juddering on the cusp between control and outright chaos.

I was serving a table of six people and had already taken out two of the plates. I had just returned to the kitchens and was stretching over for the next two plates on the pass. One of them was a beef stew. I had presumed that since the plates were on the pass, then they were good to go.

'Cheers,' I said.

'Oi!' It was Giles. He tried to rap my knuckles with a soup ladle, hitting the tips of my fingers. I jerked my hand out of the way and the beef stew slopped over my fingers. It was hot.

'Can't you just control it?' I said.

'It still needs the gremolata,' he said.

'Well, what's the point in trying to hit me with a ladle, you fat idiot?' I mopped the stew off my fingers with a handkerchief.

Monty had come over. He took in what was happening. 'Can we have one more stew?' he called over his shoulder, before saying to me, 'Let me have that.'

'Sure.' I passed the plate back over and stood there with Oliver at the pass waiting for a fresh plate to be brought over. I tried to mop the worst of the stew off the hem of my tunic, but only spread the brown stain up to my waist.

Another stew was brought over. Monty cleaned the rim and Giles sprinkled on some of the gremolata. The gremolata was made from parsley, orange zest and crushed garlic; it went well with the beef stew.

I was not remotely going to leave it at that.

'Is everything to your satisfaction now, Giley?' I said.

I stretched out to take the plate, though I was well prepared for what he would do next. He lunged at me again with the ladle. He missed me. The ladle cracked into the plate, spattering stew over the pass.

'You might be able to hit me once with your little ladle,' I taunted. 'But if you want to hit me again, you'll have to move a lot faster than that, fat boy.'

I think if Monty hadn't been there, Giles would happily have thrown the plate at my head. Monty charmingly defused the situation. 'Giles, you couldn't get some more gremolata from the fridge?' he said, before turning to me. 'I could do with a glass of champagne, Kim, old love. You wouldn't do the necessary?'

I fetched him a glass of ice-cold house champagne, and by the time I'd returned to the pass, Oliver had already delivered the offending stew to my table.

'Cheers,' Monty said, tilting his glass towards me. 'I find that in most situations, champagne is usually the best remedy.'

'You must be right,' I said. Giles scowled.

We arrived at The Bankes Arms at just after ten. I hadn't even bothered to change out of my tunic, just slipping a coat on top. Oliver, of course, had changed; for him it would have been inappropriate to have worn work clothes to the pub.

There was a horse outside the pub. I remember thinking how unusual it was to see a horse tethered onto to a tree, as if some cowboy had turned up to his local Wild West saloon. Though I knew nothing about horses, I realised that it was a fine gelding, at least sixteen hands high and probably more. The horse was saddled up and had a nosebag. It seemed quite content.

The pub was buzzing. Oliver was getting the drinks and I recognised a few of the hotel guests. I smiled at a girl who was staying at the hotel with her parents. I like looking at people in pubs while I am waiting for my drink; it's almost impolite to start scanning the crowds when you are in company. But when you're waiting for your drink, you can stare all you like.

Over in the corner, I saw Cally. She was wearing her riding gear and I realised immediately that it was her horse out at the front. She was talking to a man in a jacket, though he was facing the wall and I could not see him. Her brown, voluptuous hair was coiled about her neck, but not overly so. She looked sexy.

I had only been looking at her for a couple of seconds before she looked up and stared at me. She smiled and flashed the palm of her hand. I gave her a wave back.

Oliver came over with our two pints. We squeezed onto the end of a table right in the middle of the pub. We chinked and looked each other in the eye. Oliver approved.

'It is important to look somebody in the eye, when you toast,' he said.

'Why's it important?'

'Otherwise, seven years bad sex.'

'Bad sex?' I said. 'What's bad sex? I'd certainly take bad sex over no sex.'

'I am not very good at sex.' Oliver said, announcing it in the same way that he might say that was no good at football. 'I have not had much practice.'

'Just find yourself a nice girl and—'

Roland had just come into the pub. He pulled up a stool and squeezed in between us. 'Whose round is it?' he said.

'It's mine,' Oliver said. He got up to fetch Roland a drink.

'You got a girlfriend?' asked Roland. He had tousled light hair and silver-rimmed glasses, but the most striking aspect of his face were his full lips. They were fleshy and made him look slightly debauched.

'I haven't,' I said, 'but I'd like one.'

'Anyone in particular? Janeen's taken a shine to you.'

'I don't think I'd be quite right for Janeen. Besides, she's seeing Darren.'

'She sees Darren when there's nothing else better on offer.'

The four drinkers at the end of our table left. We were just moving our chairs, when I felt a puff of cold air from the front door opening, and then a thump on my back.

'Kim! I hoped I'd find you here.'

I looked round. Everyone looked round. It was Ed McKenny. But it was the person with him who had me transfixed. He'd come to the pub with Annette. She was so very different from his now ex-girlfriend Liz: bare legs, white sneakers, a grey skirt to her knees and a baggy green jacket. Effortlessly gorgeous. There might have been a trace of make-up, but she was in full bloom and her skin just glowed. She smiled at me.

McKenny had made some effort. He was in full rock star regalia with tight jeans and a white silk shirt and necklaces and bangles and rings and all the other rubbish with which a man can try to turn himself into a peacock. Yet next to Annette, he was like a tatty old crow who'd sidled up next to a swan.

'Can we join you?' McKenny asked.

'Be my guest,' I gestured.

'I'll get us something to drink.'

He bought two magnums of Moet and paid in cash. I introduced Annette and McKenny to Oliver and Roland. I did not mention that McKenny was a rock star, and to my delight, Oliver had no idea who he was. He gave McKenny a brief handshake and then turned his full attention on Annette. He was pleased to meet her.

'We are the only two foreigners in the hotel,' Oliver said to Annette. 'When England plays football, we will have to support the other team.'

She laughed. Do you know, it's only now, in my forties, that I have realised there is nothing so sexy on a woman as a smile and a genuine laugh. 'And will you support Sweden at the Olympics this summer?'

'Of course,' Oliver said. 'I have always supported Sweden. I even support Sweden over Germany, because the Swedish women are, without question, the most beautiful women on earth.'

Annette giggled and sat down next to Oliver. I don't know what McKenny made of it, but he found himself perched on the end of the table between Roland and me while Annette was entirely monopolised by Oliver.

We drank very fast. Annette and McKenny were drinking out of flute glasses, but Oliver set the lead for the rest of us. He drained his pint of beer and then, after giving his glass a swill, filled the entire thing with champagne. He knocked off the first half pint in less than five seconds.

'I am thirsty!' he said.

I was not to be outdone. I filled up my pint glass with champagne and downed most of it in one.

'Rock on!' said McKenny. 'Annette, do you want a pint?'

'I'm fine with this.' She sipped from her glass.

Roland was in awe of the rock god who was sitting next to him and said not a word; but I, on the other hand, felt as if I had been released from my fetters. For the first time I was on equal terms with McKenny. I liked it also that he had spent hours on his clothes, while I was still wearing my stained tunic.

'So you didn't hang around long after Liz left,' I said to McKenny.

He looked at Annette and smiled. 'Just trying to make the most of all the hotel's amenities.'

'So what happened?' I finished the rest of my champagne and took the second magnum. We'd already emptied the first. I topped up everyone else's glasses and poured myself another pint. 'Annette was making your bed this morning and just happened to find you in it?'

'I like you!' McKenny clapped me on the shoulder before bellowing, 'I like this guy!'

'I said goodbye to Liz,' I said.

'Did you now?'

'She told me to give her a call just as soon as I'd made my fortune.'

'That'd be Liz,' he said. 'I hope you get that fortune. She's well worth it. When she turns it on, she's dynamite.'

I looked over at Annette. She and Oliver were laughing about the British. Being outsiders, they were able to observe all of the British ticks and foibles.

'Your date tonight might give Liz a run for her money,' I said.

'We're just out having a pleasant drink – I like to make new friends,' McKenny said. He stared at Annette as he spoke and you could see the seedy lust dripping off him. Oliver's desire for Annette seemed much more wholesome. For the rock god, Annette would just have been another notch on the bedpost.

McKenny was quizzing me about my plans for the future.

'Well, Plan A,' I said, 'is to get myself a girlfriend.'

'Shouldn't be a problem.'

'It shouldn't be a problem, but it has nonetheless been a problem.'

'And what's Plan B?'

'Plan B is to keep the girlfriend. I haven't been very good at keeping girlfriends in the past. It would be interesting to see if I could hold onto a woman for, I don't know, a year. A year would be great.'

'A year?' McKenny mocked me. 'Why does a young guy like you want to be tied down for that long?'

'Why not?' I said. 'I've never given it a go.'

McKenny bought more champagne and swapped seats with Roland so that he could sit next to Annette. He was trying to work his way into Oliver's conversation with Annette, but he was having no luck. Oliver still had no idea that he was sitting opposite a rock god. In Oliver's eyes, McKenny was just this lusty old goat.

I saw Cally leave the pub. In her hand, she had a packet of cigarettes and a silver lighter. Even though this was long before the smoking ban, Cally loved the tranquillity of smoking outside. As she walked out, she looked at me and raised one elliptical eyebrow, as if to say, 'What on earth are you doing with Ed McKenny?'

I went to the lavatory. I pressed my forehead against the tiles above the urinal. I liked the coolness and the quiet after the madness of the dining room.

From outside the window came a slight squeal. The sound was muffled. I ignored it.

I washed my hands and looked at myself in the mirror. Not bad, but certainly not great either. Just indifferent.

Back at the table, Roland was holding the fort.

'Where are the others?' I asked.

'Annette and Ed went out for a cigarette a while ago. Oliver's just followed them.'

I went outside. I couldn't see any of them. The horse was still tethered.

I walked around the side of the pub. It was dark with only a little light beaming out from one of the upper windows. I rounded the corner and the first thing I saw was Oliver's feet. He was lying on the ground. It took me a second to understand what I was looking at. He was out cold. I stooped down. He'd been hit on the head.

A noise. The sound of ripped fabric. I peered into the darkness. Several yards off, I could see something dark against the white wall.

I walked over, treading on the balls of my feet. Whatever was over by the wall was moving. The black outline was now quite clear against the white, but I still did not know what I was looking at. There was a short feminine shriek, cut off instantly, and I realised that it was McKenny. He had Annette up against the wall.

'Stop that!' I ordered. Nothing happened and I rushed towards McKenny. I grabbed him by the waist and dragged him sideways. I glimpsed Annette. Her ripped skirt was riding high round her waist and her white shirt was torn at the front.

McKenny rolled with me on the ground. He bounced back onto his feet and while I was still on the ground, he gave me a thundering kick to the stomach. He took a step back and then kicked me again in the guts, and I've been in fights before but I have never been so comprehensively bested. Two kicks and I was finished. I could barely breathe. I lay curled up in a ball. I couldn't say a word. But even if I could have spoken, I would not have known what to say.

Annette made to move away, but McKenny caught her easily by the wrist and held her.

He looked at me, very cool, and shook his head. The old lion had seen off the young pretender. His belt was unbuckled and his fly buttons undone. He shook his head. 'No hard feelings, kid?'

I still couldn't speak, but I did what I could and I gave him the finger. He laughed and turned to Annette.

McKenny had his arm round Annette's waist, and I don't know what he was planning to do next. Suddenly, there was a blur of movement. Against the whiteness of the wall there was something moving very fast. I saw a flash of lightness and then this soaring leap and McKenny's head was jerking to the side, as Cally delivered a flying kick to the side of his face. He toppled to the ground. Cally landed on her feet and stood over him, very light on her feet. She was ready for anything. But McKenny was out for the count. A trail of blood oozed from his lips, some of his teeth were broken.

Cally was helping Annette. She tugged Annette's skirt back down over her hips and helped do up her jacket. She gave Annette a hug. The girl was in tears. I got to my feet. My ribs were tender.

Cally turned and looked at me. 'You'll live,' she said.

We had a last look at McKenny. He was still unconscious. 'Useless piece of shit,' Cally said. 'I've half a mind to geld him.'

'Should we call the police?' I said. 'Or an ambulance?'

We turned to Annette. A sudden look of alarm on her face. 'But what about Oliver?' she said. She broke away and ran towards the front of the pub. We followed. We found Oliver still lying on the ground, but now with his head cradled on Annette's lap. He was conscious but bleary.

They didn't speak, but just gazed at each other. She stroked his hair and then, very gently, leaned forward and kissed him on the cheek. It wasn't quite love at first sight, but it was pretty close. Oliver had done his best to be Annette's knight in shining armour, and though he had failed miserably, he was about to receive his reward.

CHAPTER 7

We went back to Cally's house, McKenny abandoned in the pub's garden.

Oliver was still woozy. We helped him onto Cally's horse, and there he sat, clinging on tightly to the horse's mane as Annette took the horse's reins and led the way down the road. The horse's hooves clip-clopped on the tarmac. Occasionally Annette would look up and smile at Oliver. Nothing was said between the pair of them. There was nothing that needed to be said.

Cally and I followed a few yards behind.

'You better come back for a drink,' she said. 'Where did he get you?'

'In the ribs,' I said.

'I should have known it would happen,' she said. 'McKenny is a monster. Charming some of the time. But underneath, he's always a monster.'

'How do you know that?'

'I just do.' She shrugged and sniffed. I wondered if Cally and McKenny had had some history together, but I never asked and Cally certainly never told. Best not to go there.

Cally's house was a mile from the pub at the bottom of a cul-de-sac. There was a turning circle outside the house, and as you went up to the front door, the place seemed old and ramshackle, with moss on the tiles and ivy growing up the walls. But inside, it was quite different – warm and airy; it was only when you were halfway through the house that you realised it was much bigger than you'd expected, and that you were walking through to a large spacious room, with rugs and sofas and floor-to-ceiling windows that looked out to the sea.

'Kim, can you sort out the drinks?' said Cally. 'I'll just see to Dapple-Down.' She smiled as I looked at her blankly. 'My horse.'

I found a bottle of cognac in the drinks cupboard and poured out four triples. She had lovely cut-crystal glasses. I flicked one with my nail. It had pinged like a bell.

Oliver and Annette had slumped onto the sofa. They were holding hands and were staring out into the darkness. There was a light out towards the sea, though I was so disorientated that I could tell if it was a ship or a plane or even a house.

I looked at the pictures on the walls. Birds cartwheeling in the air; horses stampeding; seals on rocks and hares boxing: all was action. Not that I have any eye for pictures, but they were very good. I could see that they would sell well and sell for a lot of money.

Cally came into the room. She had taken off her jacket and there was a wisp of straw in that lovely chestnut hair of hers. We chinked and she sipped and savoured. 'Brandy,' she said. 'I don't drink nearly enough of it. So how are you all? Anything terminal?'

Annette shook her head and smiled. She looked very happy as she sat there on the sofa holding Oliver's hand. 'I'm fine,' she said.

'And you?' Cally said, nodding to Oliver.

He touched his scalp, winced, and then looked down and realised all over again that he was holding Annette's hand. 'I am happy,' he said.

'What about you, then, Kim?' said Cally. 'How's your chest?' She stood by the window smiling at me – competent and confident. It was the first time that I had ever really realised that I was staring at a very sexy woman. Not that anything could come of it, but I could see that Cally had really got it. She oozed it.

I fingered my chest. 'I don't know,' I said. 'He got me in the ribs.'

'Let's have a look,' she said. 'They might be cracked. There's not much I can do. It might help if I bind them.' She looked over at Annette and Oliver. Neither of them had even touched their brandies.

Cally led me upstairs to her bathroom. It was handsome, with another floor-to-ceiling window. Right in the centre was one of the largest claw-foot baths that I had ever seen. Two people could lie in it in comfort, fully outstretched. The floor was carpeted in inch-thick oatmeal pile and in the corner was a power shower that sparkled silver. Next to the bath there was a reading light and an armchair in purple velvet. It was opulent. Adult. The bathroom of a woman with taste and style – not to mention money.

Cally pulled a first aid box out from the cupboard underneath the sink. 'Take off your top and sit on the ottoman,' she said.

I winced as I unbuttoned my tunic. It was even more painful peeling off my T-shirt. I sat on the ottoman by the window.

Cally had a roll of cotton bandage in her hand. 'Let me see,' she said.

With light fingertips, she started to feel my chest.

'Nasty bruise,' she said, as her fingers worked her way down my ribs. I flinched. It was not erotic, but I did like having her fingers on my skin. There is something quite relaxing about being pampered after you have done yourself an injury. It is that contented glow that comes from a total surrender of control. 'Must be two or three broken. I'll bind them.'

She wrapped the bandage tight around my chest, starting just underneath my armpits and working her way down. And as she wrapped me, she talked; but it was almost as if I was not there.

'It's been a long time since I've touched a young man like this,' she said. 'So trim. Not an ounce of fat on him. Very different from any other chest that I have touched in the last decade.' She gave my shoulder an affectionate stroke and laughed to herself. 'Listen to me! I'm thinking I'm a twenty-year-old again, when in fact, I must be twenty years older than him!'

She stopped in front of me and smiled. 'Sorry if I carry on,' she said. 'I am marvelling at your chest – sinewy and lean and with just the perfect amount of chest hair. You don't mind, do you?'

'I don't mind at all.'

'Good.' She plucked up a couple of safety pins and secured the bandage.

I stood up. 'Thank you.'

'You're very welcome.' We were so close that I could feel her hair touch my chest. She smiled up at me. As I held her gaze, a dart of light seemed to pass between us. It was more than just a connection; it was the recognition that there was an affinity between us. I had an urge to kiss her, but I stamped it down. The moment passed. Cally turned to pack up the bandages and scissors in her first-aid box.

She drove us back to the Knoll House in her Mercedes. I sat next to her, while Annette and Oliver sat in silence in the back, still holding tight onto each other's hands.

She dropped us off and waved out of the window as she thundered off into the night and the three of us tramped back to our little concrete cells, each hurting in our own way, and yet also awed by the evening's revelations.

For myself, that night was the first time that I had ever really considered the possibility of dating a much older woman. Over the years, I had of course fancied many women who were older than me: superstar women in pop and showbiz; the mothers of friends and the friends of my stepmother. But I had always perceived these women as untouchables. I knew my place. I understood that this attraction was a one-way street and that it could never be mutual. I could look and I could admire, but under no circumstances would I be allowed to touch or kiss.

But with that one single look between us it was as if the door had opened, and I could glimpse a glimmer of burning light in the room beyond. All this from looking into her eyes. Some friends, when I've told them this, have thought it ridiculous. But others have got it. They've understood that looking into someone's eyes can, on occasion, be every bit as charged as a kiss; it can speak volumes.

As I tramped back to my room, part of me was green with envy that my awkward, clumsy German friend had managed to pull the most beautiful woman on the entire staff. I hid it well and after a while, I was delighted for them. How could I not be?

Oliver bided his time. He wooed her with hand-picked posies and they would go for long walks in the afternoon, holding hands every step of the way. A week later, on his first night off, Oliver took her out for dinner in Swanage. They took a taxi there, waving as they went just for the sheer pleasure of being in each other's company. That night, they kissed for the first time. I had never seen a couple quite so inseparable. If they were both off work at the same time, then they would be with each other – simple as that.

Occasionally, Oliver and I would go alone for a manly drink in the pub, but more often than not Annette would accompany us. She was lovely. If she was beautiful when she started working at the hotel, after she started dating Oliver, she took on a glow of pure love.

After that extraordinary night at the pub with Annette and Oliver and McKenny, I did not see Cally again for at least a week; and I did not see McKenny again either, come to that. He skulked from the hotel early the next morning. A few days later, Oliver showed me one of the tabloids. There was a half-page picture of McKenny, along with a quote from his spokesman saying that McKenny had slipped over while he was running. He looked awful. He had lost some front teeth, and the side of his face was this swollen, livid bruise, the colours mixing from black and brown all the way through to aubergine and lime green.

'Certainly gave him something to remember us by,' I said.

'I will not be forgetting it either,' Oliver said. I called him a lucky dog and he told me that it was about time I acquired myself a girlfriend. It was.

We'd just finished serving lunch at the hotel and so I went for a walk along the coast. When the Studland beach runs out, you hit the white cliffs of the Jurassic Coast, packed with chalk and fossils and all things ancient. The cliffs are high and the drop is lethal and as I have vertigo, I kept well clear from the edge. Even if I'm flat out on my belly, it still makes me giddy to peer over the edge of a cliff. I stare into the abyss and feel this primordial tug willing me to jump. So instead of walking by the cliffs, I stuck to the path on the rolling grassland high over the sea.

The cliffs are famous not just for their fossils but also for their smugglers' dens. As the wind flapped and the waves roared, I only had to close my eyes to imagine the smugglers shipping in to some quiet cove and hauling their booty up to the Dancing Ledges and all the other hidden crags along the coast.

The cliffs rise gently from Studland until at their peak, you reach Old Harry, a massive chalk archway carved out by the sea. I had seen pictures of these age-old clumps and pinnacles that had been chiselled from the cliffs, but this was the first time that I had ever seen them for real. Old Harry was much bigger than I'd expected, bigger and higher and absolutely petrifying. I did not go near the edge. There was another chalk pinnacle that was nearby to Old Harry. It was on a thin peninsular, a white spike that was connected to the cliff face by a very narrow path. In fact, it was so narrow that it didn't really qualify as a path at all: it stretched for perhaps eight or nine yards, and in places was not even a foot across. On each side of the path there was a sheer precipice that dropped fifty, sixty yards to the rocky beach below. I stayed a good distance from the cliff edge; just looking at the path made me feel queasy.

I looked out towards the sea. The top of the pinnacle was covered in lush grass. It was home to hundreds of seabirds. I watched them gliding through the air before they corkscrewed into the sea.

I almost completely missed her. I was about to continue my walk when I saw that that there was someone sitting on the edge of the rock. Her painting stool was perched just three inches from the cliff edge.

Even though she was quite a long way off, she instantly knew I was there. She looked over her shoulder and when she saw me, she waved. She left her easel and paints and came over. I watched as she walked right next to the cliff; a single slip and she'd have been over the edge. She was sauntering along as easily as if she'd been striding down Oxford Street. When she came to the foot-wide strip of path, she just walked straight over. She never once looked down. It was not in her nature to look down to the jags and snags that might yet finish her; instead, she always had her gaze level and looked dead ahead.

Cally came towards me with her hands outstretched. She placed a hand on my hip and kissed me on the cheek. 'Hello Kim,' she said. 'How are the ribs?'

'Fine,' I said. She was in her painting gear, daubed jeans and a flecked fleece and she smelled of paint and turpentine. 'Are you really painting out there?'

'It's magical,' she said. 'No one ever goes there.'

'I can believe it.'

'Come on,' she said, tugging at my elbow. 'Come join me.'

'No,' I said. 'I'm terrible with heights.'

'Come on,' she said. 'You'll like it.'

'No, seriously.'

She pulled at me again. I had never experienced this sort of womanly persistence before.

'I'll make it worth your while.'

'How?' She looked lovely. There was quite a gale and her hair was blowing out almost horizontally to the side.

'Come over and you'll see.'

'I've told you, I hate heights.'

'You're too young to be saying "No",' she said. 'Come on. I'll look after you.'

'This is a really bad idea.'

'Hold onto my hands,' she said. 'I'll lead you.'

Cally took my hands. My fingers were in her palms. 'Look only into my eyes.' She briefly looked behind her and then started walking backwards. I followed, my feet shuffling forward little by little. I gazed fixedly into her eyes, though all about me I could sense the hostile elements as they tried to drag me off the cliff, the wind buffeting at my side and the waves thundering in beneath me.

She paused momentarily. 'I'm enjoying this,' she said.

I didn't smile, I didn't say a word. My life, my world, revolved around her gaze, every sense and sensation focused on Cally's bewitching eyes. We were standing toe to toe, our faces just a foot apart. I could feel the connection forged between us, thin threads of silk that looped through our eyes and plucked at our hearts. I had never before realised how a woman's eyes are the very window to her soul or that if a man would woo her, there is no call for words and no need for smiles.

'Shall we go on?' she asked.

'Okay.'

'You're doing great.'

She continued to walk backwards and I followed her over, still holding her gaze. She stumbled and fell, yelping with fear, and then looked up at me and laughed for the path was already way behind us and we were walking onto good solid ground.

'And how was that for you?' she said.

'Hair-raising.' We walked to her easel; as ever in her life, Cally strolled right by the cliff edge. It was as if she were almost daring herself. Sometimes the toe of her shoe would splay right over the edge of the precipice.

'Why do you walk so close to the edge?' I asked.

'I like it,' she said.

'Ever tried walking down the middle of the motorway?'

'No, but only because of the traffic.'

'Did you say you'd make it worth my while?'

'I did,' she said. 'I've got some sloe gin. Do you like sloe gin?'

'Sure.'

'But I have only one glass. I didn't know anyone was going to be joining me.'

'Or would be foolhardy enough to join you.'

'Grabbing life by the throat,' she said. 'I'll have to put you in my picture now.'

'Just so long as you don't want me to sit anywhere near the cliff.'

'No, Kim; it is always me who has to sit next to the cliff. Sit on the grass, watch the birds, sip some gin.' I cleared some of the stones and the guano and made myself a nest in a little hollow, out of the wind and yet with my head slightly raised so that I could stare out to the sea. There was a weak spring sun, though the wind made it cold. Cally was close enough by for us to talk. I watched her as she painted. She was painting in oils, working in broad, sweeping brush-strokes. She had her back to the sea and I could not see her picture. I liked watching her. She was beautiful and talented and she was utterly absorbed in her work.

She looked up again at the birds overhead. 'It is funny to think that long after I am gone, those birds – or at least the next thousand generations of them – will still be there, will still be nesting on Old Harry, and will still be diving into the sea for the limitless fish.' She went back to the painting and for a while was silent.

'I can feel when you're looking at me,' she said, her paintbrush darting.

'How do you know?'

'I don't know,' she said. 'I just do.'

'And do you have any other extrasensory perceptions?'

'I do, as it happens.'

'And what are they?'

She pointed at me with her paintbrush. 'One day...' She trailed off and smoothed the hair from her forehead. 'You might find out. One day.'

I took another sip of the sloe gin. Cally had made it herself, she told me, plucking the sloes from the autumn hedgerows, before spiking them with a fork and adding sugar and gin and leaving them to mulch over the winter. It was much stronger than the shop-bought sloe gin that I was used to, both sweet and astringent, and with the bitter bite of the sloes. I liked the colour of it. It was a vivid pink, bordering on crimson. I held the glass up to the sky and squinted through the gin and the brown dregs and up to the sun. I'd had a few glasses.

Cally was concentrating on a small detail of her picture, working in small dabs with a tiny brush. Without taking her eyes off the canvas, she asked me one of the most unanswerable questions that a man can ever be asked.

'What is it,' she said, 'that a woman really wants?'

I swirled my gin and watched the pink diamonds form on the edge of the crystal. 'I don't know,' I said. 'What do women want?'

'It's not going to be that easy,' she said. 'Think about it.'

'Give me a moment,' I said. I thought back to some of my past loves – not that there had ever been that many. As I thought back to India, and to Estelle, and to those other great loves who had once been capable of snatching the very breath from my throat, I discerned that they might have had something in common. 'I guess a woman wants to be loved,' I said. 'But she must be loved unconditionally. She can be as capricious as she pleases. She can blow hot, she can blow cold; she wants you and then she doesn't want you. She wants to settle down; she wants to party. But if you are a man, and you love her, you must accept all that, because that is what she is, and that is what you have to do. Your love must be without ties or conditions. No matter what the provocation, and no matter what a woman says, your love must be deep and loyal and last for ever.'

Cally broke away from her painting and looked at me. Her eyes were smiling. 'Not far off.'

'But I'm still not even close.'

'Well, of course we want to be loved unconditionally,' she said. 'But we don't want our men to be doormats. We don't want to be trampling over them as we please, and then having them get up and ask for more. So the love must be there. But we want a man who knows his own mind.'

'So it's still just this riddle that is wrapped in a mystery inside an enigma?'

Cally painted. I sipped sloe gin. The gulls dived and the sea throbbed; it was very soothing. Cally was working at the top of the picture. She seemed to be concentrating on her work, but very softly, she started to speak.

'Did you know that King Arthur was once captured in an ambush?' she said.

I shook my head.

'I'll tell you about it. He was captured by a king, and he was given a very difficult question. He had to find out what women really want; he was given one year to do it. If he didn't do it, then he was going to be executed.'

'Okay.'

'So the young king went round quizzing women, girls, ladies, princesses. He still couldn't find an answer. And then, when his year was nearly up, he was told that there was one woman, a hideous crone, who knew the answer. But she would ask a heavy price.

'In the end though, he didn't have any option, and so he went to see her. She was just as ugly as everyone had told him. The crone said that she did know the answer to his riddle, but that she would only give it to him if she could marry his most handsome knight, Sir Lancelot.

'Arthur thinks that this is too much for his friend, but Lancelot says that if it means saving Arthur's life, he'll marry the hag. So Arthur agrees to the deal, and he finds out what it is that women really want.'

I topped up the glass and took it over to Cally. She rolled the gin in the glass and sipped, before handing it back to me. 'Thank you.'

'And the answer?'

'What a woman really wants is… to be in charge of her own life.'

'Right.' I didn't know what to think of the answer. 'Is that it?'

'No, it's not it. Arthur gets his answer and announces it to the king, and it is generally agreed that he has delivered the right answer—'

'At least for that day.'

'That he has delivered the right answer,' she continued smoothly. 'So Lancelot has to marry the hag, and surprisingly it turns out to be a great wedding and all of the knights of the Round Table are there to give him a good send off. On the wedding night, Lancelot is a little nervous as he goes up to the bridal suite, but as he walks into the room, he finds this beautiful woman lying on the bed. She smiles at him. She is pleased to see him; she is in fact his bride. Because Lancelot had been so lovely, she had transformed herself into a beauty.

'Lancelot is very pleased. And then she gives him a question. She can be a beauty by day, or a beauty by night. Which would he prefer? Would he prefer to have all his friends going green with envy in the day? Or would he prefer to be making love every night with this beautiful woman?'

'Tough call,' I said.

'What would you do?'

'Well, it's a tough call. I think I'd duck it. Just throw the question right back at her.'

'Correct answer!' said Cally. 'Lancelot dithered and then, since he probably couldn't make up his mind, he told her to do whatever she wanted.'

'And she was very happy.'

'And she was so happy that she decided to be beautiful all of the time.'

'But that still didn't stop Lancelot from running off with Arthur's Guinevere.'

She nodded in acknowledgement. 'He was a guy, wasn't he? It doesn't matter what a guy has, eventually he's always going to want more.'

Cally was beautiful. I gazed at her curves and the swell of her bosom, and her jeans skin tight on her thighs. Her age meant nothing; at that moment, all I was looking at was an incredibly good-looking woman.

'Do you know what you want?' I asked Cally.

She didn't look up. 'I do.'

'And will you get it?'

'Maybe. I usually do.' She broke off and looked at me quickly. I noticed her lips. They were very full. I wanted to kiss her. 'But this time I'm not sure.'

I helped Cally pack up. She swigged the last of the gin and tossed the dregs over the cliff edge. Just before she packed the canvas, she scribbled something on the back with a black pencil.

'What are you writing?' I asked.

'A reminder,' she said. 'The day, the company. What I drank. Would you like to see the picture?'

I liked it. I hadn't expected to. I'd expected the sort of student daubings that I'd seen from my friends. But this was good, very good. She had captured the gulls and the bride white cliffs against the grey sky. And there, tucked in the corner, was a figure in red, lying slouched on the grass, one arm behind his head and the other holding up a glass of sloe gin to the sun.

'It's wonderful,' I said. 'I like it.'

'Thank you.'

'One day, when I have the money, I'll buy one of your pictures.'

She smiled at me easily. I carried her easel and stool, while she took the canvas in its leather carry case.

I had forgotten about that thin strip of pathway that connected us to the mainland. I think that Cally had also forgotten that those cliffs and those precipices absolutely terrified me.

She sauntered over the pathway, one hand holding the case. Her other hand was in her pocket, like a boulevardier in the spring.

I followed. I had had a bit to drink and I thought that if I didn't fuss over the pathway, I'd be able to take it in my stride. No big deal at all. Just walk over, keep your head up, and don't for one moment contemplate the prospect of the precipice and the awesome drop. I was looking firmly at Cally. She'd turned round and was watching me.

'Very good,' she said. She clapped her hands.

I didn't look down. I was determined not to look down.

When I was young, about thirteen, I saw a piece of film footage. It was from the Flying Wallendas. The Wallendas were famous high-wire artists who would never have thought to use a safety net, and for years and years they enthralled audiences all over the world. But one day in 1962, disaster struck. There were seven of them in a pyramid and the front man lost his balance, and down they went and at least two of them died. The team never really recovered, but there was one Wallenda, Karl, who continued to ply his trade until he was well into his seventies; his last moments were recorded on film. In the footage, his hair is slicked back and he still looks quite spry. He has a long pole and is crossing a high wire that has been stretched between two skyscrapers in Puerto Rico. A sudden gust of wind catches him unawares. Karl starts to wobble. Very slowly, he lowers himself until he is almost kneeling on the wire. And then, as the crowd surges forward beneath him, he topples to the side. He snatches at the wire, misses and then he falls. He had always said that it would be the wind that caught him in the end. The wind is the nemesis of the tightrope walker.

And for me. Just as I was feeling sure of myself, a freak gust caught me flat abeam, and I was almost blown clean off the path. I tilted the other way, viciously trying to keep my balance. The path was only about a foot wide. I stared into the abyss; terrifying and yet also so inviting, the jagged rocks like a Siren to my senses, urging me ever downwards.

My arms flailed. I was trying to kneel, but like the last Wallenda, I was already too far gone. I was still desperately clutching onto Cally's stool and her easel, as the rocks and the cliffs heaved in and out of my view, like a storm-tossed sea.

I caught a flurry of movement to my side, as Cally rugby-tackled me, hard around the midriff and slammed me onto the path, punching the breath from my lungs. I was laying face downwards, my legs waving wildly over the edge. I watched as the easel spiralled down, catching the cliff face once, twice, before shattering on the rocks below. The little stool was caught by the wind. It flicked onto a grassy ledge on the main cliff and stayed there. I clung to the cliff face. My face was pressed into the chalk path. Eyes shut. I was violently trembling, my legs and my arms and my back all quivering with terror.

Cally had me, I think, by the belt. She was sitting astride the pathway, as if she were riding a horse. She didn't say anything for a while. Neither of us said or did anything at all. I lay there shivering.

I heard her lighter strike. After a moment, I could smell her cigarette smoke.

I stayed with my eyes shut and my cheek pressed against the chalk and breathed in the cigarette smoke. It was all right, so long as I did not think about what had happened.

Cally flicked her cigarette into the dusk. 'Okay, Kim,' she said. 'I am going to stand up and I am going to hold onto your collar.'

She got to her feet and I felt her hand tight at the back of my neck.

'You are going to keep your eyes shut and you are going to sit up.' She was leaning over me, all but whispering into my ear. 'You are going to keep your feet either side of the path. Your hands are going to hold onto the edge of the pathway. Can you do that? Just nod.'

I nodded.

'Okay, do it now.'

I pushed myself up until I was in a sitting position. My thighs were tight on each cliff face. I was astride the path.

'Eyes still shut,' she said. 'You are facing the wrong way. Now you are going to work your way backwards. Push up with your hands and then move backwards. Okay?'

I nodded.

'Let's go.' She sensed my intransigence. The wind rippled through the cliffs. How I longed to cling to the rock. 'Do it now!'

I started to shuffle backwards, a few inches at a time. 'Good,' said Cally. Her hand was still tight on my collar. 'It's starting to get wider now. You're going to have to spread your legs.'

Spread my legs? A foolish thought drifted into my head and I started to giggle.

'You liked that, didn't you?' said Cally, her tone light. 'Now I'm going to pull you.'

She dragged me forcibly backwards. Though she was much smaller than me, she was a strong woman. I was bumped along a few yards, my legs dragging along the path.

'And rest,' she said.

I was lying on the ground, on good, proper terra firma. I opened my eyes. Cally was standing above me. She was grinning. 'Are we having fun yet?'

I laughed at her; such delirious release now that I was away and free from that hellish precipice. Then and there I vowed never ever to do anything like that again.

I got to my feet, but I was still very shaky. She put her arms round me and with relief I held her tight. It is what you do when you have looked death in the face: you want to touch and be touched. And the more terrifying the experience the greater your appreciation of everything that it is to be a human being. I opened my eyes and looked out at the roaring sea. It was still that same roaring sea and that same piece of chalky headland that it had been ten minutes earlier, but now I saw it all through fresh eyes. It was good to be held.

After a while I even forgot my shivering. Cally looked at me, and we stared and we stared, and then she lifted up slightly on her toes and she kissed me; her kiss seemed to come as naturally as breathing.

The kiss was not mentioned when we walked back to the Knoll House. Instead, Cally was regaling me with how I had looked when I had been on the verge of falling off the cliff edge.

'It was like slapstick comedy,' she said. 'Everything was exaggerated – your arms, your legs, even the look on your face.'

'What was the look on my face?'

She thought for a moment, her leather bag swinging back and forth. 'Panic, I think, tinged with horror. Like you were going to some really smart wedding and you'd trodden in the most enormous dog's mess.'

'That's a very stirring image.'

'It wasn't just horror, you see,' she said. 'Your face was also mixed with annoyance and incredulity.'

'And you saved my life.'

'In some circles, that means I now own you.'

'I can think of worse mistresses.'

She laughed at that. 'And I can think of worse slaves.'

We were coming up to the road that led to her house. 'You moved very fast to save me, didn't you?'

'I had to!' she said. 'If you'd fallen off, I don't think I'd ever have forgiven myself.'

'I'll bet the picture would have sold for a fortune.'

'You're probably right,' she said. 'The papers would have loved it: "Painter's Muse Plummets to His Death".'

'Anyway,' I said. 'Thank you.' I gave her a light kiss on the cheek.

'See you soon, I hope.'

'I hope so too,' I said. 'When you're around, Cally, I have adventures.'

CHAPTER 8

The next two months were torture. I longed to see more of Cally, but at best I only saw her once a week when she came for her lunch in the hotel. We would laugh and we would talk and I would gaze at her from afar like some love-starved kitten. Cally just seemed quite oblivious to it all. Not that I ever flirted with her – that would have been *inconceivable*. But when I waited at her table, I would do my level best to be alluring: happy and busy and full of good cheer and good energy. For even in my youth, I still had the wit to realise that no woman could ever fall in love with a dull dog; rather, what is sexy in a man is vigour and optimism. So unwittingly, I was presenting the exact same front to Cally that she herself was presenting to me: the most robust indifference.

I found that I was thinking about her almost all the time. If I were not in the dining room and not actively involved in some activity, then up would swim Cally's image. It was a new experience for me. If Cally had been the same sort of age as me, I would have asked her out. But the age gap between us, while it didn't necessarily seem wrong, it did make it seem inappropriate. I don't know why I didn't just declare my hand. After all, what was the worst that could have happened? She could have laughed in my face and told me not to be so stupid. But actually, now that I think of it, Cally was much too kind to have done something like that. Instead, my mind only half in gear, I mooned about the dining room pining after her.

By now, the staff in the dining room had settled down into their various camps and allegiances. There were allies and there were enemies and there were also the non-combatants who didn't register very much one way or the other. Chief among my allies was, of course, Oliver; his girlfriend, Annette, also became a dear friend.

Roland was up there, though his miserliness did tend to grate after a while. It wasn't just money; whether he was dealing with emotions or time, Roland was tight. I always got on well with Michelle and Tracy, and Janeen was an on–off ally, depending on how her relationship was going with Darren.

There were two people who actively wished me ill. The first was Giles the cook, though since he was in the kitchens, he was limited as to the amount of harm he could do me. I found that what vexed him most was to present an attitude of the most sublime cheerfulness, seemingly unaware of the Neanderthal taunts that he directed at me.

'Good morning, Giles,' I'd say as I picked up the day's first order of eggs and bacon. 'And how are we on this wonderful Monday?'

'I'd be doing a lot better if I didn't have to listen to you.'

'Get out of the wrong side of the bed again, did we, Giles?'

'Go screw yourself.'

'Or should I do what you do so well, Giles – and start playing with myself?'

Dealing with Giles was mere knockabout stuff. He would still occasionally try and hit me with a ladle or whatever else came to hand, but I was much too quick on my feet.

Darren, however, was of a different category altogether. He was much more sharp and much more dangerous. But seeing as he had a small but pivotal role in the development of my relationship with Cally, I suppose I ought to be grateful to him.

It was May, I think, and Cally had come along for another of her lunches with Greta. Cally was in a tight black skirt and a creamy silk top. She really knew how to carry herself. Greta, as always, was done up like some exotic fruit cocktail. I'd already delivered their first bottle of champagne and was biding my time at the central station. Even if nothing much was happening, a waiter would still keep an eye out for his guests. I may have been looking at Cally and Greta, but I don't really remember. I was polishing a glass with a white napkin.

'You fancy her, don't you?' Darren had sidled up to me. He was also looking at Cally and Greta.

'Fancy who?'

'That woman who you've been staring at for the last month.'

'What are you talking about?' I continued blandly to polish the glass.

'You must think I'm blind.'

'Not blind, no. Though, other words do spring to mind.'

'She's not bad, is she?' said Darren. 'At least not bad for someone in her forties.'

'Is she now?' I dead-balled the question. As so often in my life, the closer that someone gets to touching me on the raw, the more seemingly indifferent I become.

'You fancy her rotten.'

'Though I'm sure she'd just love to become a member of the Darren harem.'

'Maybe.'

I did not think anything more about it, until the next time that Cally came over. It was for dinner and she was with one of the middle-aged men who so loved to court her. She beamed at me as I brought over the menus, and then introduced me to Hugh, an antiques dealer from Wareham.

'Good evening, sir,' I'd said as I handed him his menu. He wasn't much interested in either the menu or me.

It was a busy night and I had a lot of tables. By now at the Knoll House, I was competent enough to be able to handle them all, but it did take concentration. It was like keeping twenty plates forever spinning in the air, this whirlwind of charming activity. I had just been getting some wine for a table and had returned to the dining room to find that Darren had insinuated himself onto Cally's table. He was clearing away their plates and Cally was laughing at something that he had said. I wondered, at first, whether to go over, but then another table was waving at me for the bill and so I left them to it. The next thing I noticed, Darren was trotting off to get Cally another bottle of wine.

I waited until he came back. 'Thanks very much, Darren,' I said. 'I'll take over from here.'

'No I'm fine, mate,' he said and made to continue walking to Cally's table.

'No, *I* am fine, mate,' I said. 'I can handle my tables.'

'Sure you can.' He pointed to some elderly woman by the windows who was holding up her water jug. 'She looks thirsty,' and off Darren went to give Cally her wine.

That was the start of it and by the end of the evening, Darren had all but wormed his way into her affections, or so it seemed to my love-drugged brain.

It was a few days later, after I'd had a day off, that Darren accosted me again in the dining room. 'Cally was sorry not to see you yesterday,' he said.

Immediately, I realised that Darren must have been waiting at her table. 'I'm sure you looked after her as best you could,' I said.

'I'm meeting her for a drink tonight,' he said. 'Should be fun.'

Now this I had not expected. 'I'm sure you'll have a lovely time,' I said.

'I'm sure *she'll* have a lovely time,' said Darren. He sleeked back his hair at the sides. He was a good-looking guy, very smooth and he had the patter. It was all too possible, I realised, that I had met my match. After all, why should Cally have been interested in me? It was ludicrous to even think that this sophisticated artist would want anything to do with me. But Darren? Even Hugh the antiques dealer from Wareham would have been preferable to Darren.

But on the other hand, why shouldn't Cally have been interested in Darren? He was earthier than me. He dripped with raunch. A number of the waitresses were a little in love with him. Why not Cally?

I was in two minds as to whether to go to the pub. I certainly didn't want to be forced to look at Cally cosying up with Darren on one of the corner tables. But a part of me was also fascinated to see what would actually occur between them.

She couldn't…

It wasn't possible…

And then in an instant, I had realised that although Cally might not, Darren most certainly *would*.

I went to the pub with my usual little coterie, the two lovebirds, Oliver and Annette, and Roland. Cally's horse Dapple-Down was already tethered up outside the pub.

I put on my most gregarious mask as I walked in. I bought four pints of lager and was so focused on being Jack the Lad having fun with his friends, that I did not even look round the bar.

We chinked and we looked each other in the eye, and Oliver and Annette held hands under the table. They were so loved up it only served to highlight the lack of love in my own life.

'You two are sick making,' Roland said.

'We are in love,' Oliver said. Annette giggled. She truly was a woman in love; she radiated it.

'Do you have to paw each other in public?' Roland said.

'Do these public displays of affection disgust you, my friend?' Oliver said.

'He's just jealous, aren't you, Roland, you old stoat,' I said. He did not like it when I ruffled his hair.

'Get off me.'

'I'll find you a nice girl, Roland,' Annette said. 'There are lots of pretty girls among the housekeepers.'

'Yes,' Oliver said. 'That is a plan. We must get a girlfriend for Roland. And that will make Roland happy and then we can all double date in the pub together.'

'And what about Kim?' Annette said. She looked at me, and I wondered if there had ever been that sort of spark between us.

'You don't need to worry about me,' I said.

'So what's it like being in love?' Roland said.

I was pleased that Roland had changed the subject. I was a little too chary to bring up the matter of my unrequited love for Cally. At the thought of Cally, I instinctively looked up. She was at her usual table in the corner. Wherever she was, whether in the pub, her own kitchen or the Knoll House dining room, she always loved to be able to survey the room. Darren was at her table, facing the wall. His hair gleamed with wet gel. The very moment that I looked up, Cally caught my eye. It was instantaneous. She raised her wine glass in greeting, and then she gave me a elliptical raise of an eyebrow. I was not sure what it meant, but I liked it. It was a private intimacy. I winked at her.

Oliver and Annette were gazing at each other, exuding love from their very pores.

'What is it like being in love?' Oliver repeated. He was still gazing at Annette. 'I have never been in love before. It is… it is the best thing, the nicest thing, that has ever happened to me.' He brought her hand to his lips and kissed her on the wrist.

'And you, Annette?' Roland said.

She gave a shy smile. 'I love being in love with Oliver. He makes me very happy.'

'I am going to marry you,' Oliver said.

'Are you proposing to me?' Annette said.

'Am I?' Oliver said. 'I think I am. Annette, will you marry me?'

'Yes, please,' she said. They laughed and they kissed, and we none of us knew whether they'd agreed to get hitched or whether they were just larking around, but it was fun, and they were happy.

'My fiancée,' Oliver said to me. 'My fiancée, Annette. We are going to be married.'

'And how many children are you going to have?'

'Lots of them!' Annette said.

'We can only hope that they inherit their looks from their mother,' I said.

'And what will they inherit from me?' said Oliver. He drank almost three-quarters of a pint in about ten seconds, his Adam's apple the size of a plum as it joggled up and down. We all of us watched.

'From you?' I said. 'The children will inherit your pleasing personality—'

'And your amazing dexterity and sure-footedness,' Roland said.

'Me?' Oliver said. 'Clumsy?'

Annette laughed and kissed him. 'I don't want a ring,' she said. 'All I want is you.'

'Of course I am going to get you a ring,' Oliver said. 'Are you saying we Germans do not know how to do things properly?'

Michael, the publican, came over with a bottle of white wine and four glasses. It was decent white wine too, Sancerre. It was in an ice bucket, with the cool condensation deliciously dripping down the side.

'What have we here?' I said.

'From a secret admirer,' he said. 'And this is for you.' He gave me a note that had been folded over several times and then crossed in the middle, so that it looked like a pretzel.

'Thank you,' I said.

On the side of the note, was written, 'For Kim'. Black ink and with a very thick nib; I think the thickest nib that I had ever seen. It was large, florid writing, and with the thick nib was almost a version of copperplate.

As Oliver poured the wine, I discreetly opened the note. Already I had an inkling that I would want to keep it secret.

First I noticed the picture. It was a very simple sketch, done with the same ink pen. It was undoubtedly Cally sitting at her table. She had a glass of wine in front of her and a large Dunce's cap on her head.

Underneath, in words so big that they filled the rest of the page, she had written, 'Kim, can you kindly come and rescue me. Please!'

I looked. I read it again.

'What does it say?' Roland said.

'It says that you, specifically, should not have more than one glass of wine,' I said as I folded the note up and tucked it into my pocket. 'Otherwise you are likely to get drunk and abusive.'

'Again,' Oliver added.

'Yes, again,' I said.

'So who's it from?' Roland said.

'That's the point about secret admirers, isn't it?' I said. 'They kind of want to remain secret.'

'So you don't know, or you're not telling me?'

'Is it likely that I'm going to tell the biggest blabbermouth in the hotel?'

'What if I said please?'

'Okay. Say please.'

'Please?' Roland said.

'Say it like you mean it.'

'Pretty please?'

'No,' I said. 'I'm still not telling.'

The wine was delicious. We were all of us big drinkers in those days, but we were still capable of recognising decent wine when we drank it. As I drank, I pondered just how I was going to go about rescuing Cally.

Oliver swirled the wine in his glass, letting it breathe before he took a small sip.

'Very good,' he said. 'I am afraid that the French produce much better wine than the Germans.'

'And much better women!' Roland said. 'All that hair! Hairy armpits, hairy legs! Why don't they ever shave?'

'They shave their moustaches,' Oliver said.

'Too bad,' Roland said. 'I'll bet those German *Fräuleins* would look really hot with a little Hitler 'tache.'

We cackled at the idea of these comely German girls sporting dainty little toothbrush moustaches. A germ of an idea was filtering through. As the others continued to chafe each other, I slipped on my coat and excused myself.

I went outside. It was a lovely night, cool but not cold. Cally's horse was still standing stolidly by the side of the pub. I waited for a minute, breathed the air deep into my lungs, and then hurried back inside. I went straight over to Cally's table. Darren was talking and Cally was drinking. She looked up as I came over.

'Hi Cally,' I said. 'Sorry to bother you, but I think there's something up with your horse.'

'My horse?' she said. 'Right. I better…' She downed her wine in one. 'Excuse me,' she said to Darren. 'Thank you for a lovely evening.'

It all happened very fast. Cally gave Darren's shoulder a squeeze and a moment later she was flying out of the pub.

Darren caught my eye. I tried to look bland, bored, indifferent, just a humble minion who had duly passed on a piece of information to an acquaintance. I gave him a shrug and dickered for a second at the door before following Cally outside.

She had already untethered Dapple-Down and was waiting for me by the side of the pub. 'Quick thinking,' she said. 'Thank you.'

'Any time,' I said.

'I should never have come.' She scratched at Dapple-Down's cheek. 'At least, I should never have come with Darren.'

All words, words, meaningless words, and the tension crackled between us like so much static. I could smell the horse and the sea, and in the dull light of the porch I looked at Cally and she looked at me, and nothing was said. Yet what a welter of thoughts kaleidoscoped through my mind, this incredible longing to stretch out and touch her, kiss her, and aware that she was so much older than me, knew so much more about the ways of the world.

'Would you like to give Dapple-Down a carrot?' she asked.

'I'd love to.'

She pulled a carrot from her pocket and gave it to me. I offered it up to the horse on the flat of my palm, with my thumb tucked low.

Dapple-Down leaned forward and kissed my hand with his lips. I could feel his teeth smooth on my skin. We listened in silence to the sound of the horse contentedly champing. Our eyes were locked. I had a sense of our faces, our lips, moving closer to each other, but maybe that's just what happens when you look long enough into a woman's eyes.

There was a bang from the pub door. It was Roland.

'There you are!' He bumbled over. The spell was broken. Cally stepped in towards the horse and stroked its nose.

'Saved by the bell,' she said softly, and we looked and we stared, and she gave me this calm nod, as if to say that we must accept whatever it was that the fates decided to throw at us.

'Hi, I'm Roland.' He stretched out his hand. 'I work at the hotel with Kim.'

'Hi Roland. Yes, I've seen you often at the hotel. I'm Cally.' They shook hands. 'So how's your evening going so far?'

'Not bad,' he said. 'Though everyone round here seems to have got a girlfriend, except for me and of course Kim.'

'Not for want of trying,' I said.

Cally looked from me and then to Roland and then back to me again. 'I'm going now.' She put on her riding hat. 'Would you like to ride with me?'

'I…' I paused, for I had some history with horses. I have always been quite diabolically bad at riding. 'I'd love to.'

'Great,' she said. She was like an acrobat as she swung herself up onto Dapple-Down. It was a big horse, but Cally, as ever, made it look effortless. 'Tomorrow after lunch? How's that suit?'

'That would be lovely.'

Roland and I watched her as the horse clip-clopped sedately down the road.

'She likes them young, doesn't she?' Roland said.

'What do you mean?' I said

'First Darren; now you.'

'I'm sure you'll get your turn eventually.'

'She'd do just fine,' he said. 'I'm not picky.'

The next morning, as I shaved and showered and served full English breakfasts to the holidaymakers, there was only one thought running through my head. In six hours I would be seeing Cally and we would be riding together. It was the most breathless anticipation, but combined with it was this seasick queasiness that comes over me when I have to mix with horses. I did not have any idea what was going to happen that afternoon, though I did fear the worst.

My tortured brain managed to produce every conceivable scenario, most of which revolved around my horse somehow being startled and then bolting off at high speed. From there I could picture myself with my fingers entwined in the horse's mane as it galloped hard over the heath, flying over ditches and dry-stone walls, before finally catching its fetlock in a rabbit hole. I was almost positive that it was going to end badly for me. I didn't even know where the nearest hospital was, but hospital certainly seemed on the cards, and there I would rest up for a week or three as Cally brought me books and grapes and tenderly nursed me back to health.

In the morning after breakfast, I played golf with Anthony. The hotel had a pitch-and-putt course, which was small but lethal. There were no fairways, and if you did not land your ball plum on the green, then you were stuck thrashing for ever in the heather. Every drive was either a hit or a complete miss; there was absolutely no margin for error.

I was playing like a donkey. Anthony was four up after four holes.

'Something on your mind, Kim?' he asked as he teed up.

'Nothing,' I said. 'Nothing at all. You're playing out of your skin.'

'Don't think so.' His ball looped high into the air like a mortar, before trickling onto the front edge of the green. 'How are you enjoying it at the Knoll House?'

'Very much.' I teed up my ball.

'You seeing anyone?' he asked.

'Nope.' I swiped at the ball and shanked it into some bushes. 'Nobody.'

'Won't be long before you're snapped up.' He tossed another ball to my feet. 'Have another go.'

I sent the next ball straight into the same bush.

'And again.' Another ball dribbled to my feet.

I could not believe it. For the third time, I smacked the ball into the bush.

'Remarkable,' said Anthony. 'I've never seen that done before.' He tossed down a fourth ball. 'So what's on your mind?'

My normal reaction would have been to hide anything that even remotely touched on an affair of the heart. I wouldn't have dreamed of mentioning my passing passion, even to a friend like Oliver. And yet there was something so utterly disarming about Anthony's blunt, cheery face that I opened up to him.

'Cally,' I said. I twirled the club in my hand.

'Cally,' he said meditatively. 'Cally is lovely.'

'I'm going riding with her after lunch.'

'Ah,' he said. 'That's what's wrong with your golf. I'm sure you'll have lots of fun. But...' He trailed off and gazed out to the grey sea and the grey horizon. For a long time I waited for him to finish speaking, but he said nothing more.

'But what?' I asked.

I don't know if he was going to say anything more, but he just shrugged and laughed. 'But I'm sure you don't need to be told that!' he said. 'You young whippersnappers never do anything else but have fun!'

I teed the ball up, focused, drilled it to the back of the green.

I remember how the sun shone. Anthony was whistling Lilliburlero as he merrily went on his way; now there, truly, was a man who didn't have a care in the world.

CHAPTER 9

I don't recall much of lunch that day, because I was so desperate to leave. After we were done, I flew back to my room. I had a lightning shave, and I nicked my cheek, and do what I might, the cut would not stop bleeding. I was furious with myself, and spent minutes trying to stem the blood before plugging the cut with some toilet paper. I pulled on jeans and boots and my coat and then stumped off to Cally's house.

It was the first time that I had seen her house in the day; it was beautiful, just exactly the sort of holiday home by the sea that you would dream of. Set off to the side was a garage that I hadn't noticed before, as well as two stables and a small barn for chickens and bantams and horse feed.

Cally was already outside with the horses. Dapple-Down was saddled up, and she was just working at the buckle of a second slightly smaller horse. It was a black mare, at least a couple of hands smaller than Dapple-Down; it seemed docile enough.

'Hello Kim.' Cally was in her tight britches and cream shirt and a very trim grey jacket. She had a silk stock, held in place with a gold tiepin; the brown leather of her boots absolutely gleamed. In comparison, I was a ragamuffin.

'Hi,' I said. Now that I was confronted with the reality of Cally, in person and in the flesh, I was of course rendered into clodding inarticulacy. It was like I had blundered into mental quicksand that had dulled my synapses and turned my gushing words into a rancid little trickle.

She looked at me quickly and smiled.

'Come and meet Scampi,' she said.

'Good name for a horse.' I went over and gave the horse a stroke.

'You have ridden before, haven't you, Kim?' said Cally.

'A long time ago,' I said. 'I'm very rusty.'

'You'll be great,' she said. 'Need a hand up?'

'I'll be fine.'

I put on some black leather gloves. She had found me a substantial helmet; in my mind's eye, I was already preparing myself for the inevitable fall that would occur some time that afternoon. I wondered if I'd even make it out of the yard before the horse managed to buck me.

I put a boot into the stirrup and hauled myself up. From years back, I vaguely remembered how to hold the reins. Cally inspected me. I knew enough to know that I should sit straight with my shoulders back, like a cavalry officer on parade.

'You look good,' she said, swinging herself up onto Dapple-Down. 'Shall we go?'

We ambled at a slow walk through green fields and down towards the sea. Cally was riding next to me. We were almost knee to knee. I was no longer quite so edgy now that I was concentrating on not falling off.

Cally was smoking. She had crop and reins in one hand and her cigarette in the other. She looked very stylish. 'Can't be too long today,' she said. 'I've got a boring appointment at four thirty.'

'An hour will be perfect,' I said.

'See how we get on,' she said. 'Shall we trot?'

My heart sank. Despite a dozen riding lessons during a teenage summer, I have always been particularly inept at the rising trot. As the horse moves, you rise up out of the stirrups. But the movement is almost syncopated, like a Scott Joplin rag, so that you're rising not on the beat but just a fraction of a second afterwards.

Not that Cally noticed, or if she did, she didn't care a fig. She was always happy when she was out riding.

'She's a very easy ride, isn't she?' Cally said. 'That's why I chose her. She's my daughter's horse.'

'Your daughter?' In all our encounters, I had never once heard mention of a daughter.

'Fiona,' she said. 'She's studying in America at the moment.'

'Wow.' I was momentarily taken flat aback at the idea that this beautiful woman had a daughter who was practically my own age. 'You must have been a child bride.'

'I don't know about that,' she said. 'Married and pregnant at twenty-two. It worked out – for a while. I was very happy when we split up.' She had started on another cigarette and puffed on it as she opened the next gate. 'I won't marry again.'

'Who knows,' I said, 'you may yet get swept off your feet.'

She was smiling, almost laughing, as she closed the gate. 'I'm certainly hoping to be swept off my feet again, thank you, Kim darling,' she said. 'But marriage is not for me. You, on the other hand, I think marriage might suit you very well.'

'We'll see.'

The bridleway was narrow and uneven, cracked with narrow gullies where the streams of rain had carved through the chalk. I thought about getting off my horse, but the mare seemed steady enough. On all sides, we were hemmed in by trees and hedgerows so thick that they all but arched over our heads. I could already hear the sea on the sand, and as the flies droned in the hazy afternoon, the horses' ears flickered and their tails switched from side to side. Just a few yards ahead of me was Cally, a horsewoman to her very bootstraps. Even from behind she was a picture of easy elegance, a little stream of cigarette smoke eddying above her helmet.

The hedgerow dwindled to scrub and the chalk bridleway turned to sand and suddenly the sea opened up ahead of us. We rode at a leisurely pace through dunes and marram grass, and then we were on the hard, compact sand of the beach, and the horses pricked up their ears and cantered towards the sea. Cantering is easy; anyone can canter. Just bend your knees, lift up out of the saddle and lean slightly forward and, of course, hold on tight to the horse's mane. I dug my fingers deep into the mare's thick hair.

The tide was out and the horses' hooves tore up a hail of wet sand. Cally pulled up in the shallows and we stood in the sea, exuding exhilaration and verve and life.

'You ready for a gallop?' she asked.

'I think so.'

'Let's go.'

With a slight squeeze of her thighs, she turned Dapple-Down's head and we started cantering up the beach in the direction of the Knoll House. And then, imperceptibly, she gave her horse a tweak and it was like flooring the accelerator in a sports car, for suddenly we were thundering along the beach at an all-out gallop. I had forgotten the extraordinary thrill of being astride a horse at full throttle. You can sometimes get a bit of it when you're skiing a black run on the very edge or when you're surfing. But the sheer speed and power of being on a horse at full gallop is something else altogether.

I don't know how fast we were going, but perched eight, nine feet above the ground, it was terrifying. Ahead of us, way ahead of us, we could see a couple walking hand in hand towards us through the surf.

It seemed like only a matter of moments before we were upon them. In a flash, I recognised that it was Oliver and Annette. I raised a hand as we tore past. 'Hola!' I called. A glimpse of Oliver's amazed face as he recognised me.

I'd never ridden on a beach before; I don't think I'd even galloped on a horse before. But it was a total revelation. I think beforehand I'd always associated riding with prissy girls and haughty women and fat men in hunting pink, drinking cherry brandy. Well, I'm sure there is a bit of that. In any activity, there will always be people who grate. But it was the first time that I ever truly experienced the joy of riding, that heady rush of elation as we galloped along the Studland beach, with the sand and the surf spattering beneath our hooves.

Eventually, Cally eased up. She pulled a silver hip flask from her pocket and offered it to me. I took a swig. It was Grand Marnier, very cold, and I could feel it pumping heat into my core. 'Thank you.' I passed it to Cally. She didn't wipe the top, but just put it straight between her lips and drank. A tress of wet hair lay on her cheek and she smoothed it away. I couldn't take my eyes off her lips. There was still some liqueur on her mouth and her lips glistened in the sun. I wanted to lean over and kiss her.

'What about that then?' she said.

'Brilliant.'

'Brought a bit of colour to your face.'

We were facing each other, our horses side to side. She offered me the hip flask again and I took it and I drank.

'I think I'd die if I couldn't ride,' Cally said.

I smiled and tried to think of something pleasant to say. My brain stalled. I busied myself with rubbing the horse's neck. What does one say to a woman when there is nothing left to say and all that you want to do is kiss her?

We looked at each other. If a picture can sometimes be worth a thousand words, then that one gaze contained a whole book.

Without using her hands, she turned Dapple-Down around, and as she did so, her knee brushed against mine. As the whole of this delicate manoeuvre was performed, her eyes never once left mine.

We cantered back, nice and easy. Cally eased up so that we were side by side, riding knee to knee; she carried herself like a jockey.

Annette and Oliver had already left the beach. In silence, we rode up the bridleway, out of the sunshine and into the shade, and each of us alone with our thoughts. I wondered if I'd blown it. Sometimes, with a kiss, you can miss the moment, and there may never be another one.

We rode into the yard, and then led the horses through to the stables. I was relieved that the ride had passed without mishap. The stables were wide and airy, thick with fresh straw and with two cast-iron mangers bracketed onto the wall. There was a deep water trough, and a small orange feed bucket by one of the stalls.

I watched as Cally unbuckled saddles and bits and reins. There was nothing I could do to help, but when she picked up some straw and rubbed down her horse's flanks, I quickly followed her lead. I started at Scampi's neck and moved down to her flanks and legs. She was wet with sea and sweat and her underbelly was dusted with sand.

Cally had finished and came over to admire my handiwork. I could not see her but I was aware that she was standing quite close to me.

I gave a last sweep across Scampi's back and tossed the straw onto the floor.

'Very good,' said Cally.

I smiled at her and made to walk out of the stall. But there was not much space and I planted my foot into the bucket of feed. I lost my balance and staggered into Cally. She caught me, her arms full about me. Without even a moment's hesitation we were kissing each other, hard and urgent and with all the open-mouthed ardour of a passion that had been denied, defied, for so long.

For a second we broke off, looked at each other, smiled and, still staring into each other's eyes, we kissed each other again, very softly at first, until eyes closed and lips parted and our tongues tasted and dabbed. We were locked into each other's kisses. I opened my eyes briefly, and saw Cally's mouth open underneath my own. I couldn't believe it that this was Cally, straining up beneath me, and that my mouth was upon her lips.

We explored each other's mouths and cheeks and faces, and for a moment Cally drew back and kissed my eyelids. I felt like I had been blessed.

'I love your kisses,' she said.

'I've been wanting to kiss you for a long time.'

'Not half as long as I have wanted to kiss you.'

'Really?' We had not kissed for all of ten seconds, and we were already eager for more. I kissed her again, very gently.

Still holding onto me with one hand, she looked at her watch. 'I'm so sorry,' she said. 'I've got to go.'

'Your four thirty appointment.'

'But perhaps later we will be able to continue where we left off?' Her eyes twinkled as she stretched up to kiss me again.

'I hope so,' I said.

'I wondered if you might be around tomorrow?'

'I am.' I kissed her. How could I not kiss those lips that were but six inches from my own, especially as, in that moment, I was free to kiss her lips just as and when I wanted? 'It's my day off.'

'Oh good,' she said. Another look and another kiss. When lovers first start kissing, they can never have too much of each other's mouths. 'I'll cook you some lunch.'

'Perfect. What time?'

'Say...' She kissed me. 'Say noon. On the beach.'

'I'll bring my trunks,' I said. 'Whereabouts on the beach?'

'Where you see the smoke, that's where my fire will be.'

Back at the hotel, I ate my tea dreamily. I, Kim, was going to be seeing Cally the next day. I couldn't help wondering, speculating, if there might be more than kisses on offer. But I was in no hurry. Besides, Cally was much older than me; she knew her own mind and would know exactly how slowly – or how fast – she wanted to take things. Yes, Cally could call the shots, and I would happily, delightedly, go along with whatever she suggested. She was obviously experienced, sophisticated; she had been married, had a daughter. How long, I wondered, would it be before she wanted more than my kisses? Would it be a quick burn, heady, fast and furious, or would it be a languorous, slow courtship, delightfully paced over many months before we succumbed to the inevitable?

I couldn't tell. Slow or fast or perhaps it might even be a no-go altogether, a 'terribly sorry, big mistake, alcohol and idle curiosity, and the huge age difference between us, and so do please forgive me, but I do not wish to kiss you ever again' sort of thing.

As we were having tea, Anthony came to talk to us. He stood there, slightly awkward, rubbing the back of his hand with his fingers. He was already dressed for dinner in dinner jacket and bow tie. Gradually the chatter dwindled and Anthony had our attention.

'I'm afraid that somebody has been stealing some of the wages from my office,' he said. 'I'm sure that it's none of you. But, in the unlikely event that it is, could you kindly desist, otherwise there will be some general unpleasantness which will almost certainly involve the police.' His face lapsed into a smile; that was his natural default. 'Thank you. I know it won't be any of you, but seeing as I've discussed it with the rest of the staff, I could hardly avoid mentioning it to you lot.'

Anthony walked away, and there was a momentary lull before we all started talking at the same time.

'So that's why you're always so flush with money,' I said to Oliver.

'You are right,' he said. 'My little secret is out.'

'No more buying drinks for the entire pub, then?'

'There may have to be some cost cutting'

'And no more going off to Swanage for dinner with Annette?'

'Ah,' he said. He tried to prong a roast potato. It shot off his plate and onto the floor. He picked up the potato and, without even looking, ate it with his fingers. 'I do not mind not paying for your drinks. But Annette will still have to be taken out for dinner.'

'She'll love you whatever you do.'

'I am sure she will. But a woman like Annette deserves the very best,' he said. 'I am not prepared to compromise on either flowers or dinners.'

'Where are you going to get the money if you don't nick it?'

'All right,' he said. 'I will not steal from Anthony any more. I will just take it straight out of your wallet.'

'My door is always open.'

'That is kind of you.'

Michelle and Tracy had been listening to our conversation. They both looked thoroughly bemused.

'So it was you who stole the money?' Michelle said to Oliver.

'No, no, no!' I said. 'It wasn't Oliver, it was me!'

Roland joined in. 'It was neither of you two clowns. I was the thief!'

Janeen piped up, 'I stole the money!'

It was not long before everyone was at it. 'I was the thief!' 'No, I was the thief!' 'No, I stole the money!' Oliver was louder by far than anybody else. 'I stole the money!' he shouted.

Anthony popped his head round and stared at the madness. He was about to speak but thought better of it and with a shake of his head he left us to it. I had not realised how, over the previous two or three months, our tight-knit team had developed the most incredible *esprit de corps*.

It was early on in the evening and I was loafing around with Michelle and Tracy when I saw a young couple come in. Anthony gave them his usual effusive welcome, they chatted, and then the couple looked over at the cluster of waiters and waitresses. They peered at us, sizing us up, before the woman smiled. She seemed to point at me. More banter from Anthony; they were led to one of my tables.

As I walked over to their table, I was quite sure that I had never served them before, but there was something oddly familiar about the couple; I had this tingle, the slightest shake of a rattlesnake's tail, that told me to tread warily.

They were a youngish couple, just a little bit older than me; he was clean cut, in a blazer and tie, and she was a blonde, with big hair, Margaret Thatcher hair, perhaps even a little Sloaney. Her pearls and silk shirt made her look older than she was. They were married and she had a large diamond solitaire.

But I just couldn't place them. Where had I met them before? Was it London? It didn't seem likely that I'd met them in the local pub.

'Good evening,' I said, menus in hand. 'Welcome to the Knoll House.'

The woman smiled at me. Scarlet lipstick and not a line on her face. But the look on her face was that she had the cards; she knew something that I did not.

'Good evening, Kim,' she said. That was fair enough. I had my dog tag on. 'How are you?'

'Just great, thank you.'

The woman's smile got wider. She's got me, I thought, scanning through memories of places and parties, and lunches and pubs, but it still wasn't coming through. I've definitely seen her before somewhere.

'You don't know who I am, do you?' she said.

I gave the standard riposte. 'Of course I do.'

There was no let up.

'Well, tell us then, Kim,' she said. 'Where did we meet and who are we?'

I temporised. 'You don't think I know, do you?'

'No,' she said. 'I don't. And to think you've forgotten us so soon.' She was enjoying herself. Was a silent slithering hiss of sexuality in the air? I don't know, but there was definitely an edge. We had certainly gone way, way beyond a normal waiter–guest relationship.

The man edged into the conversation. 'I don't think you're being strictly fair, Ju, dear.'

I seized on the name. Ju? It had to be short for Julie, or Juliet, or Julia, but none of those names were quite right. And then, even as I was talking, it all came back to me.

'I know exactly who you are, Julienne,' I said. 'You and Mark very kindly gave me a lift to this hotel just before Easter—'

'You're good,' she said.

'Just a humble waiter going about his business,' I said. 'And how is your little boy, James?'

Very lightly, Mark clapped his hands. 'I think that's checkmate, darling.'

She smiled. I noticed her eyes sizing me, raking me from top to toe. 'You're wasted on a place like this,' she said.

'That's exactly what my stepmother says.'

I gave them the menus and got them some wine, but apart from the usual civilities we didn't really talk again until I was clearing away the main course.

'You'll be after some of the pudding, won't you now?' I said. 'I remember how you were raving about the hotel's puddings. But perhaps I could tempt you to a half-bottle of chilled Sauterne – I am told it is delicious with chocolate.'

Julienne did a double take. 'You're up-selling!' she said.

'Up-selling?'

'Selling us more stuff.'

'Is that terribly naughty?'

'You must meet my sister.'

'You said that the last time we met. So what's your sister's name and when am I going to meet her?'

'Her name is Louise. She's just finished her finals.' Julienne primped her hair. I quite liked her, though her make-up, her hairspray, her pearls and earrings were too much for a woman in her twenties. She didn't need any of it; all this artifice was merely gilding the lily.

'Well, if Louise can't think of anything better to do, then send her to the Knoll House,' I said. 'We're always on the look out for bright young things.'

'You never know,' said Julienne. 'She's coming to stay soon. I'll bring her here.'

'And has Louise lined herself up some fancy job in the City?'

'Perhaps. She wants to be a lawyer.'

I staged a very elaborate yawn, fluttering my fingers over my mouth.

'My sentiments exactly,' Julienne said. 'Do you think you might be able to dissuade her?'

She looked at me. She played with her earring. As I watched her, I caught myself wondering whether there just a part of her that yearned to be nothing but a carefree young woman, with no house, no husband, no career, and with nothing whatsoever to prevent her from kissing just exactly who she pleased.

CHAPTER 10

By now, the hotel was in full swing. It was early June and still term time, so it was going to be a month or so before the real action started with the mums in their designer gear, and the dads with their tums and their newspapers and the precocious teenagers in search of drink and love and sex and adventure. How little our tastes change over the decades.

I shaved before breakfast, and I shaved again three hours later. I'd been thinking about what to take Cally; obviously not anything that could be bought, so instead I wandered into the woods and started collecting a posy of wild flowers. My stepmother Edie would have known the names of every single one of them, and probably the Latin too, but beyond the dandelions and the buttercups and the honeysuckle, I knew the names of none of them. They looked pretty though. I was going for the most colourful flowers that I could find, snatching up bulrushes and marsh herbs and slender twigs from trees as accents.

'What are you doing?'

It was Michelle out for a walk with Tracy. I was trying to snap off some heather, but the gnarly shrubs were much tougher than I'd expected.

'Just picking some heather,' I said.

The girls came over to have a look and saw the other flowers that I had already picked.

'Sweet,' Michelle said. 'Getting some flowers for your girlfriend.'

'Not really,' I said.

'Come on,' Tracy said. 'He's shy. He doesn't want to tell us.'

'I wish I had a boyfriend who picked me flowers.'

'Why don't you just tell him?' I asked.

'It'd be even nicer if I didn't have to ask.'

'A flower in the hand is worth two in the bush.'

'What's that?'

'Guys don't know a thing,' I said. 'They know nothing. The only time they know what a woman wants is when she tells them.'

They waved as they went on their giggling way. Tracy peeked at me over her shoulder. Now there was a woman who was destined to make someone a wonderful wife.

I found an old piece of bailer's twine on some barbed wire and tied up my flowers. It was now more of a bouquet than a posy, with the bulrushes in the middle and the more delicate flowers on the outside. The flowers were pleasingly rustic, all set off by the orange twine.

I had wondered about putting on aftershave, but then decided against it. I guessed that Cally was an *au naturel* woman.

And then: to the beach. It was about a fifteen-minute walk from the hotel and meanwhile my guts were concertinaing at the very prospect of seeing Cally again and what exactly, if anything, would happen between us. Maybe we'd kiss. I hope we'd kiss. But I was all too aware that, in a fledgling relationship, twenty-four hours is an absolute aeon. Cally might well have come to her senses.

I was certain that I wouldn't be able to eat. New love seems to shrink my stomach to the size of a walnut. I can't even eat a mouthful of bread. I can still drink, but the alcohol just goes straight to my head, making me burble the most absurd inanities.

I got to the beach and looked for the tell-tale trail of smoke that would lead, rainbow-like, to my pot of fairy gold. I could not see the fire itself, but I could see the smoke, and I grinned when I saw it, because it meant that Cally was waiting for me. The fire was about half a mile away, in the dunes behind some beach huts.

I walked along the wet sand, the surf sighing in and licking over my boots. I didn't dawdle, but I was not in a hurry either. Now that I knew that Cally was waiting for me in the marram grass, these delicious waves of anticipation washed over me and I wanted to eke it out for as long as I possibly could. How could the reality ever match up to my ridiculous expectations? It was turning into a lovely day.

I put some Vaseline on my lips. I like to have moist lips; I also like to kiss moist mouths.

Cally was some way in to the dunes, at the bottom of a large crater-like hollow, and her fire was well out of the wind. She saw me the very moment that I appeared over the top of the dune, and waved enthusiastically.

I coasted down the dune. She was sitting on a tartan rug and had obviously been there for some time, because the fire was at least an hour old. Cally was wearing tight jeans and a paint-spattered Musto fleece. She had a notepad in hand and was drawing the fire itself. She had turned it into a Hieronymus Bosch-style picture of hell, packed with tortured souls and demons; tucked over in the corner was a wanton posing as the very she-devil herself.

I stooped down to kiss her. I had intended to kiss her on the cheek, but she moved her face and we kissed on the lips. Her fingers cupped my smooth-shaven cheek. I sat down next to her on the rug.

She looked very demure with her legs tucked almost underneath her. I gave her the flowers.

'Thank you, I love them.' She put them by her side and for a while she just gazed at them with a huge smile on her face. 'Like a beer?'

'I'd love one.'

She flicked the tops off two bottles of Dos Equis. The beer was beautifully cold. We chinked and sipped. I looked at her picture.

'It looks hellish,' I said.

She smirked. We sipped again and stared at each other, and ever more slowly, but now synchronised, we took another sip from our bottles, our eyes never once leaving each other, and then as one, we leaned in and kissed each other.

We kissed and we kissed. Most of the time my eyes were closed as I wallowed in the texture of her lips and the light dab of Cally's tongue, but sometimes I would open my eyes and I would look, just for the sheer joy of seeing Cally's cheek next to mine and her lips working languidly against my own.

I was very careful to follow Cally's lead. It was a type of kiss that was new to me, for although our lips were parted and tongues occasionally touching, there was none of this open-mouthed plunging; it was a much more delicate type of kiss than I had ever known before. I liked it. I liked it a lot.

When we broke off, Cally stared at me with this smile on her face before throwing her arm around my neck and kissing me on the cheek.

'That,' she said, 'was a kiss.'

'It was a wonderful kiss.'

'I'm glad I experienced it before I died. What a miss that would have been.'

'Who's talking about dying?'

'Where, I wonder, did you learn to do that?' She looked at me dreamily. 'Kiss me again. I want you to kiss me again.'

I kissed her again. And again I followed her lead. It was then that I realised that what she wanted was the texture of my mouth, and to bite gently at my lips, to lead slowly and for me to follow. She stretched behind her and put her bottle into the sand and now with both hands about me, she lay back on the rug and drew me on top of her. She worked her hands under my shirt until her fingers were cool against my back. I could feel the dry paint on her hands.

My face was just a few inches above hers. I could see specks of sparkling gold in her eyes. Gradually the rest of our bodies synchronised with our lips and I could feel Cally straining against me.

'God in heaven,' she said. 'I want you so much.'

'I want you.'

'Not outside though. At least not yet.'

'Don't want to scare the horses.'

'And they scare very easily.' She continued to look at me and gave me a peck. 'Come with me.'

We got up. She tucked the flowers under her arm and took my hand.

'And the fire?'

'And the fire and the cooler can take care of themselves for a little while.'

'We might come back and find that Goldilocks has eaten our sausages.'

Cally led me to the top of the dune, through the fringe of marram, and we scampered down the other side. 'Goldilocks is welcome!'

I didn't know where we were going. I assumed we were heading for Cally's house, but instead we made for the long line of beach huts. Her hut was a lovely, light pastel blue with a tiled roof. Unlike most of the beach huts, she had a small wooden veranda with a couple of deckchairs. On the walls and on the balcony rails were shells and seaweed and bits of gnarled wood that had been sucked by the sea. As she went up the stairs, her fingers caressed a large piece of glass, forest green and pebble-smooth.

She pushed open the door and we went inside. It was just the one room, small and exquisite, with a window at the back and a much larger window looking out towards the sea. And as she took the flowers over to the sink, I took in this new world. One long wall bristled from floor to ceiling with shelves full of books and games and pictures and a treasure trove of mementoes, driftwood and pebbles and starfish and ocean-worn glass. At the back was a kitchenette of sorts, with a sink and a small cooker and a dainty breakfast table and two wooden chairs. Leaning against the wall was an easel as well as a number of canvases, some blank and some halfway there.

In the middle of the room, looking out towards the sea, were two large pillar-box red leather armchairs. From the ceiling hung a kite and a mobile of seashells, and a landing net and two old cane fishing rods.

Most striking of all was one of Cally's paintings, which took up almost the entire wall. It was a raging seascape, with white horses on waves and the wind blowing hard through a vivid patchwork of the sky at dusk.

Cally kissed me as her hands stroked my chest.

'Could you help move these chairs?' she said. We moved the armchairs right up next to the window. Cally then tugged at a black leather strap at the top of her seascape picture, and as it started coming towards me, I realised that behind the picture was a foldaway bed. It was a massive double bed, with a sumptuous foot-thick mattress, cantilevered so that it glided easily to the ground.

The picture disappeared and in its stead, the bed took up almost half the room, with white pillows and a white down duvet.

'It's from Malaysia,' she explained. 'I took a fancy to it and had shipped it back home.' The frame was substantial, each side as thick as a telegraph pole; it was built to last. 'Centuries from now, that bed will still be being used for sleeping and for loving.'

The wood was very dark, perhaps teak, but what made it so extraordinary was that it was covered with hundreds of words – English, German, French, Spanish, along with other languages that I didn't recognise. The words had been carved out, to different sizes and depths, all about the bed frame, and had then been underscored with white lime. At the head of the bed, carved deep in formal eight-inch letters, was the word 'Love', and this was the Queen Bee to all the other words that sprawled and wandered about the bed. I can still see to this day the most extraordinary mix of words 'Tenderness' and 'Mercy', through to 'Grease' and 'Canvas Bag' and towards the bottom, 'Futility' and even '*Todt*', the German word for death.

Cally undid the three buckles, smoothed the duvet and plumped the pillows, and when all was pristine, she sat on the edge and patted the bed next to her.

'Come here and kiss me,' she said.

I sat down next to her, a parody of primness, my hands cupped on my legs. She kissed me. It was rather nice. With our lips, we pecked very slowly, very languorously, at each other, our knees tight together, but our hungry hands still tucked tidily away. Here, now, it all seems like the most unbelievable luxury. A whole afternoon, a whole night, to make love, to roam free about each other's bodies, and not a thing in the world to stop us. And not befuddled with drink and not heavy from food and with none of that reckless urgency that comes from having not enough time and not enough patience.

So I took my time. On that afternoon, I decided, I would submit to being led wherever Cally wanted to take me. Even from the first, I think that she knew exactly where she wanted to go and was intent on showing me all of the sights along the way.

'May I?' She tugged at my jumper. It was an old white Aran that my grandmother had knitted for me after I'd left school. It was not as clean as it had once been, but each wine stain, each scuff mark was a story of my life.

I stretched up and she pulled the jumper over my head.

'That's better.' With deft fingers, she started unbuttoning my shirt. Her eyes were focused on my torso and her fingers strayed onto my dusting of chest hair.

'You're not asking permission?' I said.

She looked up and I smiled at her.

'I should have, you're right,' she said. 'I was just…'

Her eyes strayed back to my bare chest. She kissed my shoulder blade as she eased the shirt off my back.

'I was mesmerised,' she said.

She kissed my shoulders and her kisses moved from my neck to my lips and then back to my heart.

'You're mesmerising me,' I said. I could not take my eyes off her lips against my naked skin. 'And I, can I help you—'

She stayed my wandering hands. 'No, Kim,' she said. 'Leave me be. I'm enjoying myself. It's been a long time.'

So I submitted.

The window was slightly open. I could see the sea and hear the waves rumbling into the shore; who needs music when you have the sounds of the ocean?

My boots were untied and taken off and my socks followed, and Cally kissed my toes, every one of them. 'I like your smell,' she said.

She worked her fingers at my belt, and old brown belt with a thick brass buckle that had been given to me by my father.

She stroked my jeans and raised a coquettish eyebrow. 'May I?' she said.

'Would you?'

One by one, she popped the rivets on my trousers, and then as I straightened my legs, she took the trousers by the hem and pulled them off in one dextrous flick.

Standing beside the bed, she looked down at me. My body wasn't buffed or ripped and I certainly never worked out, but as I remember it, when Cally looked at me, I think she liked what she saw.

'I think I'll leave it at that for the moment,' she said. 'I'm going to join you.'

And as she started to take off her top, she was singing very softly. I'd heard the English variation of the song before, but this was the first time that I had heard Charles Trenet's original French version of 'La Mer'. She knew every word of it; I could not take my eyes off her. She stood just a few feet in front of me and took off her fleece before letting it fall to the floor. She kicked off her espadrilles, and then pulled off her trousers. I don't know how she did it, but she managed to make it all look so unbelievably sexy. Firm, solid thighs, a rider's thighs, well-muscled and used to hard work. She was wearing simple white cotton knickers. I loved that. I longed to stretch out and touch her, and to taste her skin, but I knew that in this first dance, Cally had the lead.

She had on a white cotton shirt and was still singing in French as she unbuttoned it. She unbuttoned the cuffs and then she stepped out of her shirt and towards me. I marvelled. She was quite unlike any of my other lovers. In Cally, there was no rake-thin flesh, no obsession with diet and drink and no absurd quest for the Perfect Size Zero like there is today. Her hips rolled out from underneath the elastic of her knickers, and as for her breasts, they positively strained against the confines of her bra. She was sexy as hell.

She stretched behind her, undid the clasps, and her white bra fell to the floor.

'How am I doing so far?' she said.

'Pretty well.'

'Can I join you?'

'I'd like that.' I stretched a hand up to her. 'I'd like that very much.'

WILLIAM COLES

I lay back on the bed and Cally lay on top off me, her warm skin pressed hard against mine. She kissed me, our legs locked with each other and for a moment we writhed.

We kissed again and she broke off and she smiled at me. 'I don't know about you,' she said, 'and this may sound a bit previous. But I'm...' She kissed me again. 'I'm very excited at the prospect of making love with you.'

'Are you now?'

'Very,' she said. 'But, actually there is one thing: the *petit mort*, if you don't mind me calling it that.'

'I don't mind you talking about my little death.'

'The other words for it are all so coarse.'

'I've never thought about it like that, but you're probably right—'

'Will you humour me?' she said.

'How.'

'When it comes to your petit mort, you must first have my permission. Okay?'

'Okay.'

'Good.' She clapped her hands. 'But let me tell you now, Kim, that that permission will not be given lightly.'

'But there is going to be some tit for tat isn't there?' I asked. 'You're also going to be asking for my permission?'

'Of course,' she said.

'Excellent.'

As we kissed, our hands roamed free about each other's skin. For a moment her fingers strayed teasingly beneath my boxers. There was something incredibly erotic about the thin strips of cotton that still divided us.

Slowly our lips strayed from mouths to necks and chests and belly buttons and knees, with lingering tongues that promised so much yet never quite touched.

I don't know how it would have turned out if I had had my way that afternoon, but I think that after perhaps an hour or so of licking and stroking and teasing, then I might have suggested that it was time for the *coup de grace*. But not Cally. Her kisses had wandered all about my body and she had come back up for air, while I was burning with desire, like a tinder-dry forest that needs but one single spark to start an inferno.

'Fancy a beer?' she said.

It was not remotely what I'd expected to hear, but I submitted.

'I'd love a beer,' I said.

I watched as she sashayed over to the icebox by the sink, her gorgeous rolling hips lilting from side to side. She stooped deliciously and retrieved a single bottle of beer. She opened it, brought it back, and then straddled me as she took a deep sip from the bottle. She leant forward, her full breasts trailing lightly on my chest, and kissed me, the beer trickling from her mouth into mine.

What a way to drink an entire bottle of beer. I was as putty in her hands.

I smelled something in her hair. It was like pine resin in a verdant Spanish forest on a hot summer's day.

'Is that turps in your hair?' I asked.

She took a lock of hair and sniffed. 'It's like artist's turpentine,' she said. 'It's Damask resin, a varnish. It's a bit more gummy, like a globule of tree sap.'

'A globule of tree sap?' I echoed. 'That's a nice turn of phrase. And what other smells do you have about you?'

'Let me see,' she said. And she started to sniff at her hands and her forearms. 'There's the white spirit, rather acrid, chemical, gets you right at the back of the throat.'

'For cleaning your brushes?'

She nodded before sniffing her wrist, and when she could find nothing new there, she stretched to the floor and picked up her Musto. She put one of the sleeves to her nose and inhaled.

'Ah!' she breathed and she inhaled again. 'Musty and sweet. Linseed. Useful for diluting the paint mix.'

She thrust the sleeve under my nose and the smell brought back memories of summer holidays in the Cotswolds and fields of grey-blue pastel flowers. 'Cricket bats,' I said.

She'd found another smell on the collar of her fleece. 'And beeswax.'

'Like honey mixed with turps.' I'd never dreamed that a single item of clothing could have held such a wealth of smells. 'What's that for?'

'Makes the paint more opaque. Gives it a soapy texture.'

I had the front of her Musto to my nose now and was picking up the smells of the paints themselves. I'd thought that they would smell the same, but each had its own peculiar aroma. The creamy sweet smell of titanium white and the more acidic smell of Indian yellow, which was the colour of bright turmeric.

Towards the zipper, where she'd leaned against the easel, I came across a rich vein of umbers. 'I like these.'

She took the Musto back and held it to her face. She knew the oils without even having to open her eyes. 'Burnt sienna,' she said. 'Raw umber. Oh, and that's burnt umber, redder, chocolatey.'

She thrust the fleece back under my nose. 'By the zipper. It's like damp undergrowth.'

'Mulchy wood chips.'

Cally looked at me, arch. 'All this talk of paint. It reminds me that…' She kissed me. 'We need some oil.'

She broke off to start nosing through a cupboard by the sink. 'Olive oil?' she asked. 'Sesame oil? That might be nice. White wine vinegar? Red wine vinegar? Or even malt vinegar?'

She squatted down and I gazed at those solid, firm thighs. She was rooting through a cupboard under the sink. 'Never seen this before,' she said, holding up what looked like a small brown medicine bottle. 'It must be Fiona's.' She squinted at the stained label. 'Coconut oil! Perfect!'

She asked me to lie on my front and, well trained and obedient, I submitted. I could hear her rubbing the coconut oil into her hands and then Cally's strong fingers began working at my neck and my shoulders and down the spine of my back.

'It might be easier if I helped you off with your boxers,' she said.

'I thought you'd never ask.' I lifted up and my boxers were eased down my legs. Her hands lingered for a moment at the bottom of my spine before moving to my legs and the backs of my knees. She was humming to herself, very happy with her work.

'And turn over,' she said.

I turned over. She had taken off her knickers and she was naked and she was lovely.

She was sitting astride my legs. We both admired each other, eyes dwelling on supple skin and curves that dimpled.

She leant forward and took a pinch of my stomach between thumb and forefinger. 'What it is to be young,' she said.

I cupped my hand round her waist. 'What it is to be beautiful.'

She laughed and busied herself with more coconut oil. 'You're a charmer.'

'Kiss me.'

Cally looked at me in query. 'I thought I was in charge.'

'So you are.'

And this time, with the oil and with her lips she led me to the very brink. But not quite over the edge. I was only just coming to appreciate what a skilful practitioner she was in the art of love.

She gazed at me.

'I like that look of hunger in your eyes,' she said.

'I'm hungry.' I stroked her breast. I wanted her.

'Oh you're hungry?' she said in mock surprise. 'Well, let me make you a sandwich! I have ham. I have pickles. I have tomatoes and lettuce and mayonnaise and several pots of mustard!'

I groaned and I smiled. I don't know how long we'd been in the beach hut, but it must have been several hours.

But my darling Cally knew what all women know: when a man is hot with desire, you can lead him any which way you please. You can do with him what you will. He is a rubber band that you can wind around your fingers and knot and stretch and play with to your heart's content. It is an extraordinary power, and a woman knows it. But once a man is spent, once that rubber band has snapped, that power dissipates in a moment. We men are like balloons. You can blow the balloon up with all your might, and you can let the air out, and you can keep on blowing until the very fabric of the balloon is quivering with tension and you can let the air out again. And, if you have a mind for it and if you have the patience, you can string it out for hours on end. But when, finally, you've had the explosion and the hot air and all the noise, as we all know, the game is over.

Cally was rummaging by the sink. I watched her.

'I can feel your eyes on me,' she said.

'I can't look at anything else.'

She came back to the bed with a tray and on it were two rolls, some home-cooked ham, tomatoes, lettuce and, just as she'd said, a selection of pickles and mustards. She sat cross-legged at the end of the bed with the tray in front of her and would look at me occasionally as she made me a ham sandwich.

'What do you want on it?'

'I want everything.'

'I'll bet you do.'

Cally's strong thumbs peeled the roll open, and then with a fine French blade she smeared on butter and pickled walnut and mustard and mayonnaise, and topped it off with two thick slices of ham.

She passed me the roll on a plate. 'Eat,' she said. I waited until she had made her own roll.

I was suddenly very hungry. We ate in silence, looking at each other, her feet straying up towards me to stroke my knee. It was one of those sandwiches which needed two hands to keep it all under control, and even then the mustard still dripped onto my chest. She watched it, her roll suddenly forgotten.

'I like that look of hunger in your eyes,' I said, echoing her words back at her.

She nodded at me. 'Very good,' she said. 'I am hungry.'

She took another small bite from her roll, but she was now watching my every move. I sensed a turning of the tide. Because although I was not spent, I was quite deliriously content, with food in my belly and the promise of all that was yet to come. Cally watched as I swallowed down the last of the roll. I wiped my lips with my fingers. She put her half-eaten roll onto the tray, put the tray onto the floor, and then she pounced. She was a very strong woman. She was on top of me and she was licking the mustard off my chest.

And so it started all over again, with the teasing and the dinking, only this time, for the first time, it was I who took Cally to the very brink.

'Please?' she said.

'Are you begging me?'

'I might be.'

Our eyes were but a few inches apart. She had this lazy smile on her face.

'I'm begging you,' she said. 'Please, Kim.'

'Very well.'

And hand in hand, over the edge of the abyss we went, freefalling through the air to our little deaths as the sea rushed up to meet us. And when we were done, and when all that we were left with was that calm sweep of the sea, we lay on our sides and cupped each other in our arms.

Cally stroked my nose, her forefinger running along the bridge of my snub. 'That was something.'

'That's an understatement.'

'All right,' she said. 'That was quite something.'

'That was quite exceptional.'

She kissed me, moistly, lovingly, on the mouth. 'And I hope it will be the first of many other somethings.'

I looked at her and then I stared out of the window. It was late afternoon by now, and our fire in the dunes was long burned out and our food long ago eaten by Goldilocks and the bears. I smiled to myself in perfect ecstasy. This woman, this calm, confident beauty, she wanted more of me; and I most definitely wanted more of her.

CHAPTER 11

We spent the night together in her beach hut, with candles on the shelves and the breeze blowing in through the window. We made love again, though this time without quite so much time taxiing down the runway, and once again we were airborne and laughing and gazing at each other with such utter adoration.

What a splendid thing it is to be in love, when the slate is wiped clean and when all those past hurts and shattered dreams are forgotten in an instant.

We ate rolls and ham, and when the ham was finished, she opened up a tin of sardines, eating them whole and the olive oil dripping down her chest and I licked off every drop of it. I don't know whether it was our love making or Cally herself, but I was suddenly ravenous. I ate a tin of corned beef with my bare fingers, dipping it into one of the chutneys and then tearing off great chunks with my teeth. It was not elegant, far from it, but it was in keeping with the general earthy mood of the evening.

And when we'd drunk the beer, we started on the red wine, and had drunk nearly two bottles of it before we made drowsy love for a third time, and yet again, she showed me sights that I had never seen and things that I had heard tale of, but had hitherto believed were the most fantastical fictions.

What I remember about it was that it was all so very good natured. There was no shyness, no awkwardness, no desperation to please; right from the first, it felt in the natural order of things to be there lying in bed with Cally beneath me. And how refreshing it was to find a woman whose libido matched my own. Cally revelled in sex for its own sake. Never once did she use sex as a carrot and as a reward for good behaviour, and nor, indeed, did she ever withdraw her sexual favours on account of behaviour unbecoming. Rather, sex was there to be enjoyed, savoured, and in our time together, we gorged ourselves upon each other until we were sated to the last drop.

Before we fell asleep, we had cleared the bed as best we could of all the debris of bread and oil and ham, and then with Cally soft in my arms, we lay there as the candles flickered in the wind, and I watched as she closed her eyes with a contented smile upon her face.

We made love again in the middle of the night. The rapture of waking while it was still dark, and as I fumbled to get my bearings and work out where I was I realised that I was with Cally, and that she was in my arms and that we were by the sea, and that, very simply, everything was on offer. I kissed her and kissed her again and gradually she groaned and opened her eyes, and remembered that it was me, and then she grabbed at me and she took me with all the earnest energy of a woman consumed by desire.

I was in love.

Cally woke at sun up. She always woke early. She kissed me awake, and I squinted at her and at the scene of our debauchery. One candle was still burning.

'Good morning,' I said.

'Hello,' she said.

I looked at my watch. It was not even six.

'Do we have time?' she asked.

I loved that. Oftentimes with a new love, there can be some awkwardness in the morning. But with Cally, there was none of that. We started our day in the best way possible way by reaffirming each other.

Afterwards, we raced naked into the sea, and though there were dog walkers about on that early morning beach, we waved at them as we charged delirious into the sea. It was cold and it was heady and it was good to be alive. The saltwater washed away the alcohol and the night's depredations. By the time we walked back hand in hand to the beach hut, we were reborn.

We towelled each other down and we kissed, and then Cally sat naked on the edge of the bed and watched me dress.

'I like you,' she said.

'I like you, too,' I dusted the sand off my toes and pulled on a sock.

'I like being with you. You give me energy. And I've not had so much of that recently.'

'No?'

'No. I want to see more of you.'

'What about in three hours' time, after I've served breakfast?'

She laughed at me. She had finished towelling her hair and was brushing it with an elegant Mason Pearson hairbrush. I remember the name; they'd been making hairbrushes for over one hundred and twenty years. My mother used to use them.

'I'd love to see you after breakfast,' she said, 'but I've got to sort out the horses and I've got to go up to London. Some essential pieces of necessary boredom that I have to do, and an exhibition that can't wait any longer.' She tugged at a knot in her hair. The knot wouldn't give. She gave another tug and then ignored it and went on to another shank of hair. 'I'll be three days. I wish it was less.'

'I'll be waiting for you,' I said. 'Brimming with ardour.'

'How do I get in touch with you?'

'You could write,' I said. 'The only person who's written to me in the last three months is my father, how sad is that?'

'Or you could call me,' she said. 'I'll give you my numbers, here and in London. If I'm not in, just leave a message.'

'Sounds good.'

As I tied up my laces, she wrote her numbers on a piece of paper, along with her address. She lived in Holland Park.

'Thank you,' she said. She stood next to me and stroked my hair. I liked her doing that almost more than anything else that had occurred between us. I stayed quite still and closed my eyes. I don't know what long-forgotten memory she had tapped into, but I luxuriated in the feel of her fingers upon my scalp.

'Yes,' I said.

Her hand trailed to the nape of my neck.

'In three days?'

'I can't wait.' I stood up and hugged her. Cally was naked, while I was now fully clothed. I cupped her breast and kissed her and then I walked out of the beach hut and strode off along the sand. After a short distance, I turned back. She was watching me.

I was overcome with adoration for this extraordinary force that had come into my life. 'You're the best!' I called out to her.

She flapped her hand down in mock disparagement, then blew me a kiss and waved, and when I next looked back, she had gone.

I'd never known a woman like Cally before. As I walked up the hill to the hotel, I was sated and serene. There was dew light on the leaves and the sand crunched underfoot. Compared to my past lovers, she was so calm and at one with herself. What I did I care about the age difference between us? It was Cally, the woman, I wanted. Whether she was forty-four or twenty-four, it made no difference to me.

Yet, no matter how hard I tried to convince myself to the contrary, Cally's age *did* make a difference. I wasn't ashamed of her. It wasn't that I didn't want to be seen out in public with her. But I was nevertheless aware that I was not quite ready to start trumpeting my love to the world. It would be different, I thought, if I'd fallen for a girl my own age. But as it was, with this woman twenty years older...

I had already divined the need for circumspection. I think that Cally knew that too. It wasn't that we weren't proud to be in each other's company; and neither of us were ever much swayed by other people's opinions. And yet, right from the start, we both of us knew that as soon as our love became public knowledge, then it would lead to complications. Of course, these complications could all be dealt with – true love conquers all – but certainly at first we both of us realised that it would be easier all round if we kept things quiet.

At least that was my intention.

But in that tiny little goldfish pond that was the Knoll House Hotel, I was rumbled almost immediately. Looking back, it now seems utterly ridiculous: young Kim endeavouring to sneak unseen into his hotel room, only to be accosted at almost every turn.

It started as I was walking back on the main road to the hotel, with my head still filled with the night before.

A large black Citroen drove past. I didn't even notice it until it pulled up a few yards ahead of me.

The passenger window rolled down. It was Anthony.

'Give you a lift?'

'I'm fine thanks, Anthony. Just going for a walk.'

He inspected me slowly. 'And don't tell me: you've been walking right through the night.'

I laughed him off and continued on my way. But then, as I walked up the hotel drive and past the staff entrance, who should I see but Tracy, bright eyed and cheery as she went in for her breakfast.

She laughed when she saw me. 'Dirty stop-out?' she said.

I grinned innocently. 'What a wicked little mind you have in that pretty head of yours, Tracy,' I said.

'Those flowers must have worked a treat,' she said.

'Tracy, darling Tracy. I am shocked – shocked – that you see me out for a morning walk and automatically think that I've been with a lover.'

'It's a lot more likely than you getting up early to go for a stroll.'

I waved her on and stole quickly to my room, only to be hammered by Janeen just as I got to the door.

'Been out shagging have you?'

I looked at her. She was just off to the dining room, looking good in her waitress' uniform, brazen and brassy.

'If only.'

She came over and sniffed me. She was so close to my neck that she almost kissed me.

'So who was she?'

'What, you can smell her on me?'

'Smell her? You reek of it!'

I wasn't sure whether she was bluffing. But it made no difference; I was never going to admit that I'd spent the night with Cally, or anyone else.

'You're just judging me by your own depraved standards.'

'I don't know about that,' she said, and then she flicked my crotch with her middle finger. 'But I certainly know there's a good reason for a guy having his flies undone first in the morning.'

I looked down, amazed. And of course my flies weren't undone at all. 'Made you look!' Janeen crowed with laughter as she went on her way.

By the time I had showered and shaved, it would be fair to say that news of my tryst was all round the dining room. By the time breakfast was over, it was right round the entire hotel.

Annette and Oliver ran me to earth as I stumped back past the playground. In truth, although I had offered to see Cally after breakfast, I was now relieved that she'd not taken me up on my offer because I was absolutely shattered. I had gone through breakfast in a daze and all I could think of was getting back to my grey bunker and sleeping till noon.

'When are we going to meet her?' Annette said. As ever she was holding hands with Oliver. She had a wild rose tucked behind her ear and looked quite beautiful. They were sickeningly in love and did not care who knew it.

'When I'm good and ready,' I said.

'Is it Cally?' Oliver asked.

'Cally?' I was striving for a tone of slight bemusement. 'Oh, Cally. No, it's not Cally.'

'Really?' Oliver said. 'I thought Cally was sweet on you.'

'She's very attractive,' Annette said.

'Yeah, well,' I said. 'Cally is hot, and maybe she is sweet on me, but it's not her.' I wonder now why I fought so much to keep Cally's identity hidden. I suppose I thought that once Oliver and Annette knew, then the rest of the staff would know. Then it wouldn't be long before I became a figure of fun, mocked for dating not just a guest but a much older woman, and then mocked a again when she eventually dumped me (which I was sure that she most assuredly would).

'So when are we going to meet her?' Annette said.

'I told you,' I said. 'When I'm ready. When she's ready.'

'I think it is Cally,' Oliver ignored me completely and spoke to Annette. 'It is not one of the staff, so it has to be a local woman.'

'Why does she have to be local?'

'I don't think you went up to London yesterday,' Oliver said. 'The last time I saw you, you were going down the drive at lunchtime with a big bunch of flowers.'

'Okay, so I didn't go to London.'

There was no respite. 'But if she is a local, which she must be, then why would you not want to introduce her to your friends?'

'He's a bit shy,' Annette said. 'It's definitely Cally.'

'It's *not* Cally!'

'Swear on your father's life?' Annette said.

'All right, it's Cally.'

'So it is Cally?'

'Maybe it is and maybe it isn't.' I was floundering, a young buck wallowing in quicksand. 'Anyway, is this any of your business?'

'Of course it's our business,' Oliver said. 'You are one of our closest friends.'

'I suppose so,' I said. 'Okay, it was Cally.'

'Cally?' Oliver said.

'Cally!' Annette said. 'I think she's lovely.'

'Yes.'

'I am surprised it has taken you so long to get together.'

'Some of us didn't luck out quite as quickly as you two did.' I said. 'Look, please don't tell anyone.'

'We won't tell a soul,' said Oliver.

And, to my immense surprise, they didn't.

I called Cally from the hotel payphone after lunch, but she wasn't in. I left a stuttering message on her answerphone.

I had two days by myself, buoyed up on this wave of euphoria, and I did what any other swain does when they are alone and in love, and played back my most magical moments with Cally. That first kiss in the stable; the way her hands had snaked under my shirt; how for a whole afternoon she had teased at me; her body, naked, available and charged with desire.

It did not take the other waiters long to notice the change.

'Are you on drugs?' Roland said.

'He's not on drugs, are you, puss?' Tracy said. 'He's in love.'

'I wish I could find someone to love,' Roland said.

'Not for want of trying,' I said.

'We'll find you someone nice,' Tracy said.

'What about you?' Roland said.

'I've got a boyfriend, as you well know, Roland,' she said. 'But if I ever dump him, I'll give you first refusal.'

'I thought I was on first refusal,' I said.

'Saucy!' she said. 'You've got your own girlfriend now. Who is she?'

'I don't have a girlfriend,' I said. 'And even if I did have one, I certainly wouldn't be telling the hotel radio.'

They looked at me and then both fell about laughing. 'So have I really got first refusal, then?' Roland asked Tracy. I was, for the moment, already forgotten.

So after months of wandering alone through love's Gobi Desert, it seemed for once that I was in an oasis. I had a modest but enjoyable job; I had time to myself in the mornings and the afternoons; and, although it was still early days, it seemed that I had somehow acquired myself a girlfriend. An affable, kind, easy-going, low-maintenance girlfriend, who just happened to enjoy sex just as much as I did.

But would it last? Well might I have asked, because inevitably – just as night follows day – shortly thereafter another very desirable woman was to enter into my life. But the timing of Louise's entry into my world was not great.

It was supper time in the hotel and I had been busy with some sportsmen when Roland directed my attention to three people being escorted to one of my tables. I recognised Mark and Julienne immediately. The woman who was with them was striking. I first saw her from behind. She was tall, at least as tall as me, but she held herself like a Hussar, broad shoulders, very squared. Sheer silk tights, a short dark skirt and elegant court shoes set off her amazing legs. She wore a tight floral basque; her lovely brunette hair in a gamine crop gave a delicious glimpse of tanned skin at the top of her back.

I waited a minute for the three of them to take their seats before going over. I still hadn't seen the woman's face, but I knew that I wanted to; I couldn't take my eyes off her legs.

I sauntered over to their table. They were by one of the windows. Mark was in ebullient form, joking to the women.

'Good evening,' I said. 'Hello Julienne; hello Mark.' For the first time, I turned to their guest. 'And hello Louise.'

We looked at each other.

She was an absolute knockout. Her face was a perfect match to her sensational figure. Her cheekbones were flawless, while her lips formed a laconic smile. Her level green-grey eyes never left mine.

'Hello Kim,' she said. She extended her hand, and we shook. I'd never shaken hands like this before with a guest; it was as if to say that we were meeting as equals. 'I've heard a lot about you.'

'I'm afraid it's all true,' I said. My eyes never left hers. I don't think I even blinked.

'And you have some career advice for a young graduate?'

'Come and work at the Knoll House, but only if you're absolutely desperate.'

'It looks like great *craic*,' she said, using the Irish.

'We do have that,' I said. 'And a fair amount of alcohol.'

We had not let go of each other's hands. I continued to look into Louise's eyes. She had poise, that's what it was. She was serene; not placid, but a woman who would for ever remain unruffled.

'And you drink here?'

'We usually go to the Bankes Arms.'

'Where I had my first drink.'

'Where they've got the world's smallest snug.'

'I know all about it.'

'Do you now?'

Before she finally let go of my hand, she gave it a light squeeze. I didn't know quite what it meant, but I guessed that it meant she liked me.

Throughout the transaction, I had barely looked at Mark or Julienne. They wanted to drink claret, but Louise wanted a spritzer. As I went away to get the drinks, I could overhear Julienne saying, 'I told you.'

As a waiter, it is very easy to strike up a quick, frothy relationship with a guest. That is our stock in trade. We have smiles and banter; our sole purpose is to ensure that dinner is convivial and good natured.

But although we can quickly learn to lark with our guests, it is difficult to move from that stage onto weightier matters. It's like making a fire. You first start off with the kindling and the little twigs, and then when the fire is drawing well, you move onto larger pieces of wood. And if you don't move onto larger pieces of timber, the fire will never generate any real heat. That's how it is in conversation. We waiters are very good with tinder and kindling, but we never move on from that and it means that our workaday conversations rarely have any bite. We are for ever locked in the light and the frothy.

So I delivered the various plates and drinks to Louise's table and I busied myself topping up the glasses.

'What's the best thing about working here?' she asked.

'Talking to people like you,' I said.

'Really?'

'I love it,' I said.

'You're quite good at it.'

'Good at it?' said Mark. He drank his wine. 'How can you be good at chatting to people?'

'Louise's right,' Julienne said. 'He's very good.'

'You could be a politician,' Louise said.

'Or a door-to-door salesman.' I winked at her.

In the kitchens, hostilities between Giles and me had recently abated, though there were still the occasional outbreaks of verbal hostility.

That evening, when I went in to fetch the mains for Louise's table, it was Giles who was at the pass. Even though it was summer, Giles was still as white and pasty-faced as ever.

'What do you want, Little Boy Blue?' he said.

'The mains for Table Five, my little dumpling,' I said. 'Would you like me to come blow your horn?'

Janeen, who was behind me, joined in the badinage. 'It'll be the only thing he gets blown this month.'

We laughed. I took the two ladies' plates out to Julienne and Louise.

When I returned to the pass, Giles pushed a plate of shepherd's pie towards me. 'There you go.'

I took the plate. It took about a second for the pain to register. The rim of the plate was burning hot. I let out a short, sharp curse and dropped the plate. The pie cascaded over my tunic and the plate smashed on the floor.

'Clumsy,' Giles said.

I waved my hand to ease the burn. 'Thanks very much, Giles,' I snapped. 'Well done.'

Oliver was already on his knees cleaning up the debris with a dustpan and brush. He picked up a plate shard. 'This is hot!'

'That's because the Russian dough boy has spent the last two minutes with it in the oven,' I said. 'He's such a wag.'

'You should take more care,' Giles said.

I blew him a kiss with my red, raw fingers. 'You've been a naughty, naughty boy, haven't you, Giles?'

'Haven't you got work to do?'

'Now apologise properly, Giley, or you'll be going onto the naughty step.'

It was another five minutes before I returned to Louise's table, with the lower half of my white tunic now stained brown. They were all aware of the delay and eyed up my tunic, but they were too polite to say anything.

'Trouble with the natives,' I said, brandishing my spoon and fork for some timely silver service. It's the perfect way to linger with the guests that you like. 'How many potatoes for you?'

'Three, please,' said Louise. They watched as I went about my well-honed craft. I served the potatoes in one fluid, easy movement. 'You make it look so effortless,' said Louise. 'I'm sure it's not.'

'Just a bit of practice.'

'I'll bet.'

I looked at her. A spark passed between us. Whatever there was, it was at that moment that we definitely clicked.

They had their puddings and their coffees and then paid their bill. I helped Louise back with her chair and for the first time, she stood next to me; with her in her short heels, we were exactly the same height.

'Thank you,' she said. 'Goodbye.'

'Nice meeting you, Louise,' I said. I touched her on the elbow.

Just like a politician knows a kiss is inappropriate, a light touch to the elbow with just the fingers is perfect: not too forward, but nonetheless a very delicate stroke. It forges a subtle physical connection, and it's real beauty is that it is equally effective on men and women.

Mark and Julienne waved as they walked out, though Louise did not turn round. I watched her as she curved out of the room.

And that was that. I had a met a beautiful woman, and I fancied her and there was chemistry. However, the timing was awkward. She would be off to London soon. And there was Cally, delectable Cally, and there was much that still had to be explored between us.

As I watched Louise sashay out of the room, I felt a pang of regret. But I certainly knew it was not something that I was going to pursue. I could recognise Louise's beauty, and acknowledged that there was chemistry between us. But that would be it, wouldn't it?

The usual mob went to the pub that night. The Bankes Arms must have been packed out with at least half of the hotel's waiters and waitresses.

I was standing at the bar, buying yet another beer for Roland.

'She was lovely,' Roland said. 'How come none of the good-looking guests ever sit at my tables?'

'Cos you're too damn ugly,' Janeen said.

'Looked like you were getting on really well with her,' Roland said. 'You were even shaking her hand.'

'You ought to try it some time, Roland,' I said. 'Women like it.'

'So I just go up to the table, say hello to the guests, and then shake them all by the hand?'

'That's about it. I'm not saying it works every time, but when it works, it works like a charm.'

'I'll try it,' he said.

'You could try telling them a few jokes,' I said. 'Knock-knock jokes can go down very well.'

'You tell jokes?' said Roland.

'Depends,' I said. 'Sometimes I give them a bit of poetry. Shakespeare, Shelley, that sort of thing.'

'And they really like that?'

'Why do you think I always get the biggest tips?'

I was just about to pay for the drinks when I felt a touch on my elbow.

I turned.

It was Louise, still wearing exactly what she had been wearing in the dining room, but now with a long black coat. She had put on fresh lipstick.

'Hello,' she said. She smiled at me and instinctively I stepped towards her and kissed her on the cheek.

'Hello Louise.'

'Can I buy you a drink?'

'I'm in the chair, Louise. What can I get you?'

Introductions were made. Louise took off her coat, hung it up by the door, and joined our table.

It was a glorious night. We had new, beautiful blood at the table, and as ever when that happens, the guys were doing their mouthy best to shine. In particular, I remember how we were teasing Louise over her future career.

'You're going to be a lawyer?' Roland said. He was horrified. 'What a waste!'

Louise laughed at him. 'What would you rather I do?'

'Well, anything!' he said. 'Anything at all! But please don't be a lawyer!'

'What about a waitress?' she said.

'That'd be great,' Roland said. 'With a short skirt and roller skates.'

'Or a bartender—'

'Making cocktails!'

'Or a chauffeuse—'

'I like that word!' Roland said. 'Chauffeuse!'

'You're very easily pleased,' I said. 'But what's wrong with being a lawyer?'

'Kill all the lawyers!'

'It's a steady job, swimming in money—' I said.

'It'd bore the hind legs off a donkey!'

'Louise,' I said. 'Roland is being wilfully provocative because he fancies you—'

'I fancy everyone!'

'I know you do. Anyway,' I continued. ' I must apologise for his behaviour.'

'No need at all,' she said. 'Law can seem a little dull.'

There were about eight or nine of us sitting around a table that was meant at best for six people, and it was a tight squeeze. I was sitting between Louise and Annette; both had their legs firmly pressed against mine. As we talked and as we drank, there stayed an unspoken awareness that, from thigh to knee, our legs were squeezed tight together. Shoulders and arms, too. We were so hug-a-mug around that tight table that we could not help but touch each other. Annette, of course, was with Oliver, and I knew that, but it felt good all the same to feel her leg pressed to mine.

As for Louise, this was a different experience altogether. Throughout our hour in the pub, I did not give one single thought to Cally.

She sipped her spritzer and at the same time I sipped my beer. Our elbows nudged. In silence we looked at each other, as neurones fizzled and connections were made.

'My round,' said Louise. It was a huge round and she bought drinks for the lot of us. She remembered everyone's drinks first time. I joined her at the bar.

She smiled at me.

'I'm glad I came,' she said.

'Bit of a squeeze round the table,' I said. 'Sorry about that.'

'That's the best bit.'

Now, if you give me enough time, I can always come up with some sort of riposte for any situation. If somebody insults me, they'll get it right back in their face, with a bit of extra spite for good measure. If somebody compliments me, then that'll be returned with added topspin. I am very rarely lost for words. But there, at the bar with Louise, I could think of nothing to say.

She took three pint glasses to the table and I followed with the rest of the drinks on a tray.

I sat down at the table next to Annette and Louise squeezed herself in next to me. But this time, immediately, she pressed her foot firmly next to mine.

We looked at each other. We drank and our eyes never left each other, and the drinks were returned to the table.

'You're right,' I said. 'It is the best bit.'

'What would it be like if we were all sitting at a table for two?' she said.

'Probably even better.'

'I'd have to sit on your lap.' She tilted her wine glass to me. 'Cheers.'

The subject returned, yet again, to Louise's career. She was planning on having a couple of months off before spending a year at Guildford Law School. After that, she had set her hopes on getting a job with one of the big London solicitors.

'That'll be back breaking,' I said. 'Do they start you off on seventy-hour weeks?'

'Eighty, minimum,' she said.

'That's my big problem with the law,' I said. 'Doesn't matter how high you get up the tree, you still have to put in the massive hours. Even when you're senior partner, you—'

'What are you going to do?'

'Ah,' I said. 'You have found out my weakness. I don't know what I want; I don't even know how to find out what I want.'

'What's the hurry?'

'That's what I keep on telling my stepmum, though she doesn't seem to be quite so receptive as—'

I broke off. Louise had kicked off her shoe, and her stockinged foot was very softly stroking my ankle.

'Me?' she said. 'Now what are you going to do?'

For the rest of the night, we looked; we connected. We both knew that we wanted each other.

I was flooded with a tumult of conflicting emotions, questions. Would it be there, then, that very night? Would it be right, would it be wrong? We had only just met. Should we? Could we?

Time was called and we were thrown out of the pub, and with that last lingering warmth on my thighs I stood up together with Annette and Louise.

We said our goodbyes outside the pub. Louise kissed everyone on the cheek. The rest of my motley crew stumbled off down the lane, their shouting laughter drifting into the night, as Louise and I stood alone in the darkness.

'Thanks for coming,' I said.

'I'm going to South America with my parents,' she said, before adding, 'I'm sorry to say. A last family holiday.'

'What a shame. You'll come back to the hotel when you're home?'

'If you're still there.'

'If, of course, I'm still there.'

We were both suddenly tongue-tied and awkward.

'Well, goodbye,' she said. 'You're just what Julienne said you'd be.'

'Very sweet of her,' I said. 'But you're the gorgeous one round here.'

We moved together and we clung to each other, like lovers who know they are about to be parted for a long time. She kissed me, but not quite on the lips. Two firm solid kisses, one on each cheek, missing my mouth by millimetres.

'Can I give you a lift?' she asked.

'No, I'll be fine thanks.'

I watched as she went over to her Mini, but I did not follow. She opened the door. 'What's it like being a warlock?' she called.

'What's it like being a temptress?

'Have I cast a spell on you?'

'You certainly have.'

She waved as she climbed into the car. I had never seen such a tall woman get into such a tiny car. She made it look both effortless and sexy, and I could feel wave after wave of raw desire washing through me.

CHAPTER 12

I don't do guilt. I don't know if it is a bad thing. I don't know if it is a good thing. But I do know, I do not do guilt.

I know plenty of people who do feel guilt: men, women; practically every Catholic that I've ever met. They not only feel guilty for their sins, but they feel guilty for even *thinking* about the mere possibility of sin. What a wretched time they must have of it, with this constant mental self-flagellation, as if life isn't tough enough already without having to beat yourself up over something as fantastically subjective as a misdeed.

I, however, have never suffered from guilt. This doesn't mean that I am without moral compass. But for whatever reason, there is no guilt gene within me. I mess up, I do the wrong thing, say the wrong thing, and I move on. There is no insidious demon inside me that forever whispers that I have behaved badly.

But although I do not do guilt, I'm also not very good at lying. I'm not an actor and don't have the skills to make my lies look breezy and effortless. Lying is especially difficult when you are telling stories to a woman who is possessed of some uncanny sixth sense.

So the next day, I woke up knowing that Cally was coming back to Dorset, and knowing that I would be seeing her. But I also allowed myself to revel in the memory of Louise in the pub, her leg pressed against mine and the beautiful hug when we parted.

I called Cally after lunch and, as ever, I got through to her answerphone. I was leaving a long, rambling message, when she suddenly picked up.

'It's you,' she said. She sounded tired.

'It's me. How was London?'

'Full of disease and back-stabbers. How are you?'

'I am so looking forward to seeing you again.'

'Nice to hear that my feelings are reciprocated. So what mischief have you been up to while I've been away?'

A fleeting thought of Louise, beautiful, available, wanting me to kiss her.

'Nothing,' I said. 'Nothing at all.' Perhaps I said it too quickly; perhaps it just came out wrong. 'Just playing with Darren. Just the usual.'

She sighed. I wouldn't have put it past her, even at that very early stage in our relationship, to have divined that only the previous night I had been dreaming of another.

'Dear, dear Darren,' she said. 'He means well.'

I was suddenly piqued. 'Why did you go to the pub with him that night last week?' I asked.

'Why do you think?'

'Do you fancy him?'

'Dear me, Kim, you know so little!' She laughed. 'Maybe I went to the pub with him so that you might finally be goaded into action!'

'Really?' I was incredulous.

'Didn't you know that is we women who call the shots?'

'You… you schemer!' Here I was imagining that we'd got together through happenstance and coincidence, yet Cally had had it all planned out from the very first.

'So are you going to tell me what happened last night?' she said.

'Happened last night?' I said. I could sense immediately that my voice had started to sound rather hollow. 'Nothing happened last night.'

'I'll believe you,' she said, before adding. 'Though thousands wouldn't.'

'What's that supposed to mean?' I said. I was still nettled by the thought of her drink with Darren just being a ruse to ensnare me.

'It means whatever you take it to mean.'

'That's not a very nice thing to say.'

'Oh, well…'

There was a silence between us, as we both paused, like a couple of heavyweight boxers, a little bruised and now taking stock of each other.

'Can I see you?' I said. 'Can I see you tonight?'

'Ah,' she said, and again there was a pause. 'Don't come today. I've picked up something vile and I'm shattered. I want to be at my best for you.'

'I'll take you any way I can get you.'

She gave a very soft laugh. 'Let's end this conversation now,' she said. 'Call me tomorrow, and we'll see if we can be any nicer.'

It wasn't what I'd hoped for. I'd hoped, I don't know, for an urgent call to action, and an insistent demand to be at her home or at her beach hut within the next ten minutes.

Instead we'd had our first tiff, and Cally did what I would learn she always did when there was bad blood. She withdrew to wait patiently for the heat to simmer down.

I wondered if I should have told her about Louise, if I should have confessed straight up. But it was always going to be sticky and I disliked confrontations with women. I don't know how Cally would have taken it; though in all probability, she'd have laughed it off. She knew me better than I knew myself, and she certainly knew that a young man in love was always capable of having his head turned by the sight of a pretty girl.

So I had been told to stand easy, and my ardour had to be put into cold storage for the next twenty-four hours. It's never a great feeling when you're primed and full of expectations only to be told that your shot at the moon won't be happening after all.

When tomorrow came Cally tried to fob me off then, too.

I called her after breakfast. She sounded like she was still in bed.

'How are you feeling?' I asked.

'Not brilliant.'

'I'll bring you some fruit.'

'No please don't,' she said. 'I look dreadful.'

'I don't care about your looks. I just want to see you.'

'Do you really want to see me?'

'Yes, very much.'

'I'm going to have a bath,' she said. 'I'll leave the back door unlocked.'

My feet had wings. No other words could have got me moving so fast. A young man in love will stop at nothing when he is on a promise and the very thought of Cally naked in a bath had me scuttling back to my little breeze block snug for fresh clothes. I stopped off in the dining room to filch some apples and grapes. One of the chefs spotted me as I was putting them into my knapsack. I gave him an airy wave, and then I was out in the sun and loping down the road towards Cally's home. By the time I got there, the sweat had soaked through to the back of my shirt.

I rolled into Cally's courtyard with my anticipation sky high. The very last person that I expected to see was Greta. She had obviously just rung the doorbell and was now walking back to her car.

'Oh,' she said. She was quite taken aback at seeing me at Cally's house. 'Kim. What are you doing here?'

'Just popped over,' I said.

She was wearing black boots and white trousers and a pink cashmere top, coiffed hair, perfect make-up. She was sort of sexy, but she didn't do it for me.

'She's not in,' she said. 'She's probably out painting.'

'Oh well,' I said. 'I'm sure I'll see her around.'

'Do you come here often?'

'No.'

I could sense her probing me. She wanted to know if we were lovers.

'Can I give you a lift somewhere?' she asked. She had a slight pout. 'Buy you a coffee in Swanage?'

'I'm good thanks,' I said. 'I think I'll…' I was about to say I was going to the beach, but I realised that she would immediately want to join me. 'I'll be on my way.'

I walked off down the road and took a turn down a footpath that led to the beach. Greta watched me as she drove by. She was in a sporty little GTi, white, and she was driving too fast.

I gave Greta five minutes before looping through the fields round to the back of Cally's house. I jumped over a dry-stone wall and walked up through the garden; it was in immaculate order, but with a lush hint of the wilderness in the borders. I don't think that Cally was ever much of a gardener, but she had a man who looked after it all.

Just as she'd said, the back door was unlocked. I let myself in, took off my trainers, and silently padded up the stairs in my stockinged feet. I was excited; not quite a thief in the night, but I did feel like a trespasser.

I knew where the bathroom was. It was where she had bandaged my ribs all those months ago. The door was closed. I had not made a sound, but she already knew I was there. I was about to knock when she called out to me. 'Come in,' she said.

I turned the knob. I eased the door open and the dark of the corridor was flooded with daylight that spilt out of the bathroom. I looked in. Cally was in the bath, hair tied up, sipping at a mug of black coffee. She held the cup with both hands as if it were a two-handled *quaich*. She looked at me over the rim of the cup with she-devil eyes. The bath was full and thick with bubbles. I could see her face and her neck, but all else was hidden from view. Two candles burned by the sink. The window was open and the room smelt of citrus. It was heavenly – so clean, so spacious, so very different from everything about my life in the hotel.

'Hello,' she said.

I put my bag on the ground, knelt by the bath, and kissed her. Her lips moved underneath mine. 'Hello,' I said.

She set her coffee cup on a table, snaked her wet arms around my neck, and kissed me again.

'Would you like to join me?' she said.

'I'd love to.'

'There's coffee on the side if you want. Pour yourself a cup.'

I poured coffee from the cafetière and quickly peeled off my clothes. I left them scattered on the floor.

She laughed at me. 'I like that,' she said. 'You just throw your stuff wherever you want and dive straight in. Too few people do that.'

'Really?' I got into the bath. The water was hot, but not piping. 'I thought most women liked to keep things neat and tidy.'

'Not me,' she said. 'As for *most* women – well, they may like things one way today, but tomorrow, they may also have a fancy for spontaneity and hurling your clothes any which way you please.'

I lowered myself into the bath. The water was very close to teetering over the edge. Cally watched with amusement. 'Is he going to do it?' she asked.

'Of course he's going to do it.'

Ever so slowly, I eased my head back until it rested against the rim of the bath. Our legs were interlocked at the knees. The water was so high that it tremored at the edge.

We gazed at each other.

'Still as gorgeous as ever,' she said.

'There's only one gorgeous person round here and that's you,' I said.

She smiled and cocked her head.

'Let me look at you,' she said. 'Don't talk, don't say a thing, don't do anything. All I want is to look at you.'

'Okay,' I said. She stretched a long finger to her lips and urged me to silence.

I had never done that before, just looked and looked into a woman's eyes without time constraints and without a word being said. Although nothing was being said, a myriad thoughts and thrills were constantly running through our heads as we forged this intense connection. It's very different from the connection that you have when you make love; it resonates on a much deeper level, like the subsonic boom of a blue whale that travels for hundreds of miles beneath the sea. I realised that if I had fifteen minutes with a beautiful stranger, and if I could only gaze into her eyes, then we would become much more closely connected than we would by any amount of conversation.

I have no idea how long we had been gazing at each other. Occasionally, she sipped her coffee, but her eyes never left mine. My thoughts ranged from girlfriends, to jobs, to dreams of my travels, but gradually these thoughts coalesced into the single knowledge that I very much wanted to make love to this woman.

But I wasn't going to be the first to break. It was Cally's call, her show, and if she wanted to carry on gazing at me until the evening star had first glimmered in the west, then I would go along with that.

Under the water Cally was stroking my calf with her hand and I started to do the same. Her skin was so smooth it might have been oiled. Gradually, my hand, our hands worked towards the middle, and our fingers touched and clasped and we lay there in the bath, still staring but now holding hands.

The phone rang. We could hear Cally's brief message, and then we heard the unmistakable voice of Greta. 'Cally, hi, it's me,' she said. 'Came round to see you earlier and who should I discover here but our young waiter friend. I hope you haven't set your sights on the poor boy. At your age, you really ought to know better.'

Cally sighed and broke off from my hand and let her fingers trail up the inside of my thigh. 'Well, that's told me,' she said.

'Especially at your age.'

'Perhaps, but I find it very hard to resist you.'

For a couple of minutes now, the water had been draining from the bath, until little archipelagos of knees and torsos and breasts emerged out of the soapsuds.

She leaned over to kiss me, her hands lightly about my waist, but then she pressed forward, pushing against me until she was lying on top of me, her skin warm and wet against my chest.

She kissed me. 'I've never made love in this bath before.'

'Let's do it, then.'

'How did you enjoy looking, but not speaking?' she said.

'I loved it.'

'Let's try it again, then.'

'Right now?'

'Why not?'

Once again, I wallowed in Cally's eyes, though this time it was quite different, because this time we were making love, and though we might stroke and fondle, our eyes never once left each other.

She would occasionally lean down to kiss me fondly, lasciviously, but even then our eyes remained locked, as if staring into the wicked flicker of a candle's flame. After some time, she looked at me, perhaps quizzically, and gave me a slow languorous nod as her firm fingers started to knit about my neck. She didn't speak, and neither did I, but I could hear this hum detonating deep in the bottom of her throat, and she drew her knees up and raked me with her nails, and when we were done, she kissed me again.

'Your kiss has an echo,' she said. 'Even minutes after we've stopped kissing, I can still feel the tingle of your lips on mine.'

'I can feel another kind of echo.'

'I'll bet you can.'

By now the bath had all but run dry. The foam had sculpted itself to our limbs. I thought that we were going to get out.

But no.

'Hot water's so boring, isn't it?' she said, eyes sparkling. 'It's cosy; it's relaxing. But is that we want out of life?'

I was inscrutable. I kissed the little smoker's lines that traced about her eyes.

'A cold bath on the other hand?'

She put the plug back in, and then with one twist of the tap, cold water cannoned into the bath. I gasped, my skin freezing and seizing as the water hit me. The water was bitingly cold. Cally clung to me and there was some slight warmth from her belly, but I could feel the goosebumps rippling over my thighs.

I treated it as an exercise in pain.

It hurt, but it wasn't going to kill me and if she could stand it, then I could most definitely stand it, too.

'This is nice,' she said.

'Just lovely,' I replied. 'I'm getting really turned on.'

Very delicately she kissed me on the cheek. The bath was nearly full and the water continued to torrent from the taps and my head was the only part of me that was not immersed. The feeling of cold had now moved on to a general numbness.

'I wonder if I've got any birch twigs downstairs,' she said.

'I'll tan your hide off,' I said. 'It'd be a real pleasure.'

'We're very well suited,' she said. 'I don't know anyone else who would be staying in this bath with me.'

'I'm loving it,' I said. 'I mean of course there's a good chance that I might get frostbite on my extremities, but apart from that, this is just cosy as can be.'

She purred on top of me, her lips hovering just an inch above mine.

'And are you really getting turned on?'

'Well, in my mind, yes,' I said. 'My heart is willing, though the flesh may be weak. Literally.'

I was starting to shiver. At first I could control it, but in the end there was no escaping that my whole body was shaking from the cold.

'I'm being very thoughtless,' she said. 'There's not a scrap of fat on you, you're nothing but sinewy muscle, whereas I... I have much more padding.'

I grabbed the sides of her belly, a hefty haunch thick in each of my hands. 'And I love it.'

'Let me get you out and get you dry,' she said.

With both hands she hauled me out of the bath and wrapped me in a vast white towel. I was still shivering and when I glimpsed myself in the mirror, I saw that my lips were blue. As for Cally, I don't know whether it was her natural padding, but she did not seem to have suffered any ill effects whatsoever from our ice bath.

She led me through to her bedroom, another light airy room, with a vast four-poster bed. The foot-thick posts were black with age and carved with ornate flowers and cupids. It had lush curtains, which swirled with William Morris patterns. Cally put on a white bathrobe and got me a toddy. We lay in the bed together.

'How old is this bed?' I asked.

'Over four hundred years,' she said. 'I like its history.'

'What is its history?'

'I don't know,' she said. 'But I like to think of it. I like to think of all the people who have slept in this bed, and the hundreds and hundreds of couples who have made love here...' She trailed off as her hand rummaged beneath my towel. 'I daresay quite a few people have died here, too.'

'You like your history, don't you.'

'I love it. Old cups and old coins and old sculptures – to think of all the hands that have touched them over the centuries and to know that you are just the latest in a long line, and that long after we've gone, there will be many more to come.'

'But for the moment, it's our turn in the bed.'

'It's our time in the sun.'

'If only these four posts could talk.'

'They would have a story to tell.' She swept her hair off her face. 'But I'm sure it will be nothing to the story that's about to happen.'

'Is that so?'

'I thought it might be the best way to warm you up.'

'You'll have to be quick about it, Cally,' I said. 'I've got to be back at the hotel in half an hour.'

'Yes, boss,' she said, as she went about her unique way of warming me up. Just to think of it now still sends a shiver of delight running up my spine. If I could be warmed up like that every time I was cold, then for the rest of my life, I would daily immerse myself in Cally's freezing bathtub.

I saw Cally again after lunch, when I trickled down to her beach hut, and then again in her home after serving dinner. I spent the night and was up at the crack of dawn and traipsing back to the hotel. I may have been setting a precedent, but it was a precedent that I was more than happy to keep. So long as Cally was in Dorset, I'd see her at least two or three times a day, and every time we met we made love. Her house and her beach hut were the primary places where we would eke out our ardour, but if the mood took us – as it often did – then we would make love in any discreet field or lay-by or leafy bower that came to hand.

And then there were the not so discreet places, chief of which was the Agglestone. I had been there a few times by myself, but landmarks, buildings, even trees and shrubs take on new significance when they are seen with a lover. When Cally took me there, one lunch-time on my day off, it seemed like one of the most extraordinary natural wonders of the world, with this thousand tons of sandstone perched at the top of a hill. A few decades back, the Agglestone had looked even more dramatic. The main stone had, by some freak of nature, been balanced on top of a smaller one. They looked like some miraculous hanging anvil. Then one wild winter night in the Seventies, there was a wind to end all winds and the Agglestone was tilted off its perch, and there it remains like some giant toad that is for ever staring at the stars.

It was already spitting with rain as we tethered the horses to some heather, and by the time we had climbed to the base of the rock, it was raining quite hard. We held hands as we walked around the stone, the rain drumming down, spitting off the rock. We had quickened our stride to get back to the horses, when a bolt of lightning lit up the sky followed immediately by a shockwave of thunder, which seemed to rattle the very teeth in my head. Almost immediately, we were hit by the monsoon. I had not seen rain like it in a long time. In just a few seconds I was so wet that I might as well have been dropped in the sea. Our brisk walk turned into an amble. There was no hurry because we could get no wetter. I caught Cally's eye and we laughed. 'Come on!' she said, and started peeling off her clothes. I wriggled out of my trousers which, tight and wet, were sticking firm to my thighs. And still it poured. Naked, we ran in the sand around the Agglestone, like we were taking part in an old, old ritual that had been conducted around that stone for thousands of years; we ended up against the Agglestone's rough rock, pelted by the rain and flensed by the wind, and I didn't doubt for a second that that also was exactly what the ritual demanded of us. The knowledge that lovers like us had been trysting there for millennia, and that we were just the latest link in this long, long chain, bound us both to the past and to the future.

We rode back naked, sticking to the heath and to the hedgerows, but we still had to cross a couple of roads. A car slowed as it overtook us, and the woman in the passenger seat looked at us, at first languidly and then with more interest. The car slowed as it moved on, so that the driver could inspect us in the rear-view mirror.

In spite of all that, Cally remained my beautiful dark secret.

My carping colleagues certainly knew that I was seeing someone. I didn't visit the pub so often. At sun up, I'd sometimes be spotted skulking back into the hotel. In the late afternoon, the waiters would watch as I flew back to my room to change hurriedly into my uniform.

But I kept my mouth shut and so did Annette and Oliver, and for a time no one even came close to guessing the identity of my mystery love.

It was all going to come out eventually; there was no doubt of that. In such a small community, it was inevitable that we would be found by prying eyes. Even so, when it did finally happen, I was rather surprised. Up until then, I had no idea that he knew me so well.

My father had come down to play golf with me. He'd brought my clubs. The Mini barely stopped for a moment outside the hotel before I'd hopped in and we had roared off. Darren and Janeen watched me leave. I gave them a regal wave.

My father craned his head this way and that as we went down the drive. 'Hasn't changed a bit,' he said. 'Hasn't changed in well over a decade. They still have just the one TV?'

'Only the one.'

'You get out on the pitch-and-putt course much?'

'Not so much,' I said, and that was true. Since Cally had come into my life a month earlier, I had not touched a golf club.

'I don't know what's happened to my golf these days.' He puffed away on his cigarette, tapping the ash out of the window as we screeched along the coast. 'Not hitting it off the middle. Maybe I'm just getting old.'

We had a pint in the clubhouse and ordered two lobster salads for lunch after the first nine. What a day to be out on the golf course. All those killjoys who complain that golf is just a game for bourgeois blow-hards can go suck it. On a summer's day, there is no finer way to pass the afternoon.

My father played his usual steady game, and I thrashed the ball from one bank of rough to the next, and even though I was being given strokes aplenty, he was still three up at the turn. Just a few years before he'd have been desperate to win, but on that day he was quite happy just to potter along with his cigarette trailing from his lips.

We stopped off back at the clubhouse. The lobsters were waiting for us and we had gin and tonic outside on the patio and then a bottle of white and then some Wolfschmidt kummel. I didn't know what all the booze was going to do to my swing, but it certainly wasn't going to make it much worse.

'Your stepmother has been wondering when you are going to settle down into a proper job,' my father said. There was an After Eight mint on his coffee saucer. He ate it in one.

'I have absolutely no idea. Doesn't being a waiter count?'

'It's difficult for her to swank with her friends when all their boys are beavering away in the City.'

'And what do you think?'

'If you're having fun, then who gives a monkey's cuss?' He let out a small, contented belch and massaged his broad belly. He was inspecting his glass of kummel against the clear blue sky. 'Seeing anyone at the moment?'

'Not really.'

'Oh?' He continued to turn the stem of the glass between his fingers. '"Not really." What a delicate phrase and with such a wealth of nuances. So what's she like?'

I chuckled. 'She's great.'

'But obviously not yet for public consumption.'

'Or paternal dissection.'

'Nothing ever is,' he said, 'though I suppose that's how we paters like it.'

I came out swinging over the next nine holes; I didn't know where the ball was going, but I was intent on hitting the cover off it. As my game got better, my father started to flag. I beat him two

WILLIAM COLES

and one, and he couldn't have cared a hoot. We had more drinks in the clubhouse. He'd drunk a lot, well over the limit, but he seemed to have hollow legs. Alcohol had only the most negligible effect on his faculties.

He was staying at the hotel and offered me supper there, but I didn't much fancy being inspected by the rest of the team, so we had supper in Swanage. 'What's the name of that local pub of yours?' he asked as we drove back.

'The Bankes Arms.'

'That's the one,' he said. 'Let's go for a nightcap. Your mother used to like the place. Got a very fine snug, as I remember—'

I looked at him in amazement. 'You've been in the snug?'

'Yes, with your mother, a little round table and a tiny banquette, all very cosy. Surprised you haven't tried it out.' He gave me a dig in the ribs. 'Honestly, the youth of today. Wasted on you! Wasted on you.'

I'd not seen him in such fine fettle for a long time. He bought us bitter and two whisky chasers. I was just sitting down when I saw Cally and Greta over in the corner; I'd told Cally that I would be popping round to her place later. I had not expected to see her in the pub.

I waved at them as I sat down.

'Friends of yours?' my father said. 'Shall we join them?'

The booze had turned him into a bon viveur and he was in the mood for new blood.

'Hi Cally, hi Greta,' I said. 'Do you mind if we join you?'

I made the introductions, hands were shaken, and my father went off to the bar to get a bottle of white wine. Greta was tipsy and flirty, Cally more circumspect.

'How was the golf?' she asked.

'Golf was great,' I said. 'What have you painted today?'

'I was in the mood for horses today,' she said. 'First I rode them and then I painted them.'

'And what have you been up to, Greta?'

'Busy, busy, busy,' she said, and underneath the table I felt her knee knock into mine. 'So that's your dad? Ex-army?' She eyed him at the

170

bar, where he was producing a number of notes from his wallet. 'He can come and polish my brass any day.'

'He doesn't do that any more,' I said. 'But he could probably send round his batman.'

'His batman?' Greta rolled her eyes. Her mascara was smudged down her left cheek. 'And does batman wear tight pants and a cape?'

'Only if you ask nicely.'

'I can ask very nicely indeed.' She rummaged in her bag and put on some scarlet lipstick. It was a little too thick at one side. She puckered, pouted and blew me a kiss.

I looked over at Cally. She had her back to the wall and looked very tranquil – not placid, but centred. She was a master jockey, who knew exactly when to give Greta her head.

My father came to the table with the bottle and four glasses. He'd already polished off his pint and his whisky chaser.

I was uncomfortable. As I've said, I am not an actor. I find it difficult to behave naturally when I'm in the company of a lover and I have to pretend that she's just a friend. Of course I know how I ought to behave. I should behave just as I am when I'm with Tracy or Michelle. I should be the lark, the gadabout, full of jokes and cheeky put-downs, and should have my foot firmly pressed onto the accelerator. I know how it's done. Yet when I am trying to treat my secret lover like a friend, it always comes out wrong. My voice becomes too loud or too soft. I clam up. My witticisms crash and burn. It all seems very hammy. To those that know me, I feel as if my love is writ large all over my strained face.

As my father sat down, his right hand automatically moved to his coat pocket and he produced a fresh packet of cigarettes.

'Foul habit, I know.' He flicked off the cellophane. 'Anyone like a cigarette?'

Cally and Greta both joined him, happily puffing their smoke all over me. In those days before the smoking ban, it was just seen as perfectly normal for us po-faced non-smokers to have to spend our evenings inhaling our companions' foul fumes. It would have seemed as weird and militant to have whinged about being a passive smoker.

Cally tended to smoke when she was happy – when she was out
riding, or out painting, or out drinking. I didn't much like it, though
I never told her. Her smoking was just a part of her, as immutable as
her looks or her horses.

My father was interested to hear about Cally's painting.

'Are you excited by your exhibition?' he said.

She shrugged. I don't think I ever once saw her fazed. You could
have stood her in the middle of the Pamplona bull run, being charged
down by a dozen prime bulls, and she wouldn't have turned a hair.
'I like deadlines,' she said. 'I need a deadline, otherwise… otherwise
nothing happens.'

'And it's in August?' he said. 'Where's it going to be?'

'London.' She tapped her cigarette in the ashtray and twin fumes
of smoke spilled from her nostrils. 'Cork Street.'

'Impressive,' my father said.

'I don't know about that,' she said. 'It'll be my last one. For a
while.'

Cork Street; it shows how little I knew about the art world.
I'd never heard of Cork Street, had no inkling that it was the very
epicentre of Britain's art world. Although I knew that Cally had an
exhibition that she was preparing for, it was just another facet of her
life. It was neither impressive nor unimpressive, merely something
that she did when she was not with me. But of course I should have
known that just like her horsemanship and her love making, she was
a complete expert.

'What do you paint?' my father said. He was enjoying himself, had
already tapped out the next round of cigarettes.

'Animals,' said Cally, 'movement, anything with life.'

'When my first wife died, I had a stab at painting,' my father said.
'I thought it would help. Took an art class. Water colours.'

'What happened?'

'I was outnumbered eight to one. The ladies saw me as some sort
of catch. Not a class went by when they weren't offering to take me
out for coffee or lunch or dinner.'

I'd never heard about this period in my father's life. 'And did you take any of them up?' I asked.

'A few,' he said. 'It was quite a rich seam. I'd never realised that a widower in the army could be quite so attractive, but anyway… there you have it. Couldn't paint a damn thing, mind.'

'Learning to paint is the very last reason why people go to art classes,' Cally said. My father laughed merrily to himself.

Greta had unbuttoned another button of her lilac shirt and I could see a glimpse of black bra underneath. She was drinking hard.

I felt something underneath the table. It was a foot that was worming its way up my calf and between my knees. For a moment I thought it was Cally, but quickly realised that it was Greta. She surveyed me coolly over the top of her wine glass, daring me, challenging me, to see what I would do next. I wasn't sure if she knew that Cally and I were seeing each other, or if she just fancied her chances.

I went to the lavatory. Darren was already there. He looked over at me. 'You like them old, don't you?' he said.

'I like them any way I can get them.'

'They've got to be twenty years older than you.'

'At the very least,' I said, before remembering Greta's probing foot. 'You should have a try with Greta. She'd love you.'

'Greta?' he said. 'Why would I want to go with Greta?'

'Might teach you something you didn't know.' I buttoned up and washed my hands. 'Which probably isn't saying much, actually.'

Later in the bar, I saw him staring at us. Greta saw him, too, and gave him a little wave. I shuddered as the thought of Greta and Darren together floated across my mind. What an unholy alliance that would be.

My father gave me a lift back to the hotel. We'd said our goodbyes to the ladies outside the pub; my father had kissed them each on the cheek, very suave. I'd never really taken him for a ladies' man before, but after his tales of the art classes, I was looking at him with whole new eyes.

We buckled up and the cigarette was produced from the packet. He lit up one handed as we did a tight U-turn.

'Nice girlfriend,' he said.

'I'm not seeing Greta.' I wound down the window to try and clear some of the smoke.

'Of course you're not,' he said. 'But Cally… Cally is terrific.'

It was pointless denying it. 'Cally is terrific,' I said. 'How did you know?'

'Not know when my eldest son has fallen in love? Not know when he's sitting opposite his girlfriend in the pub? Think I was born yesterday?'

'Oh,' I said, very firmly put in my place. 'I didn't know it was that obvious.'

'As for Greta, what a trollop.' He tapped his ash out of the window.

'Greta just gets a bit flirty when she's drunk.'

'That would be most of the time, then.'

CHAPTER 13

If my father had divined from one single session in the pub that I was seeing Cally, it did not take my colleagues long to follow suit. After all the hiding and secrecy, it was a relief to both of us when it was finally out there.

It was dinner time at the hotel, late July, and by now the Knoll House was in full swing, with families arriving for a week, two weeks, and with the whole operation so slick that every staff member had become battle-hardened. Even Oliver had managed to ameliorate his natural clumsiness and was no longer smashing more than a couple of plates a week. His party piece was the cuff flick, and usually occurred when he was gathering up either plates or menus. He would stretch over to pick up a plate, and as he did so, his cuff would catch a glass.

I once saw him upend a full champagne flute over a woman who was wearing a spectacularly clingy creamy cashmere dress. She was a young mum and she was revelling in having a dinner away from her children. Her husband was some corporate guy on holiday, wearing the standard blazer, chinos and natty blue deck shoes. The woman had come in to the dining room with a full glass of champagne, and had been sat down for all of one minute before Oliver handed her a menu. He knocked the glass into her lap, soaking her from her belly to her knees. The situation would have been quite hilarious if it had happened to anyone else, and if Oliver had not been so hideously embarrassed. But it all turned out all right. The lovely woman went off to change and Anthony brought them a bottle of champagne and the couple were soon laughing away and even chafing Oliver over his clumsiness.

On this night, the first person into the dining room, limping on a blackthorn walking stick, was my old adversary Major Loveridge and his wife, Jemma. Since the dry-run at the start of the season, Anthony had made sure that the major was never actually sitting at any of my tables, though I would always wave and say hello if I saw the man.

That evening, the major was seated just adjacent to my tables; Oliver was his waiter. Over the previous few months, I had discovered that he suffered from gout.

The major and Jemma had just sat down and were deciding which pie to have for dinner when I breezed over to the table next to them. I swept an imaginary crumb from the tablecloth.

'Good evening, ma'am!' I said. 'Good evening, Major! How is the gout today?'

He looked at me with weary eyes. He humphed.

'My father suffers from gout,' I said chattily. I picked up a wine glass and began to polish.

The major perused the menu.

'He swears by cherry juice,' I said. 'My stepmother got him onto it. At first he was a bit sceptical.'

The major licked his finger and, without once looking at me, turned a page of the menu.

I held the glass up to the light, admiring its gleam. 'Now you can't get him off the stuff! Cherry juice in the morning. Maraschinos at tea. Cherries on his cupcakes and cherries after dinner. He's even put in a couple of cherry trees in the garden, but they don't really produce very nice cherries. Bit bitter, you know? But there he is, still gobbling them down.'

The major's wife darted a look at me and then back at her husband, a wee timorous mouse peeping from its hole. The major was still stolidly reading his menu.

'Oh, but there I am, prattling on about my dear old dad's gout when I'm sure it's the very last thing you want to talk about. May I recommend the sole? Catch just came in this morning.'

Off to the side, I saw Anthony greeting Cally and Greta. He kissed them both on the cheek.

'My guests have arrived,' I said. 'If you will excuse me.'

Cally and Greta were at their usual table, and though Cally was usually quite reserved when we were together in public, tonight she was almost brazen.

'Kim!' She was pleased to see me. I'd not seen her for a couple of days and she stretched out her hand and cupped my arm. But she looked tired, too. I didn't really know what preparing for an exhibition entailed, but it was certainly gruelling. Every time she returned from London, she always looked a little more weathered; though it might have been the smoking. I think she smoked a lot in London and this tended to exacerbate the lines around her mouth and her eyes.

I kissed both the ladies on the cheek. 'How goes the exhibition?'

'Fraught.' She stroked my arm again and smiled up at me, and there was almost a look of relief in her face as if she was once again back in calm waters after weathering the storm. 'I'll tell you later.'

Greta gave her an arch look. I realised that if she hadn't known about us before, she most certainly knew about us now.

I fetched them their bottle of champagne.

A man had come into the room with his family. In the traditional confines of the Knoll House dining room, he looked bizarre. He was a desperate mid-forties man, in black leather trousers and cowboy boots, and a striking silk waistcoat in canary yellow over a crisp white shirt. I was not at all sure that the waistcoat worked with the leather trousers.

At first I thought that the man was accompanied by his three daughters. But when I looked at the girls more closely, I saw his hand lingering on the older one's waist and realised that she was his lover. With his clothes and his much younger girlfriend, I thought he looked ridiculous.

I should have realised that something was up when Anthony escorted the group to one of my tables, next to the major and his wife.

After the four guests had sat down, I went over to the table and went through my spiel. The man's lover was about my age and very pretty, as all trophy girls must be. She had light freckles on her nose and a healthy tan and sun-kissed hair, and was altogether way too wholesome and too lovely to be mixing with this middle-aged man in his too-tight leather trousers.

The girls seemed pleasant enough, the man perhaps a little condescending; there was some strange vibe about the table, though I was not able to place it.

'Are you regulars at the hotel?' I asked.

'The girls have been coming here for years,' said the man. He turned to his girlfriend and stroked her bare shoulder. 'But it's your first trip, isn't it, darling?'

'So how are you enjoying the show so far?' I asked, hands clasped lightly behind my back.

'I like it,' she said simply.

'Have you heard of the nudist beach?' the man said.

'Dad!' the elder daughter said, scandalised.

'There's been talk of a nudist beach,' I said, 'but we don't need permission, we just do it.'

'You've skinny-dipped here?' the girl said.

'Just this morning. It was brisk.'

'Fancy a go?' said the man to his girlfriend.

'I might do,' she said.

'You let me know what time you're going down.' I doled out the menus. 'I'll see about getting the beach cleared.'

I thought no more of it until I returned to the central station. Several waiters were agog to find out what I had been talking about with my new guests.

'Nudist beaches, or something like that,' I said to Tracy. 'What's up?'

'He's such a hunk,' Michelle said.

'Him?' I said. 'Are you joking?'

'He's not as tall as I thought he'd be,' Tracy said.

'The guy in the leather trousers?' I said. 'Why? Who is he?'

'He's Pat McNamara,' said Tracy. 'You know, the soap star. I didn't know he'd split from his wife.'

'Must have been quite recently,' Michelle said. We watched as Pat stroked his girlfriend's knee. 'But that's definitely a new girlfriend.'

'How do you know so much about him?' I said. 'When do you have time to watch TV?'

'Don't you read the papers?' Tracy said.

'Sometimes,' I said.

'You mean the *Telegraph*,' Michelle said. 'All that boring shit about Gorbachev and Perestroika!'

'And let's not forget Glasnost,' I said.

'Yes, and Glasnost, whoever he is when he's at home.'

Tracy weighed in. 'Well, if you ever sank your toffee little nose into one of the red tops, you might learn something new.'

By rights I would have responded in my usual acidic fashion, but I held my tongue. 'Maybe you're right,' I said. 'I'll give it a go. I might learn something new.'

Nothing much happened until about an hour or two later. The major and his wife had had their starter and their mains and were now readying themselves for the main event, the pudding. The major beckoned Oliver over.

'You couldn't get me some pudding?' he said. 'This gout…'

'Certainly,' said Oliver. 'What would you like?'

'Trifle,' said the major. 'Couple of brandy snaps. Some strawberries.'

'And some cream?'

'Lots of cream,' he said. 'Fill it to the brim.'

Oliver took the major at his word. At the puddings table, he spooned in a mound of trifle, placed a brandy snap on each side and then topped the whole lot off with thick Dorset double cream.

As Oliver walked back to the major's table, he held onto the bowl with both hands. As if in slow-motion, Oliver glided up behind the major, concentrating hard on not spilling a drop. At that exact moment, Pat moved his chair back to go up for a second helping of pudding. He slammed into Oliver. The tall German tottered. The bowl arced.

A brandy snap spattered onto the back of the major's neck. The bowl, brimming with cream, trifle and strawberries all ended up going down the front of Pat's canary yellow waistcoat.

For a second, the three of them just stood there, marvelling at the chaos.

'You bloody idiot!' Pat shouted. 'Look at me! Look at me!'

I looked at him. The whole dining room looked at him. The better part of his waistcoat was covered in cream and lush trifle. A stray strawberry lingered on his trousers. On the pointed toe of his cowboy boot were the remains of a brandy snap.

'I'm very sorry, sir,' Oliver said, mopping ineffectually at the yellow waistcoat. The cream smeared deeper into the brocade.

The major, meanwhile, remained in his seat, ignoring the brandy snap on his shoulder to take a leisurely sip of his wine.

'Get off me!' Pat slapped Oliver's hands away. 'Get off me!'

The two girls must have been used to their father's rages and were staring at the table, but Pat's lover was shocked.

She stretched a hand to him. 'It's all right,' she said. 'It's okay.'

'It is not okay!' said Pat.

I was enthralled. I wondered if he was actually going to hit Oliver.

Anthony bustled over. 'I am so sorry,' he said. 'Oliver, go and clean yourself up.' He beckoned to me and to Roland. 'Kim, clean up this mess. Roland, help the major. Take him to the cloakroom.'

'Don't trouble yourself,' said the major. 'Though a brandy might be in order.' He looked over his shoulder, saw the brandy snap and plucked it off his coat. He took a leisurely bite before having another draught of wine, paying no attention to the cream that was still on his coat.

Nothing much more happened during the meal. Greta had gone off to powder her nose and I was talking to Cally.

'Can I see you later?' she asked.

'I'd love that.' I removed the two pudding bowls. She'd had trifle and clotted cream, while Greta, forever dieting, had had a small spoonful of fruit salad.

'Will you take me to your room?'

I laughed. 'My room?' I said. 'It's not what you think it is, I can tell you! It's about a quarter the size of your beach hut, the walls weep when it's wet and the mattress is probably the most uncomfortable thing you've ever sat on.'

'It sounds charming.' She was tipsy and she giggled. 'Where shall I meet you?'

I looked round the dining room. We were down to the last handful of tables. 'In your car in thirty minutes?' I said.

'Perfect.'

Minutes later, I was kissing Greta and Cally goodbye. As soon as Anthony had released us, I flew back to my room, because although it may well have been small, it was also grubby. I only slept there once or twice a week, when Cally was away in London, so I hadn't actually cleaned it since I'd started working at the Knoll House.

I pushed the door open, switched on the light and looked at my room with an unflinching eye.

Clothes strewn everywhere, bedclothes that hadn't been changed in ages, various stains on the tiled floor, and all overlaid with a general hum of pheromones and sweat.

I threw open the window and the door and bundled my clothes into the laundry bag. These included all the colourful, luxurious shirts that Cally had given me. She never showered me with presents in the true toy-boy tradition, but the one thing she did like to do was buy me new shirts with cuffs and full collars. She had bought about five of them, stripy and floral and paisley – all different but every one of them pulsing with colour.

I made a trip to the laundry for fresh bed sheets. There was no air-freshener to hand so I sprayed the room with aftershave. Removing the floor stains – the mud, blood and assorted bits of scum – proved more difficult. I didn't have a brush, so I attacked the floor with a wet towel. I was like those ladies by the Ganges who scrub their clothes away to nothing on the rocks by the riverbank.

It wasn't great, but after I had borrowed a candle from Oliver the worst of it was indistinguishable in the shadows.

I put on a fresh shirt and trousers and went up to the car park where Cally was already waiting for me in the twilight. It was quite still that evening, not a breath of wind, and the pines were heavy with scent and sap.

I kissed Cally and led her back to my lair. She had a bottle of champagne. We went round the back so that there was less likelihood of being spotted. We tripped and sprawled in the darkness and ended up rolling around on top of each other, kissing and making out in the grass and the weeds.

Above us, not eight yards away, we could hear Janeen arguing with Darren. She was angry; he was placatory.

'Did you sleep with her?' she said.

'No,' he said. 'I want you.'

'All right, did you shag her?'

'Course not. Come on, baby.'

'What did you do with her?'

'Nothing happened!'

Their voices began to fade as they walked away. I could still hear Janeen's shrill voice, but I could no longer make out what she was saying.

Cally was lying on top of me. She winked at me. 'Just like every other guy,' she said.

'Oh yeah?'

'If he's got a chance of getting some fresh oats, he'll take it.'

'Just like every other guy?' I asked.

'Yes.'

'And does that include me?'

She smiled at me, her eyes appraising me. 'You, Kim? Ah yes, I often wonder what will happen when some pretty young floozy comes along and throws her cap at you. What will you do? Are you still going to be like every other guy? Will you still want to try something new?'

'I'm not every other guy!' I said.

She kissed me on the side of the mouth. 'Maybe,' she said, and then kissed me on the other side of my mouth, 'and maybe not.'

Did she know then? Had she already divined my Achilles' heel?

'I want to see your room,' she said. 'I want to christen it.'

'How do you know it hasn't been christened already?' I asked.

'Saucy,' she said with a kiss. 'But it hasn't yet been christened by me, and that's the only thing that counts.'

'You're right,' I said. 'Though actually you will be the first.'

'I should hope so too.'

She stood up and took my hand and led me to the top of the hillock. We scuttled to my room. It would have been much more cool and much more stylish to have been brazen, but I think we were both still enjoying the secrecy of it all.

I tugged her inside and closed the door behind us.

'Don't you ever lock your door?' she asked.

'Never.'

'I can come and visit you whenever I like?'

'You certainly can.'

She put the bottle on the bedside table, picked up the candle and held it up high as she gazed about the room. 'The floor's still wet,' she observed. 'The window's open and I think I am getting a distinct whiff of aftershave.' She plumped the bed. 'Fresh sheets too!' And then her hand strayed to the drawers, which she tugged open one by one to reveal the dirty clothes that had been packed inside. 'And your laundry all neatly folded too! You have been busy!'

I laughed and kissed her. 'Do you normally do that when you visit a chap's bedroom for the first time?'

'No,' she said as she sat down on the bed and dragged me down beside her. 'Normally I put on my white cotton gloves to test the picture frames for dust.'

'Well, that's me in the clear. I don't have any pictures.'

'You don't, do you?' She stared at the breeze block. The walls really were singularly depressing. 'I'll see what I can do. Do you have a marker pen?'

I shook my head.

She rummaged in her bag and seized on her lipstick. 'This will be perfect,' she said. 'Never tried lipstick before. Now sit yourself at the end of the bed, open the champagne and pour out a glass.'

WILLIAM COLES

I poured the champagne into the grubby tumbler that I had borrowed from the kitchens. The fizz was about to bubble over the top, but I did the old waiter's trick of sticking my finger into the froth. The bubbles died in an instant.

She took a gulp of champagne and then, with relaxed, easy movements, started sketching me on the wall. She was very happy; and seeing her like that, I was happy too.

I was slumped against the end wall, so I could not see her work.

'Did you see that idiot who started shouting after Oliver chucked trifle over him?' I said.

'Tosser.'

'Apparently he's some big-name soap-star.'

'Never seen him before in my life. And he's still a tosser.'

'Split from his wife and he's down here with his new girlfriend. Got to be at least fifteen or twenty years his junior.'

'How unsavoury,' she said, drily, and we laughed. I passed her the tumbler. She sipped as she continued to draw. Her lipstick was nearly finished. 'You could sell that piece of information, you know,' she said.

'Who'd buy it?'

'Just call up the *Sun*. They've even got a freephone number. Ask for the chief reporter, Mike Hamill. He knows me. If they get a good picture of Pat with his new girlfriend, you'll make more money in five minutes than you do in a month here.'

'And how do you know Mike?'

'He helped me out when I nearly had my fifteen minutes of fame.'

'Nearly? Why only nearly?' I said. 'Anything good?'

'No,' she said. 'Ask Mike.'

'I just might. So I just give him a call?'

'Any time after ten thirty. They barely start work before noon.'

'Sounds like my kind of place.'

She studied me for a while, twirling the champagne tumbler just a few inches from her lips. 'Actually, I think it is.'

'How's that picture going?'

'I'm done.'

I got off the bed to have a look. It is always difficult to assess a picture of yourself by another. But I liked it. There was a carefree attitude in that young man with his tumbler.

'Wonderful,' I said. 'Are you going to sign it?'

'Of course.' With the remnants of the lipstick she lacquered her lips and kissed the wall just beneath the picture.

I slipped my hand about her waist and we were kissing again.

How quickly I used to drink in those days. The bottle was near empty. We kissed and my room's much-vaunted christening was on the verge of taking place when Cally broke off.

'I see what you mean about this bed,' she said. 'I don't know if it's the most uncomfortable bed I've ever been on. But it's got to be in the top three.'

'Would it help if I went underneath?'

She looked at the dreary breeze block walls and the scuffed door and the flickering candle. And then she sniffed. I think it was that final sniff that decided her.

'I've got another idea,' she said. 'I'll book a room in the hotel.'

'Now?'

'I'll spend the night,' she said. 'I haven't stayed in years.'

'Cool.'

We arranged to meet by one of the side doors of the hotel, so that I wouldn't have to run the gauntlet of the night porter. Good to her word, Cally was waiting there for me fifteen minutes later with a second bottle of champagne. She took me past the nursery and the children's dining room and up the back stairs. As we skulked along the carpeted corridors, I felt as if I were breaking into the Bank of England. At every turn, I expected to be spotted by one of the managers or one of the guests who, I don't know, would instantly have blown the whistle to prevent a guest from bedding a member of staff.

Cally's room was on the first floor, just past the main staircase. We had almost made it there when she spotted the giant-sized Chippendale chair on the staircase. I'd not seen it since my first day at the hotel, in fact had forgotten all about it.

Cally was about to open the bedroom door, when she stayed my hand. 'You know,' she said, 'I've always wanted to make love on that chair.'

'You're crazy!' I said. Even at my most swashbuckling drunk, I would not have dreamed of having sex on the hotel's main staircase.

'We'll carry it to my room,' she said. 'Quickly, come on!'

I could have hemmed and hawed, but when she said it like that, I didn't have much option. She had already darted down the stairs and was busy manhandling the chair away from the wall. The chair was in the style of an old Chippendale and at least seven feet tall. It was heavy but not too heavy.

We each took an arm and Cally led the way up the stairs, while I followed four steps behind her. I was sure it wasn't going to fit through the door, but eventually we put the chair on its side and worked it around the corner of the doorframe.

Cally triumphantly shut the door. 'This deserves a toast!' she said.

We opened the champagne and then set the chair up by the window. The chair was easily big enough for both us and so we sat on it side by side, nursing our tumblers of fizz and gazing out through the open window. It all felt very daring, as if we were two young children who had set up a play-den among our parents' most prized antiques.

'How long do you think it'll be before they notice the chair's gone missing?' I asked.

'Good point,' she said. 'And since we've gone to all the trouble of getting this chair into the room…'

'It would be a shame not to use it.'

Very business-like, I eased off her top and she helped me off with my clothes and like the seasoned lovers that we undoubtedly were, we were very quickly in the saddle.

'Are you going to sit back and think of England?' I asked.

'Are you going to stand up and be a man?' she riposted, and we laughed. The laugh stretched all the way from her cheeks to her neck, to her breasts and to her rippling belly. I don't think I have ever laughed so much during my love making as I did when I was with her.

Getting that giant's chair out of the bedroom was not nearly as easy as it had been to get it in. In theory it should have been a mere matter of putting the earlier process into reverse. But for some reason, the back of the chair kept getting stuck against the wardrobe.

'Oh dear,' I said. We stared at the chair, which was now half in, half out of the room.

'Maybe it's like toothpaste,' she said. 'No way of putting it back in the tube.'

'It must be possible,' I said. 'We're just not using our brains.'

'We could just leave the chair in the room,' she said.

'At least more people would get to have sex on it.'

'Though we could always try chopping a few inches off each leg,' she said.

'Knocking down the wardrobe would probably be easier,' I said. 'Let's try something different. We'll get it out.'

'Girls like that in a guy,' she said. 'They like confidence. Even if you don't much know what you're doing, they still like a guy with confidence.'

'I'm oozing it,' I grunted as I tugged the chair back into the room and started to turn it round. 'Anything else that women like or don't like in a guy?'

'I'll tell you when we've got this piece of furniture out of the room.'

Eventually, we heaved the chair through the door, though only after a lot of scuffing. It had to go out almost diagonally, with me outside in the corridor lifting the chair high over my head.

We were so elated that we took our eye off the ball. We were bumping the chair back down the stairs. I missed my footing, stumbled and the chair hammered into the banisters. Cally held on tight and just stopped the chair from smashing into my head.

We heard a voice from downstairs. I knew it well. 'Everything all right there?'

The sound of footsteps hurrying towards the stairs.

The chair was now all but blocking the stairs. We looked at each other and we each realised there was no time to be lost. Leaving the chair where it stood, we tore back up the stairs. Anthony was already behind us – confronted by the sight of the giant chair abandoned on the staircase.

'Hi!' he called. 'What's going on?'

He was too near for us to return to Cally's room. We raced up to the second floor, Cally giggling as we ran. Anthony had stumped up to the second floor behind us. He called out again, but we never stopped and we never looked back.

I was all for holing up in a linen cupboard, but Cally was adamant that we should return to our room. 'I've paid for it!' she hissed.

Back down the back stairs. Scampering along the corridor. A brief glance at the staircase. The chair was still discarded on the middle of the stairs, just where we'd left it. Cally fumbled with the keys and we plunged into the sanctum of her room.

Except one thing wasn't quite right, and it was some minutes before I worked out what it was. When we'd left the room to return the giant's chair, the door had been left partially open. And when we'd arrived back, the door was shut.

We had been lying in bed for twenty minutes. From outside in the corridor we could hear the night porter cursing as he heaved the giant's chair back to its proper place.

We hadn't talked for some time. Cally had plucked a feather from her pillow and was stroking it on my chest.

With a pink nub of tongue, she licked my shoulder.

'We'll be ending soon, you know,' she said.

'What?' I was drowsy from booze and sex and early starts.

'I sense it,' she said. 'We'll be ending soon. Our little show is reaching the end of the road.'

'What do you mean?' I said, suddenly wide awake. 'Are you getting ready to dump me?'

'No,' she laughed. The stroking continued, but now from being pleasant and soothing, it was as if my skin had become hypersensitive. I pushed her hand away.

'But when we do end,' she said. 'Don't write. Don't come looking for me. It has to be a clean break. Anything else would break my heart.'

'What are you talking about?' I was nonplussed. I was in love with her. I was happy, deliriously happy. Why was she talking about splitting up? 'I love you.'

'It'll happen,' she said. 'I'm sorry, but it will, and I'll be even sorrier when it does, but anyway…'

'Got a touch of the black dog, have we?' I asked. 'Need some perking up?'

She turned the feather round and jabbed the quill into my chest. 'You can perk me up any time you like.'

She found another feather from the pillow and started to probe me with the two feathers' quills. 'Tell me whether you can feel one point or two,' she said. I started to feel little prickings over my chest and arms.

'That's two,' I said. 'And one. And one. And two.'

'How sensitive you are,' she said. 'At least in some places, and not so much in others.'

'Don't tell me – because I'm just a guy?'

'I'm going to tell you things,' she said. 'I'm going to make you…' She trailed off. 'Turn over, please. I'm going to try your back now.' The prickings started up about my shoulders. 'I'm going to tell you what it is that women want.'

'I don't know if I've got a spare week.'

'And your next girlfriend—'

'My next girlfriend? Why are we talking about my next girlfriend?'

'She won't believe her luck.'

'Do I get a certificate at the end of it? Maybe you could write me a reference? It might come in handy. Rather than having to go through the whole tedium of chatting women up, I could just pass them your letter of recommendation and they'll be whisking me straight to the bedroom.' A single feather was jabbed savagely into the small of my back. 'Ow!'

'Women, at least the women who are worth being with, like a guy who is reliable. They like a man who turns up on time. They like a man who, when he says he'll write—'

'Actually bothers to write!'

'So if you say you're going to do something, you do it; and if you say you're going to be somewhere, then you're there.'

'That's me,' I said. 'Mr Reliable.'

'Women also like a certain amount of unpredictability.'

'Very different, though, from being unreliable.'

'Yes.' The feathers continued to tease about my back and my legs. It was sharp and slightly painful but I didn't want to her to stop. 'Women do not want to feel that their lives are weighed down by routine. You have to mix things up. Have to be versatile. If something works once, then you can do it again; but that doesn't mean that you do it over and over again.'

'My grandad could have done with that tip,' I said. 'He never bought anyone a present in his life, except for the one present a year that he bought for my granny at Christmas. One year, he got her a bottle of Chanel No. 5; she was thrilled and she showed it. I think my dad must have been born nine months later. So the next year, what does my grandad do? He buys her another bottle of Chanel No. 5. And that was the one and only Christmas present that he gave her for the rest of his life. By the end, her dressing table was covered in all these old bottles of stale Chanel!'

'He could have tried a little harder,' said Cally. 'Women want to know that you care. Money is always going to help. We love our jewellery. But if you're going to buy, then always buy the best. If you've got a hundred pounds to spend, then buy a small beautiful ring rather than a middle-of-the-road necklace. Now, are you listening to me?' She jabbed a feather into each buttock.

'I'm listening!'

'Just making sure you're not asleep. What we want are the things which show that you've been thinking of us – that you have thought, at length, about our needs and our desires, and that at the end of it, you have divined exactly what it is that we want, perhaps, even, before we have thought of it ourselves.'

'So the perfect guy also just happens to be a mind reader?'

'It might help.'

'Any other little titbits for me?'

'Some women like surprises; some don't.' Cally had started working on the soles of my feet, sharp stabs in between my toes. 'You're not very sensitive here at all, are you?'

'If you say so.'

'I do – yes, surprises. And you quickly have to find out what sort of woman you're with, because the girls who don't like surprises are going to hate anything that's sprung on them. But obviously, they still like to think that they're up for an adventure, because we all love adventures, but if you're going to surprise them—'

'Even if it's a nice surprise?'

'Especially if it's a nice surprise, then you leave something lying around, a letter, or a receipt, just so that they've had enough time to prepare themselves.'

'So when the surprise comes, they're ready for it and they can act as if they're thrilled?'

'Presents are difficult. A lot of women like presents to be properly wrapped.'

'It shows we care.'

'But the contents is just as important. With clothes and jewellery, you have to have been given the go-ahead before you buy. Otherwise stick to classy and expensive and you should be fine.'

'Classy and expensive: good. Cheap and tatty: bad. I think I can remember that.'

'And always keep the receipt.'

Cally was trailing a feather over my back and I could feel her scratching out letters. She was writing some sort of message, and I caught the word, 'Love', but after that I was lost.

'But not showy,' she said. 'Tasteful.'

'Tell me about the sex.'

'Okay then, sex. Well, Kim, you will be surprised to hear that having sex with your partner two or three times a day is not actually the norm.'

'It isn't?'

'Surprisingly, no. It will be at first, but it will tail off. The thing is sometimes you have to take control—'

'And sometimes she wants to be in control.'

'But it's not as simple as that.'

'What now?'

The point of one feather remained buried in my spine. She paused, as if trying to remember how it had been during her marriage.

'It's like this: we want you to know before we know it ourselves. We don't necessarily know what we want, but we sure as hell know what we don't want.'

'This is sounding like a complete snap,' I said, turning over, so that she was sitting astride my chest. I had both my hands about her waist, her flesh rolling through my fingers. 'I always thought this business of knowing what women wanted was going to be really tough. I mean, you know, a whole lifetime of learning, and even then you wouldn't be halfway there. But the way you've described it, it all sounds so easy!'

She leaned forward and kissed my nose, her hair falling down across my cheek.

I stroked her stomach. 'All a guy's got to do – all I've got to do – is become both a mind reader and a clairvoyant, so that I can not only divine what it is that a woman wants right now, but what it is that she might want in the next couple of hours. Then, with the large, large fortune that I have at my disposal, I'll be able to set about making her happy.'

'And don't forget the confidence. Not cockiness. Confidence.'

'Here endeth the lesson?'

'Tonight's lesson, yes.'

She moved deliciously on top of me.

'Tell me,' I said. 'Are there really guys out there who aren't having sex two or three times a day?'

'I'm afraid there are, poor things. They have never learned what it is that a woman wants, so they must go without.'

'That's tough.' I closed my eyes, pressed my fingers to my temples, and screwed my face up in intense concentration. 'Let me see.'

I pouted and frowned. 'It's coming to me. It's coming to me! I think I'm seeing it now. I think I know what it is that you want.'

She let out a low, delicious purr of pleasure, which started in the pit of her stomach and rippled up through her throat.

'I think I'm getting it right now.'

CHAPTER 14

After university, I had travelled for nearly two years, and in that time I had found it difficult to find any decent books. In the hostels and backpacker hotels, you might find the latest potboilers, but there was rarely anything worth reading.

One day, in Madurai in India, I came across a second-hand bookshop, where – wonder of wonders – the man seemed to stock nothing but classics. For the first time in my life, I immersed myself in those thick hardbacks that can still strike a chord of terror.

Of course, at school my teachers had done their best to thrust Dickens and Hardy and Shakespeare down my throat, and that had turned out to be an unpleasant experience for everyone involved. But in India, where I was allowed to dip into these books in my own time, my love for the classics came into bloom. Part of it was just down to the fact that in those days I had a lot of time to read. I'd read at the station as I waited for the train; I'd read on ferries; I'd read at night and I'd read in the morning. And if you're reading three, four hours a day, a book soon gets its hooks into you. I read *Crime and Punishment* in ten days flat. These days, I'd be lucky to finish it in a summer. *The Idiot* – one week. *Madame Bovary* – one week. *David Copperfield* – five days. Above all others, I loved Dickens. My favourite was *Great Expectations*, ending as we know all love affairs must end with hearts broken and love unrequited. My favourite line from it: 'Pause and think of a moment of the long chain of thorns or flowers, of gold or iron that would never have bound you, but for the formation of one link on one memorable day.'

Well, I had just lived that memorable day and what a chain it would come to forge for me, though I am still not sure if it was made of thorns or iron. But for that dinner, but for that accident with the trifle, but for my late-night tryst with Cally, my life would have been oh-so different.

Anthony was in an unusually bad mood the next morning. This was not like him at all. He was the jolliest, cheeriest boss that I have ever known, and the more the guests whined and whinged and complained about the food and the service, the more he smiled and the more he laughed.

But not that morning. Halfway through breakfast, he came in glowering. He picked up some coffee, studied the waiters and waitresses for two minutes and then stomped off back to his office. I might have been wrong, but his eyes seemed to linger on me for slightly longer than the rest of the staff.

By ten o'clock, the last of the breakfast diners had gone and he called us all into a huddle. There was a long pause. He rubbed his hands together, palm to palm, as he stared up at the ceiling. His face was quite white. He was steaming.

'I'm sorry I have to mention this again,' he said. His voice was very soft. We had to strain to hear him. 'Somebody is still stealing from the staff wages and it is making me very, very angry. Now I'm not saying it's a member of the waiting staff, but if it is you, could you stop it? Otherwise we'll be calling in the police and the rest of it, and it will all get very unpleasant.'

We looked at each other, each of us sizing up which one of our colleagues could have the sheer nerve to still be filching from the wage packets.

'On another matter, as you know, we would prefer it if staff did not sleep with the guests. For God's sake! What's wrong with the rest of the staff? There must be a hundred of you!'

'The guests are better looking,' Janeen called.

'Thank you for that, Janeen. But if you are going to sleep with the guests, then kindly don't do it in the hotel and preferably not in the hotel grounds either.'

'Can we still shag on the beach?' Janeen said. A ripple of laughter flushed through the room.

'Yes, Janeen, you can still continue shagging on the beach. However, when you get caught by the police, please don't come running to me to bail you out.' His eyes roamed round the waiters and the waitresses until at last they fell upon me. 'Also, there was some horseplay last night. The giant's chair has been knocked about and the seat fabric has been torn. So could the young waiter responsible kindly confine his nocturnal activities to his own squalid room and could he desist from breaking any more of the hotel furniture.'

His eyes never left mine, and if my colleagues had ever been in any doubt as to the identity of the hotel's rogue lover, Anthony's pep talk had confirmed my identity to the last detail.

Oliver clapped my shoulder as we walked out. 'I thought I told you to stop stealing the wages,' he said.

'I can't stop myself,' I said. We were out in the sun and I was heading for the payphone. 'I think I must be a kleptomaniac.'

'And what on earth were you doing with the giant's chair.'

'Exactly what you'd like to do with the giant's chair.'

A pause and then a light bulb went on in Oliver's head and he smiled. 'Oh,' he said. 'I will have to tell Annette immediately when I see her! I think she would like that. I think she would like that very much.'

'Shame we beat you to it.'

'We do not mind that,' said Oliver. 'We do not need to chalk up these petty firsts. We have each other.'

That morning, I called up the *Sun* and asked to speak to Mike Hamill; I was very surprised. I suppose that I'd expected to be put through to this aggressive Rottweiler who would sound like one of the more ferocious characters off *EastEnders*. But I was quite wrong. Hamill was a complete charmer, very quick and very personable. From his silver tongue I would have put him down as a diplomat.

I gave him the bare bones of what I knew.

'Great story, dear boy!' said Mike. I liked that word 'story'. It conjured up an image of entertaining fact mixed with the very lightest sprinkling of salty fiction. 'Anything more I need to know?'

I racked my brain. For some reason, and I don't why, I felt like opening my heart to the man. I wanted to tell him everything I knew and everything that he wanted to hear.

'He was talking about going skinny-dipping,' I said.

'*Excellente!*' he said, swinging into the Italian. I could almost hear him rubbing his hands with glee. 'We'll get a monkey down right away.'

'A monkey?' I queried.

'One of our photographers, dear boy,' he said. 'They are called monkeys because they spend a lot of their time swinging around in the trees.'

I liked this man, and I liked the exotic world he inhabited. 'And what are the reporters called?'

'We answer to many names. "Blunt" would probably be the most complimentary. Short for the blunt pencils that we sometimes use as we scratch out our jottings.'

'So you are the chief blunt?' I said.

'We're going to get on very well!' he said. 'I do hope we catch Pat skinny-dipping with his girlfriend. I can see you are going to be a contact worth cultivating.'

During lunch that day, I was teased mercilessly about the age of my lover. For now that Cally's identity was well and truly out in the open, there was limitless scope to the jokes and the badinage.

'She must be double your age,' Tracy said.

'More like triple!' Michelle said.

'I actually think you'll find, girls, that she's about to receive a telegram from the Queen,' I said. 'She will be one hundred years old next month.'

'Coo!' Tracy said. 'She's probably got great-grandchildren younger than you.'

It was Janeen, naturally, who cut to the chase. 'So what's it like shagging a granny?' she said. 'Have these middle-aged lovers got anything going for them?'

'I'd have thought that someone like you would know all about it,' I said.

'I was asking you,' Janeen said.

'Bedroom perks?' I scratched my head as if utterly perplexed. 'Well, I mean there aren't any, not really. Apart, of course, from the fact that she's possibly even randier than I am and wants to have sex even more often that I do; and that she's got no inhibitions whatsoever; and she's up for having nookie in the most exotic places imaginable—'

'Did you really shag her on the giant's chair?' Janeen said.

I winked at her. 'Including quite possibly the giant's chair, although that is something that I could neither confirm nor deny. All I'm saying is that middle-aged women have confidence and money and cars and class; basically, they've got all the sort of things that girls half their age can only aspire to. And you know what? I reckon they're better looking too. Maybe they've got a few more lines round their eyes, but I can tell you that a woman like Cally is, for me, an absolute stunner.'

'Maybe I should get myself a sugar daddy,' Janeen said.

'They're conversation's much more interesting,' I said. 'They've got stamina and they've got style—'

'Grannies all the way!' Tracy said.

'Grannies all the way!' I high-fived her and went about my business.

Some of the staff were less generous, Giles being at the top of the list.

I was picking up some main courses, and Giles was standing at the pass, red-faced and with the usual stream of sweat dripping down his neck.

I picked up two plates of chicken. 'Thank you.'

'It's the geriatrophile,' he said, not really speaking to anyone in particular, but loud enough for me to hear.

'Geriatrophile?' I paused, the plates still in my hand. 'That's a very big word for you, Giley. I didn't know the Ladybird books stretched to words of five syllables.'

'She must be desperate,' he said.

'About as desperate as you are, dear Giley,' I replied. 'From what I hear, you're taking the term self-abuse to a whole new level.'

I was now at the exit door. I tossed him one last insult as I went out. 'I hope you're washing your grubby little fingers before you start cooking.'

I thought no more of it. To me, it was all just a part of the cut and thrust of the dining room: a dollop of charm here, a witticism there and occasionally, for the likes of Giles, the most withering and acidic invective that my simmering brain could conjure.

'It is good that this has come out, my friend,' Oliver said. 'You can now hold hands with Cally in the pub.'

'And we can go on double dates, too,' I said.

'That would be nice,' Oliver said. 'Annette and I, we would like that.'

I had just left the dining room and was returning to my room before going out riding with Cally. I was looking forward to telling her that our secret was out and that now we were free to declare our love to the world. For the first time, public displays of affection were officially permissible.

I was watching an elderly woman make her way out of the hotel. She had a walking stick and seemed to be in some pain. A man who I took to be her son was helping her towards his car. He had his hand at her elbow and he had all the time in the world for his mother. When she dropped her stick, he swooped and picked it up and with a laugh he returned it to her. It was a charming little scene.

I heard a cackle from behind me. It was Giles. He was still in his chef's whites and was having a cigarette with Darren. They were both perched on the playground fence.

'You going to have a try with her?' he said, nodding at the old lady. 'Or is she too young for you?'

I walked over to Giles. Without a word I grabbed both of his feet and in one fell movement I heaved his legs up over his head and pitched him backwards into the playground. There was a delicious thud as he hit the ground. It is not often that I get physical with another man. I wished I'd done it long ago.

I went on my way and did not look back.

But Giles wanted more.

I heard a bellow of anger from behind me. Giles was charging, his face puce, quite delirious with rage. I slid to the side and tripped him, watching quite dispassionately as he ploughed into the sun-baked earth. He'd hurt his wrist, massaging it as he hauled himself to his feet.

'You bastard,' he said. 'You bloody bastard.'

'Still want to play, do you, Giley?'

'I'll get you.'

'Try me,' I said.

I walked off and I left him standing there, a writhing heap of madness that thirsted for revenge.

Cally found me out in the pub that night. One moment I was talking to Oliver and Annette, the next Cally was bending over me and kissing me – not on the cheek, but full on the lips.

I stood up, took her in my arms. In full view of all the locals and the Knoll House staff, erasing any shadow of doubt, we kissed each other long and hard. We kissed until gradually I noticed that the conversations around us were beginning to flag, and when finally we were done Oliver started to clap, and then Roland, and the next thing the whole pub had broken into spontaneous applause. The first and only time in my life that I have ever been applauded for a kiss.

We walked back from the pub. 'We're officially a couple,' Cally said. 'Both in private and in public.'

'About time, too,' I said.

'Yes, all this secrecy and hiding was getting to be a bit of a drag,' she said. 'Anyway, I never knew what you were so ashamed of.'

'Me?' I said. 'I thought it was you who wanted me to stay in shadows.'

'Darling Kim.' She kissed me. 'I would sing my love from the rooftops.'

'We'll do a duet then.'

'Let's lie down here.'

'Right here?'

'Where do you think I mean? In the ditch? Lying here will help you concentrate on your next lesson.'

So we laid down right in the middle of the road. We were not far from the Knoll House, and although the road didn't tend to be that busy after the ferry had closed, there were still the few odd cars weaving their way back home at the dead of night.

The tarmac was warm. We straddled the white lines and held hands. There was not a light to be seen, just the moon and the firmament, and us lying there in the middle of the road waiting to be embraced by death as he swept us on to oblivion.

'Is there any particular reason why we're lying in the middle of the road?' I said.

'I've never done it before.'

'Haven't we already been down this route?' I said. 'So this lesson, I take it, is to further my development as a lover and as a human being. Why are you so sure we're going to split up?'

'I've split up with everyone else I've ever loved.'

'And why should I be any different?'

'Women like letters,' she said. 'Write to them and write to them often. Phone calls are fine. But a handwritten letter, just a trace of scent, can be treasured and it can be pored over.'

'I haven't written to you enough, have I?'

'You have not.' She pressed my hand to her lips and kissed my fingers.

'Point taken.'

'Self-deprecation, we like that.'

'Never really been my strong suit.'

'Good. You want to watch your humour, Kim. You're sharp, but you must use it more carefully; women, despite all their bluff and their bravado, can bruise very easily.'

'Noted,' I said. 'Curb all jokes which come at my lover's expense.'

'I wish my husband had had this sort of coaching,' Cally said. With her finger, she was drawing fresh patterns in the stars. 'Instead it was me who wasted years training him up, and it's his next wife who's reaping all the benefits.'

'I wouldn't bank on that. Once a tosser, always a tosser.'

'Are you comfy?' she said.

'Very. Shall we spend the night here? Tell me about the love making. What do women want?'

'Now that is difficult.' Cally rolled on top of me, kissing me as she stroked my cheek. 'Guys, as we know, can have sex anywhere, any time, and with pretty much anyone. They were born dirty. But women, at least the ones worth dating, first have to have an emotional connection. There's got to be the talk and lots of it and if you don't do that, then there will be no sex in the afternoon.'

'Painfully obvious,' I said. 'Are you going to tell me something I didn't know?'

'As regards your knowledge of women, Kim darling, I do not presume one single thing.' She kissed me. 'Try this. We adore compliments, but they must be tailor-made for the occasion. It is also impossible to tell us too often that we are the love of your life.'

'You are the love of my life.'

'Say it like you mean it.'

I looked soulfully, earnestly, into her eyes. 'You, Cally, are truly the love of my life.'

'Better. Now pay me a very personal compliment.'

'Give me a second.' I stared up at the stars. 'Here, now, I'd risk my life to make love with you.'

'In the middle of the road?' She kissed me with stunning ardour. 'Oh, Kim, that is a very pretty compliment and I like it very much!'

Hands tugged at clothes, legs entwined, skin raked over with nails and with fingers. Cally's hair fell about my face, cocooning me within its fringe. I closed my eyes and succumbed to her kisses. The texture of her lips and her warm skin was intoxicating. I was so caught up with Cally's kisses and with her warmth that I was not even aware that we were laying in the middle of an A-road at midnight.

Usually, I like to kiss with my eyes shut. I am not looking at cheeks or lips; I am in the moment, focused on the kiss and nothing else.

Something happened. Some primeval sense twitched, it was as if a pin had been thrust into my forehead. I opened my eyes and through the fringe of Cally's thick hair, I caught a faint flicker of light in the sky.

I broke off from Cally lips and heaved at her, pushing her away from me.

'No,' she said. She strained to kiss me.

'Car!' I shrieked.

What happened next happened so fast that it was all over in two seconds. I still see it in my nightmares. The car hits us full and square. The one moment we're kissing, and the next trapped by the headlights as the car roars into view. We try to move, but we can't, deer trapped in the headlights; and the car is going so fast, there's no time for it to swerve. There's a terrific blast of the horn, deafening, blending with the engine's thunder and the squeal of the brakes, and the car is so close now that I can see the flies speckled about the bumper and smell the hot engine oil and the turtle wax. I try to get up, pushing and pushing, but nothing happens. I'm stuck to the tarmac, Cally glued on top of me, my eyes locked onto the headlights and nothing else. My mouth formed into a perfect 'O' as I scream my last scream. Then the wheels, black and broad, are on top of me, mashing my pelvis to dust and, in that same moment, Cally is whisked from me, her head snatched clean off by the bumper, as her body is thrown like a ragdoll, and as she goes over the top, shattering the windscreen, I go under the wheels, pulped front and back, though not that it makes any difference, because by the time the car has screeched to a halt, our life-blood is already oozing out onto the road.

These nightmares are still capable of waking me up in a shivering sweat. My eyes flash open and I can still see that image of Cally and me, bloodied and broken, lying dead as doornails on the tarmac.

And in reality: the moment stretched into an infinity of horrific instants.

With animal strength, I forced Cally off me, pistoling my arms until she had pitched backwards. The sweep of the car's headlights reared up, huge in the darkness as the car tore round the bend. The sound of the brakes squealed as the horn klaxoned into the night and I pitched forward in a flat dive. As I crashed to the ground, my elbow jarred into the kerb. The wind of the car whipped at my feet. One wheel clipped, slightly scrunched, one of my boots. I was limping for weeks.

The car stopped; the driver got out. He was livid and as he howled out his rage, we went into the woods and the darkness. 'You maniacs!' he screamed blindly. 'I could have killed you!'

We laughed and the thrill of the adrenalin passed. My elbow hurt and I knew that my foot was also injured. We started to kiss.

'Where were we?' Cally said, and we knelt on the dark grass as she unbuttoned my shirt, and it was electrifying, erotic. We'd come within an ace of killing ourselves as we made out in the middle of the road.

But along with all my other thoughts, there was one thing that just wouldn't go away. In that first moment when I saw the car's headlights winking into the sky, for a second, it had felt as if Cally was forcing me hard down onto the tarmac, as if willing for it all to be over; for the both of us to be mown down as we conjoined in the ecstasy of the moment.

CHAPTER 15

There are many plus points when it comes to dating a much older woman. But there are also several downsides and if you would see our relationship in all its rough-hewn beauty, with its warts, its wrinkles and its libido that raged into the night, then I must acknowledge them.

If your lover is from another generation, there is no common ground with popular culture. Cally had been born in such a different era. She was a war baby, with rationing and austerity, and with not a television to be seen. She'd been there in the sixties with the pill and the Rolling Stones and the Beatles. I'd had *Watch with Mother* and *Top of the Pops* and Blondie and all the bands at which my father would roll his eyes and pluck out another cigarette. Now this lack of common ground is not in any way a big deal, but it does mean that you have to work slightly harder. Little generational jokes have to be explained before they can be laughed at.

Another niggle was that Cally always had much more money than me. I had money for beer and small baubles, but Cally had a house, a flat in London, a swish car, and always plenty of money for meals, for presents, for a never-ending supply of alcohol. She always said that she loved to buy me dinner, or whatever meal it was that we were eating, but I'm not so sure it's good for a man's soul to be kept and to be paid for. Of course, I would pay occasionally for little gifts. But I was all too aware of the size of her jewellery box and how pitiful these trinkets seemed in comparison to the diamonds and the rubies and the dazzling hunks of gold with which she would adorn herself.

But my biggest gripe was her friends. They generally treated me like this toy boy joke: doubtless pleasuring Cally senseless in the bedroom, but with nothing of interest to say and who soon enough would be sent on his merry little way. The worst by far was Greta, whose flirting would alternate with zinging slingshots as she openly mocked any chance of my ever staying faithful to Cally.

It was August, a couple of days after our interlude in the road. After what seemed like endless months of preparation, Cally's exhibition was opening. She had been spending more and more time in London, and every time she returned, she seemed more tired; it was the first time that I had ever really noticed the wrinkles about her eyes and her mouth. For the first time in her life, she was even beginning to look her age. When she did get back from London, she would always need at least a day to recover; meanwhile, I would be champing at the bit and generally behave like a lusty hooligan.

On the day of the exhibition, I'd been given the night off, so I could go up to London in the afternoon and then spend the next day – luxury of luxuries – tooling around London with Cally. I was very excited. I had only been back to London a couple of times since I'd started at the Knoll House, and with every mile in the train I could scent the city and knew that I was returning home.

I was already dressed for the party and the rest of what I needed was in a small knapsack. I always used to love travelling light. It needs discipline and grit to whittle your luggage down to a toothbrush and a pair of briefs.

I'd never been to the opening of a proper art exhibition before and I tried to imagine what it would be like – would I be ignored, or welcomed with open arms? Would Cally's daughter be there? Would her ex-husband be there? Perhaps there would be a whole fleet of exes; Cally was so lovely that I could easily imagine her staying on kind kissing terms with every one of her lovers. I wondered how Cally would be with me. Would there be that confident kiss to the lips that declared to the world that I was her lover; or would it be the peck on the cheek and the skulk in the shadows until we were alone and the last guest had departed?

We'd decided that I would see Cally at the exhibition itself. She said that she got unbearably tense before a big show and that she needed time to prepare herself.

I planned to arrive some forty-five minutes after it had started. I had no clue as to what to expect. I'd never seen Cally in full artist mode before. Up until then I'd only known her as a painter – and an artist is quite different. An artist is the show-stopping butterfly that emerges after years and years of painstaking work in the pupa. Painters do the grunt work. They slog it out in the studios, scribing away with brush and pencil. The artist, on the other hand, is full of life and verve and confidence. The artist is charming to everyone she meets; the artist drinks champagne and kisses cheeks, for she is in the business of selling pictures; and for one night, and one night only, the artist is the oracle, and her guests pay obeisance as they hold fast onto every word that she utters.

I was a little tense, aware that for the first time I was going to be on public display, and that my forty-four-year-old lover would shortly be showing off her young beau to the world. Already, I could almost picture the sneers that were being directed at this irrelevant toy boy. I arrived at Cork Street a full hour before Cally's exhibition was due to start. I'd never been to Cork Street. It is the very capital of Britain's art world; if your pictures are on display there, you're made. I was still limping slightly from our canoodle on the road.

I walked up the street then down on the other side and I marvelled at the pictures and the prices. It was beginning to dawn on me that if this was the company Cally kept, she was right out of the top drawer. I briefly looked in through the window to Cally's gallery. It looked opulent and expensive, white walls and a light wooden floor. Two willowy women were pouring out champagne.

I went to a nearby pub and started to drink. I drank because I was nervous and because I thought it might loosen me up. I drank doubles of gin and gazed at the *Evening Standard*, but didn't take in a word of the paper as I mulled over just a few of the scenarios that might occur that night. I had a sense of foreboding and also a sense of inevitability. For I already knew myself and I knew my weaknesses.

One of my very particular weaknesses is that when I am on the back foot and feeling vulnerable, I will come out swinging with barbed tongue and sneering lip, and I don't much care how it all turns out. The only thing of consequence is whether I've managed to land a few telling blows of my own.

When I arrived back at the gallery, the place was humming. I felt under-dressed. I was wearing black jeans, Chelsea boots and a floral shirt that Cally had given me; compared to this crowd, I looked like a hick. The men, even the young men, wore suits and ties that reeked of money and City jobs; the women, even the younger women, looked stylish and expensive. I felt out of my depth and I was paddling hard just to stay afloat.

Breathe in; breathe out; relax. I reminded myself that I was the king of the waiters, the master of repartee, the sprite who could charm the birds from the trees. I squared my shoulders; I may not have been wearing a suit, but I was looking good. I eased through the crowd, gliding effortlessly through the suits – and immediately knocked a woman's drink out of her hand. My wrist had caught her hand and she'd dropped her glass.

'I'm so sorry,' I said. She was beautiful, long blonde hair and in a grey wool dress that clung to her every curve.

She looked at me, very cool, sizing up my jeans and my Liberty shirt. She didn't know what to make of me, but one thing was for sure and that was that I was definitely not a City-slicker businessman.

'Oh dear,' she said. She puffed on her cigarette. She had been talking to a sharp young man who was only a few years older than me.

'You couldn't get another glass, could you?' he drawled. 'And a dustpan and brush while you're at it?'

'Of course.'

I continued to press my way through the crowd. Suits to the left of me, suits to the right of me; I realised that I was the only man in the room without a tie. My floral shirt and my jeans were similarly unique. Being one of a kind can be fine – if you've got the power and got the confidence. But at twenty-three, I didn't; all my hotel chutzpah had deserted me.

Cally was by the bar. She was sipping champagne and I had never seen her so glamorous. She was fresh out of the hair salon and her hair positively gleamed, not a strand out of place; she was in black high heels and stockings and the perfect little black dress, with diamonds in her ears and a fabulous diamond necklace about her neck. She was talking animatedly to three men. They were hanging on her every word. They seemed to be about her age, though one was a little younger. I wondered if she had slept with any of them.

'Kim!' She broke off and kissed me – not on the mouth, but on the cheek. She gave me a light hug with her hand. 'Thank you for coming!'

'What a show!' I said. 'It's amazing.'

'Thank you,' she said. 'You might recognise some of the pictures.'

I was introduced to the men; I forget their names. 'This is Kim,' she said. 'He's come all the way from Dorset.'

'And what happens down in Dorset?' said the younger of the three men. He was in his thirties, slicked back hair. I think his name was Johnny. I had taken against him from the very first.

'Well, it's wurzel country,' I said. 'Cream teas. Smugglers. And inbred farmers.'

'Oh really?' he said, with this very slight inflection which I took to mean 'I could not be less interested, now kindly leave me in peace'.

'Yes, really,' I said. I stretched past the man and took a glass of champagne from the bar. I raised my glass to Cally. 'I'll see you later.'

I saw Greta, pissed and clutching onto a man in the corner, and I also recognised Hugh, the Dorset antiques dealer who occasionally lunched with Cally at the hotel.

I did not want to talk to them. I wanted to look at the pictures. I was entranced.

I had seen one or two of them before, but I had never seen the whole collection. The paintings together had far more power than their parts, transformed from being merely good to absolutely formidable. It was as if a complete diary of my time at the Knoll House had been hung upon the walls. The paintings, now with thick frames and heavy white borders, had grown in stature since I had last seen them on the easel.

There were several portraits of the Dancing Ledges, in the wet and in the heat, when the rock was bare and when the rippling ledges had begun to dance. There was even the Dancing Ledges at night and I smiled at the memory of our midnight dip. In the corner were pictures of the Agglestone, at dawn and at dusk, and more than ever I was struck by how it looked like a giant toad that had been turned to stone upon the heath. There were some pictures, also, of the Knoll House, children playing on the pirate ship and families basking by the pool. Cally's beach hut was there too, both inside and out, along with a picture of that great Malay bed. It was painted so finely that I could even read the words that had been etched into the wood. There was a picture of the ferry, as it steamed into the sunset, with the seagulls swirling about its bows.

If I'd had the money, I would have bought every one of them.

I still had no idea what I wanted to do with my life. But as I looked at those pictures, how I wished that I had even an ounce of Cally's passion.

I sipped my drink. Over by the door, there was a picture that held my attention more than any other. It was a painting of Old Harry, with the cliffs and the sea and the birds overhead – and in the corner was a young man in a red top, sipping sloe gin and dreaming of love.

It was like seeing an old friend amid a sea of strangers. What memories it brought back of the wind and the crashing waves, and a slip on the cliffs that had cost me another of my nine lives; and of a kiss after Cally had dragged me back to safety.

There was a nudge at my elbow. 'That's not you, is it?' It was my father, in full pinstripe with regimental tie and buttonhole, complete with a silk handkerchief in his top pocket.

'Hello!' I was delighted to see him. I leaned over and gave him a little side hug, before brushing my cheek against his. As usual, he smelled of cigarettes. 'How are you?'

'Never better,' he said. 'So is that you?' he asked again, gesturing at the picture.

'It is, actually.'

'Just near Old Harry, at a guess,' he said.

'You're right.'

'I might buy it then.' He squinted at the catalogue. 'They certainly know how to charge round here!'

'So... you got an invite?' I asked, still mildly flabbergasted at seeing my father at Cally's exhibition.

'Cally sent me one after we met in the pub,' he said. 'Only popping my head in. Your stepmother and I are going out for dinner to... I don't have the foggiest. Anyway...' He looked me up and down, taking in my open-necked shirt and my jeans. 'It is a bit stuffy in here, isn't it? Nice shirt, much better without a tie. In fact, you know what, think I'll take my tie off, too. They're only useful for mopping up the soup anyway.'

Then and there, he flicked up his collar, worked his fingers at his thick double-Windsor knot, and loosed his tie. He folded the tie carefully and tucked it into his coat pocket, before undoing his top two shirt buttons. What a trooper! Greater love hath no man than to take off his regimental tie in order to slum it with his son. It was an interesting look, with just a hint of string vest showing underneath his shirt. He mopped at his face with his handkerchief and looked round at the giddy throng. 'Well I'll just go and say hello to Cally and then I think I'll push on,' he said. 'How's the Knoll House? They paying you enough?'

He dipped into his wallet and fished out some fifty pound notes; he didn't even count them, just folded them up and tucked them into my shirt pocket.

I watched him as he eased his way to Cally. He gave her a fulsome kiss on the cheek, mouthed the correct platitude and then after a brief word with one of the gallery girls he sauntered back. Always, always, it's about confidence. Even though he'd taken off his tie, and his linen shirt was unbuttoned at the collar, he had more panache in his little finger than any of those young jackanapes in their bespoke city suits. He gave me a light pat on the shoulder. 'Ghastly lot of people,' he said. 'Do you think they actually buy any of her pictures? I doubt it!'

It was the only high spot of the evening. For some reason, whether it was my clothes or my 'sod you' demeanour, women shunned me. There were quite a number of pretty women there, in their mid-twenties, killer heels, and doubtless fancy jobs too. I must have been exuding some toxic vibe, because there was no one there who wanted to chat. I even presented some champagne to the beautiful blonde in the clinging grey whose glass I had knocked over.

'Thanks,' she said, before turning back to the man in the suit. Beyond my dazzling conversation, I had nothing whatever to offer her, and we both of us knew it. She wanted reliability, dependability, and above all, she wanted me to have prospects, and in my jeans and my floral shirt, my prospects must have looked dire.

Cally was making a short speech and I lingered at the back of the room. She had made two little jokes and was now going about the business of thanking everyone who needed to be thanked.

Greta sidled up to me and slipped her arm through my mine. She was drunk and she was all but using me as a leaning post. 'She's good, isn't she?' said Greta. As usual, she was in pink and black. 'You're lucky to have her.'

'I certainly am.'

She squeezed my bicep and sighed. 'I do love young boys,' she said. 'Cally got there first.'

I blurted out the words while they were still only half formed. 'Cally was always going to get there first.'

She did not like it. She was drunk and it took a moment or two for my words to sink in, but once they had, she very quickly withdrew her arm from mine. 'You're very hoity-toity, aren't you, for a jumped-up waiter boy?'

I wish that I had heeded Cally's lesson. I wish that I had bitten my tongue. But I didn't. In my callow youth, I was incapable of soaking up an insult; rather, insults had to be met with further insults, the more hurtful the better.

'If I'm a jumped-up boy, then what does that make you, Greta?'
I asked. 'A raddled old dotard?'

It was a nasty thing to say, and it was an awful time to say it; Cally
was still talking.

'The sooner that Cally is shot of you the better,' spat Greta, and
doubtless I could have come up with an equally acidic rejoinder, but
she immediately turned on her heel and went to the bar.

I should have gone home then and there. I could have caught
the train from Waterloo and been back in my bed at midnight. Hell,
with all those fifty pound notes that my father had given me, I could
have spent the night at the Ritz. But I didn't, I stayed, and my anger
eked itself out through the easiest outlet. Anger is like that. It is rarely
assuaged on those who deserve our wrath; rather, we let it steep until
eventually out all that lush bile pours, raining down onto the head of
the benighted sap that happens to have fallen in love with us.

Cally toasted us all with her glass, and revelled in her moment. Yet
all I could think was how much I wanted to get out of there. There
was a part of me, also, who was eyeing up all those well-groomed
men and who was wondering just how many of them knew Cally
quite as well as I did.

I watched as she worked the room. She was brilliant; for every
man and every woman, there was the kiss, the laugh and the perfectly
chosen word.

She gave my hand a squeeze. 'Will you join us for dinner?' she
asked.

'I'd love to,' I lied. 'Where are we going?'

'The Caprice. There's a table booked.'

'Shall I see you there?'

She squeezed my hand. 'We'll go together...' But as she looked
at me, she tailed off. Perhaps she had already divined my mood. 'I'll
see you there.'

If I was angry before, by the time I'd been in the Caprice ten
minutes, I was scorching. I was mildly drunk. I was hurting. Who the
hell was Greta anyway, calling me a 'jumped-up waiter boy'? And
who the hell were all these suits with their show-pony girlfriends?

213

And… and… What does it matter? The point, anyway, was that I was a young man nursing a grievance.

Cally had booked a table for twelve at the Caprice and I was the first in. I took the prime position, back to the wall and in the dead centre of the table, and then set about drinking the red wine. It was beastly behaviour.

The restaurant, or what I remember of it, was very formal, with sleek waiters who seemed to glide on well-oiled casters. White linen, white napkins, flowers for every table, the quiet intense conversations of the well heeled and the well mannered. I had a sudden yearning for the Knoll House's pudding table and plump dads weaving their way over for a third helping of trifle.

By the time Cally and the others had arrived, I was already well away on the second bottle of wine.

Cally led the rest of the guests into the restaurant. She looked at the empty bottle on the table and then she looked at me. 'My,' she said, 'somebody has been drinking.'

'Cheers!' I waved a glass at her.

Cally set herself at the far corner of the table. She was looking at me as she took her seat. It may just have been paranoia, but it seemed as if the other guests were also doing their best not to sit next to me. I ended up with Greta on one side of me, and on the other was the companion of the woman whose glass I had knocked over. Opposite me was Hugh, the antiques dealer. Cally's guests were mostly men, very slick, very polished, and so wholly different from me that I might have been from another planet. Their ages seemed to range from late twenties to their late sixties. Unfortunately, I had neither the time nor the opportunity ever to discover much about them; that's rather what happens when you end up hogging the show.

Greta presented me with her shoulder and hardly said a word to me.

The man on my other side was not interested in me either, but manners dictated that he did at least have to talk to me. I had tried unsuccessfully to engage with Hugh on the other side of the table, so for five or ten minutes I sat there and seethed as I drank my wine.

The man turned to me. 'Hi, I'm Morgan.' He offered me his hand. His fingers were small and rather pointed, as if they belonged to a plump clairvoyant.

'Hi, Kim.'

'So what brings you up to London?'

There were a lot of things that I could have said. I decided to lob a small grenade into this urbane millpond.

'I'm Cally's boyfriend,' I said.

'Oh,' he said. He looked at me anew, interested despite himself. 'I didn't know she had a boyfriend, but of course she would. Where did you meet?'

'In a hotel in Dorset.'

'Were you staying there?' He'd turned to me now, lolling in his chair, arms spread extravagantly wide.

'No, I'm one of the staff. I'm a waiter.'

'You're pulling my leg!'

'Or maybe I'm not.'

'So you're a waiter at this hotel in Dorset, and Cally comes over for dinner, and then one thing leads to another! Stone the crows!'

Hugh had picked up the fag end of our conversation.

'Did I hear right?' he asked. He was tearing off bits of bread from his roll and popping them into his mouth without looking. 'You're seeing Cally?'

'I suppose I am,' I said.

He crowed to himself, rocking from side to side, before turning to address Cally at the end of the table. 'You're a cradle snatcher, by God!'

Cally looked quizzically from Hugh to me, sizing up how best to flatten him. 'Who wouldn't?' she asked. 'Miles more fun than being with a middle-aged man.'

And by now, the whole table was listening and was digesting the fact that I was Cally's lover, and although I didn't know what they were thinking, I was aware that Cally's guests were not really wishing me well. Perhaps incredulity, perhaps a slight amount of hilarity, and perhaps there was some envy mixed up in there, too. Cally was a very beautiful, very rich woman, and she had this extraordinary sexual magnetism.

Morgan's girl, bless her, piped up. She was sitting on the other side of Morgan. 'I hope I have a toy boy when I'm in my forties.'

The other woman piped up, well groomed, jet-black hair, slightly older than Cally. 'I'd have taken a toy boy in my thirties,' she said.

Hugh had finished his bread roll. He licked his index finger and very carefully swept up the crumbs on his plate. He popped his finger into his mouth. 'They never last,' he said, 'but they're jolly good fun while they do.'

'They are,' Cally said. I don't think she was overly pleased that our love affair had become public knowledge, but now that it had, she was going for it. 'If you'll forgive me, Kim,' she said, with a nod to me. 'I think that every woman should have at least one toy boy in her life.'

'And you've had plenty!' Hugh crowed.

'Thank you so much, Hugh, I can always rely on you.'

I don't know whether the man was drunk or just intent on baiting me, but as the others watched, he snuffled into his drink. 'Once tasted, never forgotten, eh?' Hugh said. 'What was the name of the last one? Was it Martin?'

'Hugh, please,' Cally said.

'Don't mind me, I'm just a middle-aged blow-hard,' he said. 'Lucky to get it up more than once a week. Not like you young bloods, eh, Kim? Eh?'

I suddenly felt liberated, relieved of an enormous weight. I didn't care what I said, in fact the more outrageous, the more shocking the better.

'Let me explain something to you, Hugh,' I said. 'Men – as you well know – are at their sexual prime when they're about, I guess, my sort of age. Maybe a bit younger, but I'm not far off it. You, on the other hand, are probably a little over the hill. But women reach their sexual prime at roughly the sort of age that Cally is now. So you can see that it makes perfect sense for Cally and me to be together. Morning, noon and night, we're at it like rabbits.'

I looked over at Cally. She drank some wine, then put down her glass and massaged her forehead.

'Are you, by God?' said Hugh.

'Indoors or out, rain or shine, before breakfast or after tea. We're at it non-stop. We can't get enough of each other. We've worked our way through the Kama Sutra, and now we're doing it with bells on.'

'Kim!' Cally said.

But it was way too late for self-restraint. The genie was well and truly out of the bottle.

The faces of the other guests were a complete picture. The men, perhaps remembering their glory days, perhaps imagining what it would be like to work their way through the Kama Sutra with Cally; the women, discreetly toying with their wine, glancing at me intermittently. But what they were thinking, I could not fathom.

'And do you do anything else apart from have sex with each other?' Hugh said.

I have noticed that middle-aged men tend to have a peculiar fascination with sex in all its forms. They may not be getting much of it themselves, but they like to talk about it, as they fancifully lust after all those ships that once passed them by in the night.

'Apart from the sex, Hugh, of which there is quite a lot?' I said. 'There isn't time for much else. We talk. We have a laugh. We drink and sometimes we eat, and then we start having sex all over again, though sometimes we do it all at the same time. Haven't had sex on a horse yet, but it's certainly on the agenda. Anyway Hugh, enough about me, and enough about my incredible sex life. When did you last have sex during lunch?'

'I – I...' He stretched for the bottle and poured himself another glass. 'Not for a long time.'

I threw the question to the floor. 'Anyone had sex over lunch?' I said. 'Any takers? You, Morgan. You must have given it a try with your gorgeous girlfriend?'

'No,' he said.

'What about al fresco sex?' I said. 'Anyone in the last year?'

'Kim, darling,' Cally said. 'Delightful though it is to parade our love life to the world, can we please change the subject?'

'Change it?' I said. 'But they're riveted! Look at them!' And one by one, I held the gaze of everyone at the table, and they were indeed fascinated. It was as though they were watching a car crash, waiting expectantly for what would happen next. 'Look at that old goat, Hugh!' I said. 'Still trying to get into your pants after all these years, and now doing it by proxy! He's loving it, aren't you, Hugh?'

'Kim, please,' Cally said. She looked at me and raised her hands in a pleading salaam.

I would have left it at that. I was done. I had caused enough havoc for that night, and it was time that the conversation tipped back onto its usual adult train tracks with talk of all that is bland and safe and anodyne.

Greta spoke. It was the first time she'd spoken to me since she'd entered the Caprice. 'But it hasn't always been by proxy, you know, Kim.'

That was a choker. The very thought of Cally with Hugh.

As ever, I did what I always do when I have been touched upon the raw: I made light of it.

'Me and you, Hugh? We're comrades in arms!' I said.

Hugh shrugged and dabbed his finger at the plate again to wipe up a last crumb. 'Taught me everything I know,' he said.

I was repelled. The very thought of Cally with this bloated carcass of a man. It was a stunning blow to the guts.

I raised my glass to Cally. 'Cheers!'

A sudden and very vivid image played through my mind; not of Hugh having sex with Cally in her old four poster – I'd never much cared for that ancient bed with all its history. No, the thought that had winded me was the thought of Cally and Hugh in that double bed in the beach hut, which over the last few weeks I had come to see as *my* beach hut. But of course, she'd have made love there. It was a fantastic spot, and it was a fantastic bed, and if she'd been seeing Hugh, undoubtedly she would have taken him to her seaside haven.

'Please,' Cally said. I think that beneath her make-up she may actually have been blushing.

I toyed with my glass, downed it in one, and then charged it right to the brim. I could feel my cheeks turning white, the blood pumping to my brain. I was suffused with anger, and like Samson would have brought the whole Temple crumbling down on my head if only to crush my enemies.

'I wonder,' I said. I was looking at Hugh, but I was directing my comments to the whole table. 'Is it something that happens with middle age – do you come to sleep with every single person that you fancy? I mean, obviously you know within a few seconds whether you fancy somebody. But most of the time, one of you is tied up.' I shrugged and drank more wine. 'But you keep them on the back-burner, don't you – so that when you're both single, or perhaps not so single, you can finally get together. And so long as you're prepared to play quite a long game, then in the end you'll have slept with every person that you've ever fancied. Am I right? Is that right?'

The men looked at me and looked at each other, some sheepish, some not so much.

Cally addressed me. 'Kim, could you stop talking about that now, please?'

'Why stop talking about it?' I said. 'Since everyone's so keen to discuss my love life, your love life, why don't we open it to the floor – why don't we go into the minutiae of everyone else's sex lives?'

'Kim dear. This is my party – this is my night. And I'm asking you, in the nicest possible way, to move on. Please.'

'You're right,' I said. 'I think I will move on.' I downed the rest of my wine and got up. By now I had managed to silence not just the table but the entire restaurant. All those smart couples, talking about what it is professionals talk about with their spouses, and there in front of them this drunk young man who was creating a scene.

I couldn't get out from the table, as I was hemmed in on either side. Instead, I stepped onto my chair and stood on the table; I doubt the Caprice had seen such ill-mannered behaviour in a long time.

As I jumped off the table and onto the floor, I clipped Hugh's glass; it flopped into his lap.

'Sorry about that, old cock,' I said.

'Please go,' Cally said.

Greta gave one last turn of the screw. 'That's boys for you,' she said.

How I hated her. I surveyed the room, the table.

'Of course I'm going,' I said. Greta was nodding comfortably at me, delighted at how things had turned out. 'I'm sure there are any number of men here – as opposed to boys – who will be more than happy to take my place between the bed sheets. They'll still be warm but, hey, Hugh, I don't suppose that's ever stopped you before.' I clapped Hugh over the shoulder and gave a wave to the table. I blew a kiss to Cally, and without a backward glance I picked up my knapsack and left the restaurant.

The air was brilliantly cold on my cheeks and I breathed it in deep to the bottom of my lungs. After the smug warmth of the Caprice, it was heaven to be outside. I was walking aimlessly, pounding out my rage on the pavement; I thought about getting a drink or going back to my parents' house, and for a while I even toyed with staying at Claridge's, but I wasn't remotely in the mood. I checked my watch. If I moved fast I'd make the last train back to Wareham. The ferries would have closed by then, but I'd just get a mini-cab the long way round to Studland. Hell, I was so steamingly angry that I could have walked through the night and would have still found room for my fury. How dare Cally try to shut me up? How dare she boss me about in the Caprice? And how could she have slept with Hugh and Martin, and God knows who else.

As so often happens after a spectacular row, I was burning with righteous indignation, but it was mostly just young hurt at being so soundly put in my place. Greta had played me like a fish; had caught me, landed me, gutted me and then merrily hung me out to dry. Cally, she was not much better. Did she say one word to defend me? Far from it – all she'd done, repeatedly, was to try and shut me up.

I just caught the train, leaping on as the last doors were slammed shut. I bought six small bottles of red wine and chugged them neat from the bottle. Over and over again, I went over what had happened that night. From the very moment that I'd stepped into the gallery to the moment that I'd left the Caprice, it had been a disaster.

I remembered the insults that I had hurled at the other guests, and they felt good. They must have stung for I knew, even at twenty-three, that there was some truth in them.

I didn't walk back from Wareham, but called up a cab, which deposited me outside the Knoll House close to two in the morning. I went to bed, still steaming, still hurting, only now also a little ashamed at how I had behaved like a spoiled brat.

CHAPTER 16

The next day I was faced with that hideous combination of a hangover tainted with the knowledge that I had been well out of order.

I hitched a lift into Swanage and leafed through the papers as I waited for a vast fry-up. I hadn't eaten since the previous afternoon.

I mooched along the coastline, wondering what to do next and if there was any way that I might be able to make amends. At that stage, I was not really ready to give the full and handsome apology that was due to Cally; but I was certainly prepared to open the lines of communication. I called her in London and in Dorset and, as ever, I got hold of her answerphones. 'Hi, it's Kim here,' I said. 'I'm sorry about what happened last night. I wondered if we could talk.' I hoped that I had set the right note of contrition.

That afternoon, I had a game of pitch and putt with Anthony and in the evening I drank in the pub and waited for my friends to join me. We drank, we talked, and I carefully avoided the small delicate matter of what had happened during my trip to London.

By the next day, I think I had left another two messages for Cally, but she still hadn't picked up or, indeed, left any sort of note.

The day after that, I went round to her house. The stable girl was there sorting out the horses; she didn't know when Cally would be back. I left Cally a scrap of a note and returned to the hotel.

It's an odd thing about contrition and forgiveness. You can know that you've done wrong, and you can be very willing to apologise and make amends. But if your apology is not accepted, and if the forgiveness is not forthcoming, then how quickly your heart can turn the other way. And that, in a small way, was what happened to me. After three days of not hearing a word from Cally, I had started to become a little tetchy.

By now, it was a full four days since I had seen Cally, and my moods were fluctuating wildly. On the one hand, I was desperate to see her and to kiss her and to do all the other things that we so loved to do; on the other, I was becoming more and more punchy. What did I want to carry on seeing Cally anyway? She was in her forties; she was another generation. And what about those appallingly starchy friends of hers?

That night after dinner, I went to the pub with Roland. It was just like old times; we were two single men about town.

'Where's Cally?' Roland asked as I got the drinks in. 'She's been away a long time.'

'Sorting out some stuff in London,' I said.

'And while the cat's away…' He nodded over to a table tucked away in the corner. I looked and I stared, and I realised that it was Louise, she of the long legs and the imminent career as a solicitor. She was having a drink with her sister, Julienne, and the very moment that I looked at her, she saw me. She smiled and she waved.

'Ladies, ladies, ladies,' I said. 'May we join you?'

'By all means,' Julienne said. I kissed the women on the cheek. Louise looked pleased to see me. I sat down next to her.

'So how was South America?' I asked. 'Have you started at the Guildford Law School yet, or did we manage to dissuade you from becoming a solicitor?'

'I'm afraid you did not,' she said. 'I've just started at Guildford.' She was so pretty. I loved her skin and I loved her hair, and I glanced briefly at those endless lush legs. Then and there I could have kissed her.

'How very dull of you,' I said. 'And you never even gave the Knoll House a chance!'

'I was tempted,' she said. 'Very tempted.' Her knee touched against mine, a very light touch, and then proper, solid contact. Our feet pressed together in silent acknowledgement of our desire. I liked that.

'Well, let's look on the positive side,' I said. 'Even if the world is blown to kingdom come, we're still going to need the lawyers!'

'Are we?' Roland said.

'They're like the rats and the cockroaches,' I said. 'Somehow they'll always find a way to survive.'

But talk of the law was the very last thing on Louise's mind. I could feel her hand stroking my thigh. Without even a thought, I took her fingers in mine. We sat holding hands underneath the table.

She drank her white wine, her eyes never leaving mine. Roland may have been chatting to Julienne, I wasn't really aware.

'Oh!' Louise said. 'I've got something to show you. Come with me.'

Directly she stood up and, still holding my hand, she led me off to the snug. Julienne had Roland's charms all to herself.

The snug was empty, as snug as ever, with a stub of candle burning on the table. I hadn't been in the snug since my first night at the Knoll House; since that first drunken snog with Janeen. All was just as it had been before.

We eased our way around the table and sat on the banquette, legs tight together and now our hands about each other's waists. Now that we knew that a kiss was inevitable, we seemed to have all the time in the world.

Our faces, our lips, were just inches from each other. 'And what was it you were going to show me, Louise, my darling?' I asked.

'Something very important,' she said.

'Oh yes?'

'Yes,' she said. 'Look.'

With her head, she gestured towards the table. I looked down. Somebody had been scratching at the woodwork, and in inch-high letters was carved 'L ♥ K'.

My fingers traced over the letters. It was a good job, carved elegantly and with precision.

'Oh?' I said. 'There's the letter K. But what could that stand for? It couldn't possibly be Kim?'

'It must be.'

'But what about the L?' I said. 'Who could that be? Could it be Laura? Or Laetitia? Or Lola?'

'Or Lyndsey? Or Lulu?' We looked at each other, her lips now mesmerisingly close to mine.

'Or Lettice?'

'Or Lakshmibai?'

Our lips so close that she is all but breathing into my mouth.

'Or could it be…' I wanted this woman more than anything; any thought of Cally had gone clean from my head. 'Could it be Louise?'

She moved forward, kissed me. 'I think it might.'

Louise held me close. She was wearing a short skirt, and she cocked her leg over mine; my eyes were shut and I was embracing the moment, loving every second of it, and wondering, also, where it might lead. My hands cupped her breast and Louise let out a low hum of desire. I liked it; I liked it very much. I opened my eyes and in the candlelit gloom I stared at her cheek, her nose, her full lips which were wide, wet and open and gliding against my mouth.

A flicker of movement from outside the snug. I looked up. Staring in at us, staring at me, was Darren. I didn't know how long he'd been there, whether it had been seconds or minutes, but he was standing there, a little smile playing on his face. I did what anyone else would have done in the circumstances. I gave him the finger.

I don't remember much of the rest of that evening. We carried on kissing until we were thrown out. Roland and Julienne were already long gone. Louise gave me a lift back to the hotel. For a while we continued to neck in the car, though nothing much can ever happen in the front seats of a car. Was there ever a greater passion killer than a gear stick and a handbrake?

'I'm going back to Guildford first thing,' said Louise. 'Into classes by nine.'

'We'll be midway through breakfast by then.'

'I'll write to you at the hotel.'

'Look me up when you're next down.'

'Don't doubt it.'

With a last fond kiss I left the car and sauntered back to my room in the moonlight. My mind, my heart, were in flux. I didn't know what I wanted any more. I wanted Cally and I wanted Louise, but I had no idea how it was all going to work out. All I did know was that kissing Louise for an hour had been fantastic.

The next day was a little strange. In the dining room, my mind was not on the job. I was forever thinking about Louise and Cally, and wondering all the while how it would eventually turn out.

I kept trying Cally's phones, but she didn't pick up. There could have been any number of reasons, but the most likely was that I was well and truly in the doghouse.

The power of autosuggestion is an incredible thing. I had spent the whole day thinking about Cally and then, as I was walking past Anthony's office, I thought I heard her laugh, throaty, deep, full of indescribable zest. The door was closed and for a moment I hung there, but then I moved on. Why would Cally come to the hotel and yet avoid me?

Later at supper, just as the first diners were coming into the room, I was staring out of the window towards the sea and I thought I caught a flicker of her Mercedes. It glided through the trees. In an instant it was gone.

Supper was just the usual flurry of activity, a mad whirl that comes to a sudden and abrupt halt. One of my tables had left two nearly full glasses of wine and Oliver came over to join me. We drank them as we stared out into the night.

'Where is Cally?' he asked.

'I don't know, actually.'

'Is everything all right between you?'

'Yeah, sure,' I said. 'Everything's dandy. And you and Annette?'

'We are thinking of going travelling,' he said. 'We might go in the autumn, in the off season.'

'How will we survive without the pair of you?'

'With very great difficulty, I am sure.'

We drank and we bantered, as men like to do with their friends. Later, we climbed onto the pirate's ship with Annette and drank whisky underneath the stars.

The next day, I served breakfast at the hotel and afterwards, as I was walking back to my room, I decided to give Cally another call. I tried her Dorset number. Almost on the first ring, she picked up. It was almost as if she'd been about to make a call of her own, and had just happened to be by the phone.

I hadn't expected to speak to her. I was momentarily stunned.

'Oh,' I said. 'Cally, I… I didn't think you'd answer.'

Cally also sounded surprised to hear me. 'Hello Kim,' she said. 'How… how are you?'

'I'm fine,' I said, and then out it all tumbled. 'Look, I'm so, so sorry about what happened in London. I was completely out of order and—'

'It's okay, it really is,' she said, and I think I believed her. 'Listen, I've just got to sort something out. Can you call later?'

'Will you be around later?'

'I'm not sure,' she said. 'Give me a call.'

'I love you,' I said.

I heard her sigh, but I didn't know what it meant. 'I'll speak to you later,' she said.

I stared, unsatisfied, at the phone in my hand. For a moment I stood, locked in position as I replayed that sigh over in my head, looking for nuances, wondering what I had said, analysing the whole conversation from start to finish. I couldn't put my finger on it, but I knew that it would have been better by far if the conversation had never happened at all.

Thoroughly unsettled, I walked back up the concrete pathway to my room. There were small scuffs of bright orange paint outside my room, but I barely paid attention to them. Inside, there were other little dabs of orange on the floor and on the bedding. I wondered if I had trodden in some orange paint and then tramped it into the room.

I flung off my tunic and lay down on my bed, and stared up at the ceiling. What was I going to do?

My natural inclination was to take action, any sort of action; to go straight round to Cally's house and have it out in person. I thought about Cally's voice on the phone; I remembered how downbeat she sounded. It had sounded like she was steeling herself to swing the axe, and if she were, then I wanted to know sooner rather than later. And then there was Louise.

A knock at the door interrupted my thoughts. I tugged at my T-shirt and opened the door.

It was Anthony, very serious; behind him, a police officer.

'Anthony?' I said. 'Good morning.'

'Good morning, Kim,' he said. His eyes were searching my face.

'How can I help you?' I said.

Anthony hemmed for a moment. I could see that he found the whole thing most unsavoury. 'I, we, have had a tip that, uh…'

The police officer, who had been standing slightly behind Anthony, stepped in. Shaven headed, peaked cap, middle aged; the plodding face of the law.

'We just want to search your room if that's all right, son,' he said.

'Sure,' I said. 'Be my guest. It's a bit of a state. I wasn't really expecting guests at this time of the morning.'

I stepped aside and the two men went into my room. And as soon as they had entered, I knew exactly why they were there.

I wondered if there was anything I could do, but somehow already knew that nothing could be done. I felt very calm. My heart rate steadied. I was done for and I knew it. I'd been stitched up.

It took them less than a minute to find what they were looking for: a great pile of ten and twenty pound notes stuffed under my mattress. The notes were traced with orange dye.

'Oh, Kim.' Anthony gave a mournful shake of his head as he quit my room.

The police officer put the notes and a pair of orange-stained socks into a clear plastic evidence bag. 'You better come with us,' he said.

Anthony led the way and we trooped back to the police car. Waiters and waitresses were craning their heads to look at me: the thieving miscreant who had finally been nailed.

Oliver, though, immediately came over. He walked along with us as I was taken to the police car. 'What has happened?' he said. 'Where are they taking you?'

'Off to the cop-shop,' I said. 'I'm afraid somebody's done for me.'

'What do you mean?'

'Somebody's stuffed a whole load of loose cash under my mattress.'

'So that's your line is it?' the policeman said. He held open the car door.

'It's not a line.' I got into the car. 'I've been set up.'

'Got a lot of enemies at the Knoll House have you?' he asked.

'One or two,' I said.

The rest of the morning was filled with the tedium of procedure. The drive to Swanage police station, the dull interview, and my repeated assertions that I hadn't got the first clue how the stolen money had ended up under my mattress.

'So somebody just put it there?' the police officer said.

'That's right,' I said. 'And then probably tipped you off that the money was in my room.'

'And how did they get into your room?'

'I guess they just opened the door. It's never locked.'

We continued to trudge round the houses. It was all so unutterably wearisome.

'So how did the orange dye get onto your socks?'

'I don't know,' I said. 'If somebody was going to set me up by putting money under my mattress, it wouldn't be too much of a stretch to put dye on my socks.'

After about an hour, we had reached an impasse. I was bored and just wanted to get the hell out of the police station.

I should have asked for a solicitor as soon as I'd been arrested. For some reason I hadn't bothered. What difference would it make?

'Tell you what,' the officer said. 'We'll give you a caution and that'll be the end of it. Your boss, the manager—'

'Anthony.'

'Yes, he doesn't want to press charges. So if you accept a caution, you're free to go.'

I was an idiot. I did not even pause for a moment. 'Okay,' I said. 'I'll take the caution.'

'Well done, son,' he said. 'It's the best thing.'

Immediately, the police officer was very happy. I signed a release form and was driven back to the Knoll House. Anthony was waiting for me in his office. My bag and my rucksack had already been packed and were sitting by the door.

Anthony, now in his dark suit, was sitting behind his desk. He looked both annoyed and perplexed.

'It's a real shame,' he said. He was playing with a cup of coffee on the desk, flicking the handle backwards and forwards.

'I've already told you,' I said. 'I didn't do it. I didn't steal anything. It's a set-up. I've been set up.'

'Why did you sign the caution then?' he asked. 'You've admitted that you did it.'

'You know what?' I said. 'I just couldn't be bothered to go through the whole palaver. If I continued denying it, there was going to be the court case and everything else, and whatever happened, my time here was finished. I thought it was best just to take the medicine.'

'Just take the medicine?' He continued to pat the cup back and forth. 'Is that so?'

'Really. I'm not a thief. I'm not interested in money, and I certainly wasn't going to steal from the hotel wages.'

'So,' he mulled this over. 'Who do you think set you up?'

'Well…' I paused. I knew perfectly well who'd done for me. 'I've no idea.'

Anthony stood up and came round to me. 'Promise you didn't steal the cash?'

'Yes,' I said. 'I promise.'

'Why on earth did you sign that caution?'

'I don't know,' I said, and I really didn't. 'I think I was done. Thank you for having me here. I've enjoyed it.'

At the door we shook hands and he gave me a pat on the shoulder. 'I don't know what to make of you, Kim,' he said. 'You always were a strange one. But I'll miss you.'

A few of the waiters were just settling down for their lunch. I gave them a wave. 'Goodbye,' I said, 'and thank you.'

Oliver and Roland followed me outside. Roland shook my hand and Oliver gave me a hug. And as ever we parted with a quip.

'I thought I warned you not to steal from the hotel's wages,' he said.

'You know me,' I said, 'never been very good at taking advice.'

He rumpled my hair, his Adam's apple quivering in his throat. 'Would you like me to get Darren?'

'I wouldn't bother.'

I cuffed him on the elbow, and with a wave I was on my way.

It was a very abrupt end to my career at the Knoll House. It wasn't even yet lunchtime. And as I walked down the drive for the last time, I felt a burning wave of exaltation. I had no idea what I was going to do next or where my life would take me. But the thought of this open road that stretched before me was quite thrilling.

I was in two minds whether to go straight to the ferry, but in the end I decided to pay a last call to Cally's house. If she was in, then all well and good; if she was not, then I would leave her a fond note.

I found her in her morning room. It was filled with light from those huge windows that stretched to the ceiling. Leaning against the wall by the door were a stack of paintings. Cally was sitting on the sofa, with a box of Kleenex beside her. She had been crying and she looked drawn, the sunlight etching out the lines around her eyes and her mouth.

I had left my bags by the front door. I did not kiss her or touch her, but sat down on one of the armchairs. For a while, we just looked out through the window.

It's funny what happens when there is so much that ought to be said. You end up saying practically nothing at all.

I wanted to tell her that I was sorry. Even though I already knew the answer, I wanted to know if it really was over. I suppose, too, I wanted to thank her for everything that she had brought into my life.

I wondered if we could still make a go of it; should I at least try?

But in my heart, I knew it was hopeless.

'I'm leaving,' I said at length.

She looked at me with tired, puffy eyes and picked up her packet of cigarettes. She studied them for a moment and then just tossed the packet over her shoulder.

'I know.'

'I came to say goodbye.'

'Thank you.' She started to cry again, the tears trickling down her nose. I could feel the tears starting to stab at my own eyes. 'I'm not very good at goodbyes.'

'Neither am I.'

We looked at each other, almost shyly, and then smiled.

'Anyway,' I said, getting up. 'Thank you. You've been wonderful. You are wonderful.'

Cally got up, and suddenly, and for the first time that I had ever known her, she looked frail. It was as if the last week had sapped the very life out of her.

She followed me out of the room and we stood in the passageway clinging to each other. 'Please don't get in touch,' she said. She was crying and the breath was catching in her throat in great sobs. 'Please don't call. Please don't write. I don't want to see you again – I can't see you again. Otherwise…' She trailed off.

I kissed her. Her lips were cracked and dry. 'It's been difficult enough bringing it to this,' she said. 'I don't think I could ever resist you again.'

She was clutching onto my arm as I walked to the door. 'I love you,' she said. Her face was wet with tears.

'Goodbye.' I shouldered my Bergen. It was hot outside, the sun beating down. I walked across the yard.

When I had crossed the yard, I turned to look back. The door was already shut.

I was once caught up in an avalanche.

I had been skiing off-piste with four friends in the Three Valleys. I was second in line and we were skiing just below a ridge. The snow was thick and deep, almost a solid block. The last skier in the line schussed straight along the ridge, cutting through the snow like a cheese wire. There was a crack and the whole slab of snow jolted downwards. At first, it started quite slowly, but within seconds it was a solid wave of snow, sweeping away all before it.

Immediately, instinct and adrenalin took over. At first I was skiing along at the edge of the avalanche, heading straight downhill, riding my luck. But the snow was starting to break up. I skied flat out to the side, heading hard for some rocks that were perched above the pounding snow.

I hit the rocks at full tilt. One ski snapped in half and the other spiralled off into the roiling river of snow that seethed beneath my feet. I banged my head and was rolling away to the side when I snatched at an outcrop. I clung to the rock as the avalanche thundered into the valley below.

For a minute, two minutes, I stayed there listening to the distant roar and watching the clouds of powder puffing up through the trees.

The adrenalin began to ebb. I had bitten my tongue and could taste the metallic tang of blood. I was still numb. Very gradually I sent probes out around my body, checking to see if anything was broken. Would it be hospital for me? Or would it be just bed rest? Maybe I wasn't hurt at all and in a few minutes I'd be hitting the bar with my friends and toasting the loss of another of our nine lives.

And that is how I felt in those first few minutes after the end of our relationship. I stood in her driveway, my ears buzzing with the roaring rumble. For a few minutes it felt as if I had been thrown violently in all directions, my guts and my heart in total turmoil. Then I turned and walked up the driveway, and slowly my brain was met with silence. Just as I did lying on that rock in the Alps I could feel myself sending out probes, trying to work out how badly I'd been hurt.

As I wandered along the road to catch the ferry for the last time, my numbed brain was in tailspin.

I slouched along the road, hands in my pockets. I looked out to the sea. I wished that I had skinny-dipped more. It was one of those things I'd always planned to do; I felt like I had missed my chance.

I was vaguely aware of a white car coming towards me. It was going too fast and I heard its engine screaming. The car weaved and sped past and I caught a brief glimpse of a driver and a passenger.

Ahead of me the car stopped. The engine revved, and I could hear it coming back towards me again. The car roared past in reverse. It was a white golf GTi. In the driver's seat was Greta, wearing a frilly purple top. By her side was, of all people, Darren.

I stopped walking and stood by the side of the road. I wondered what she was going to do next.

Greta reversed ten or fifteen yards behind me. Then, with a slight crunching of the gears, she began driving past me for the third time.

The car glided past at no more than walking pace, and as she passed, Greta blew me a kiss, lips puckered and hand outstretched. I looked down into the car; Darren had his hand on Greta's knee. He watched me through the window, his face a mask of the most perfect indifference.

Greta's GTi disappeared into the distance and for some time I remained rooted to the spot. Greta and Darren, together at last. Was there ever a couple that was more beautifully matched?

Very soon I had done my sums and had come to the only logical answer. Darren had seen me kissing Louise. Obviously, he would have shared this succulent gossip. These two facts led ineluctably to the following deduction: Greta would have not wasted one single second in telling Cally that her so-called boyfriend had been spotted kissing a beautiful woman in the snug of the local pub. Which was to be demonstrated. *Quod erat demonstrandum.*

CHAPTER 17

I was surprised. I had not expected it, but I was enjoying myself.

We had had a gin and tonic, and he had ordered a bottle of Chateau Musar. I didn't know much about wine from the Lebanon, but it was one of the most extraordinary wines that I had ever tasted. To this day, it is the only red that I could recognise in a blind tasting. But in the late eighties, Chateau Musar was still a cult wine and had yet to be established as an absolute classic.

We were at a corner table in the Royal Automobile Club in Pall Mall. My host had his back to the wall, so that he could monitor every person in the room. Not that he did though. In fact, it seemed as if all his attention and considerable charms were focused entirely on me.

He was telling me stories of derring-do, outrageous stories so downright bizarre that they were beyond fiction. He was like a favourite uncle, with an endless fund of the most extraordinary anecdotes, yet at the same time riveted by my every word.

I was utterly enthralled, captivated. I had never heard the like. It was a glimpse into a weird new world, of which I had heard tale, but had never before experienced. After just half an hour, I knew with every fibre of my being that this was the world in which I wanted to immerse myself.

Mike Hamill was red in the face and laughing. His jowly beard and thick thatch of brown hair were juddering in syncopated rhythm with his belly. He certainly didn't look anything like how I imagined a red top reporter would be. I'd thought he might be some hatchet-faced reptile in a cheap suit and the classic reporter's trench coat. But instead, he was immaculate. It is one of the oddities of Fleet Street that the more downmarket the newspaper the smarter the reporters.

Tabloid reporters will, without exception, wear smart suits. On the other hand, the reporters on the *Guardian* or the *Independent* will usually be found in jeans and a black leather jacket. Mr Hamill was wearing a perfectly tailored single-breasted blue suit, a white silk handkerchief in his top pocket, gleaming black lace-ups, a double-cuffed cream shirt set off by classic gold cufflinks.

The RAC was also not really the sort of place that you'd expect to be meeting a *Sun* reporter. I'd thought we might be meeting in some dingy pub, but this opulent dining room could have held its own against any dining room in London. It was spacious and airy, with high ceilings and flooded with light. The carpets were thick, the chairs comfortable, while the staff were easy-going and fun. It didn't have any of the stuffiness that you expect to find in the London clubs.

'So tell me one more time, dear boy,' he wheezed. 'What happened with the pudding? Don't miss out one single detail! I want it all! I want everything!'

I smiled and brushed my tie. I was looking as smart as I knew how, and was wearing a grey suit, white shirt and a blue tie that I'd filched from my father.

Mike had already heard the story once, but, as I was beginning to realise, the best stories are always worth telling twice. So I repeated the tale of how Pat the TV star had been covered in trifle and cream after shunting into Oliver.

'What a picture that would have been!' he said. 'Still! As regards pictures, we didn't do too badly, did we now?'

Indeed not. In fact, the pictures had turned out just about perfectly.

The *Sun*'s photographer must have been lurking in the dunes practically before dawn and had got the most tasteful shots of Pat the soap star striding naked into the Studland surf with his new girlfriend. She looked great; Pat, perhaps not so much.

They had made the front page and had a centre page spread, though a couple had been carefully pixelated. As I was quickly learning, the *Sun* had a number of unwritten rules, not least that bums and breasts were fine, but that full frontal nudity was most definitely not fine.

In true red-top style, the bulk of the spread had been given over to the gorgeous girlfriend. She may not have been as famous as Pat, but her coltish curves were much more to the *Sun* readers' tastes. As it would turn out, those pictures would be the girlfriend's launch pad to fame and fortune. Within a few years, she had all but eclipsed her by-then ex-boyfriend Pat.

'Quite reminds me of one of Princess Diana's early holidays.' Mike topped up my glass. When he talked, his hands were always moving, adding vigour to his words. 'We'd had a tip that they were on this deserted beach in some jungle in… I can't even remember! Might have been Chile. So I've bought a machete and I'm carving my way through the jungle with the chief photographer and finally, after about three hours, there we are! We're in pole position on these cliffs above the beach, all tucked away, and things are not looking much better. What do you think happened next?'

'She took all her clothes off?'

'Nice try,' said Mike. 'But no. We'd been there about ten minutes when there was this awful racket coming from the jungle. All this noise! We were expecting an elephant to come out. Know what it was?'

'The police?'

'No, it was the bloody team from the *Mirror*!' Mike clapped his thigh and laughed. 'They'd followed us out to Chile and then they followed us through the jungle!'

'And what did you say to them?'

'I asked him if they'd like nuts or a cigar.'

'And you got the pictures?'

'Pictures? She wasn't in the country! She wasn't even on the continent! I think she was in France for Paris Fashion Week! So we had a couple of days boozing in Chile and then shipped back home again.'

'I want this job,' I said.

'Get yourself a job on a local paper. Pass your NCTJ exams—'

'NCTJ?'

'National Council for the Training of Journalists, dear boy, you will come to love it. Then after you've had a year on an agency, you'll be ready to start shifting on the old *Curranticus Bunticus*.'

'I'm in,' I said. In a matter of minutes, I had at last seized on a career. 'I'll start applying for jobs tomorrow.'

'Call me if you need a reference.'

'Thank you!' I was overjoyed. After years of floating like so much flotsam, I at last had a plan.

'Might take you a while to get a job on a local paper, so in the meantime you could do worse than going to a secretarial college. Learn to touch type, get your shorthand—'

'I've got to learn shorthand?'

'Can't be a hack without it, dear boy. They don't allow tape recorders in court, and, if the deadlines are tight, which they always are, you won't have time to transcribe the tapes. So yes, you will have to learn shorthand. You will come to love your teeline and all those tapes at one hundred words per minute. But you may well enjoy going to secretarial college.'

'Why's that then?'

'Not a man to be seen!' His hand crashed to the table, setting the glasses ajangle. 'You'll have an absolute field day!'

'I think I will.'

'It goes without saying that should you get any more of your red-hot little tips, you know who to come to!'

'I'm in!'

Mike patted his pockets. 'Oh yes,' he said. 'Some money.'

He produced an inch-thick white envelope.

'That's very kind of you.'

'Plenty more where that came from.'

'Thank you!' I pocketed the envelope.

'Don't you want to know how much is in there?'

'How much?'

He flashed up the palm of his hand, showing all five fingers.

'Five?' I said. 'Five hundred quid?'

'No, my boy,' he said. 'We pay five hundred pounds for page leads. But for splashes and spreads, we tend to pay a little more. Five grand.'

Five grand! My mind reeled. It was more than double what I'd earned during my entire time at the Knoll House. It was an astronomical sum. It meant that I could buy something for Cally. Something splendid. Something that she'd treasure. I'd take her out for dinner, properly wine and dine her; maybe we'd spend the night at the Ritz. Then I felt this queasiness in the pit of my stomach as I realised that Cally and I were through.

'Cally mentioned something to me,' I said, shaking the thoughts of our love out of my head. 'She said you'd helped her when she'd nearly had her fifteen minutes of fame.'

'Did I?' he said. 'Perhaps I did.'

'And what was it?'

'The usual.'

'What is the usual?'

'Sleeping with someone who's famous.'

'So how famous is that? Are we talking a rock star? TV star? Movie star?'

Mike grinned at me. 'I can't tell you.'

I was very intrigued. Not jealous as such, but curious as to the identity of the famous man who had also been with Cally.

'A politician? One of these seedy cabinet ministers?'

'My hands are tied,' said Mike. 'Stories may be my trade, dear boy, but I never betray a confidence.'

'Are we talking royalty?'

Mike just shook his head. 'I still can't tell you.'

And the grin just got bigger.

We finished the wine and had Armagnac with our espressos, and then in a delightful haze of alcohol and goodwill, I walked through St James's and down to the river. It was teatime when I got back to my parents' house in Chelsea. My father was in the drawing room, feet up on the settee. He was happily puffing away on a cigarette as he read the *Telegraph*. He was in pinstripe, his tie at half-mast and his jacket flung on one of the chairs.

'Hallo!' He smiled. He was genuinely pleased to see me. 'You're looking very dapper. Been out for lunch?'

'I'm going to be a journalist,' I said.

'Splendid!' he said.

'Yes,' I said. 'I'm going to get a job on a local paper; work my way up to Fleet Street.'

'Can't say we've had any journalists in the family before now; about time we started,' he said. 'Let's celebrate! I'll get some fizz.' Away he bustled to the kitchen.

I flopped into one of the armchairs, alone with my thoughts.

A journalist. I, Kim, was going to be a journalist. It had a ring to it. I liked it. For the first time in my life, I was hungry. Better by far than any of those other dull jobs in the city. It might not pay much compared, at least, to those multi-millionaire accountants, but it had the allure of fun and excitement and adventure.

My father was still clattering away in the kitchen. I could hear the reassuring sound of ice rattling into the ice bucket.

I stared sightlessly at the fireplace. It took me some time to spot the new addition.

For a few seconds I couldn't comprehend what it was that I was looking at. Was that really what I thought it was?

It was Cally's picture, in pride of place above the mantelpiece. I went over to look at it more closely. It was the picture she had painted by Old Harry, with me in the flash of red in the corner as I'd sipped my sloe gin.

I smiled wistfully at the memory of that afternoon on the rock. And as I looked at the picture, I recalled one small detail that I had all but forgotten.

After Cally had painted the picture, she had written something on the back. What was it she'd said to me? She'd said it was a little reminder of the day and of the company.

I lifted the picture off the wall. It was now in a large black frame. It was quite heavy. I turned it round. Cally's words stretched all the way across the canvas, scrawled in thick black pencil in her usual round hand. I read it and it was the first time that the loss of Cally had really hit home – as sharp and as keen as a stiletto into my side. 'There is only one thing that I want in this life,' she had written, 'and that, my darling Kim, is you.'

CHAPTER 18

I became a journalist, starting on a weekly paper in Cirencester; then on an evening paper in Cambridge; then with an agency in Los Angeles. After some years at the pit face, I was about ready to start working on the red tops. To my utter astonishment, I found that I rather took to the trade. I flourished. I built up a bank of stories of new towns and new loves, but these are all for another time.

In stories such as this, it is difficult to round things off neatly. A few strings can be cleanly tied, but not many. The threads of Greta and Darren and Roland and Anthony and Janeen and all my other compadres, alas, cannot be wound up. I have not heard a single thing since the day that I left the Knoll House. I've often wondered about them. But though I wish them well, I have no clue how it turned out for them all.

Louise became another of those great and wonderful stories that happen so rarely but which we hold so close. Ours was also a story to be told another day.

Oliver, my closest friend at the Knoll House, remains one of my closest friends. He is the chief executive of a prosperous hotel chain. Oliver still occasionally visits the dining rooms; he visits and he may even eat, but he takes especial care never to lift a cup, plate or saucer. And his lovely Annette? Reader, he married her! I was Oliver's best man, and managed to feel only mildly envious of this friend who was marrying such an extraordinary beauty. They give every semblance of being just as much in love as they were all those years ago in the Knoll House.

This leaves Cally.

You would be mistaken if you thought for a minute that I adhered to her final command. Despite the fact as she had told me that it might make things difficult for her, I wrote. I wrote her kind cards to Dorset and loving letters. At the beginning of September, I sent her a single red rose. I called a few times too, but there are only so many messages that you can leave on an answerphone.

But I never went down to Dorset to see her again.

I never heard word from Cally. It was the most complete amputation I've ever been through. We had no mutual friends, so there was no one to keep me abreast of the goings-on in Cally's life.

That might very well have been that. Our summer together would have become one of those beautiful memories that are preserved for ever in the amber of the moment.

Then: a house-warming party in London in 2008, south of the river. I was there with Elise and with the girls. My three daughters are the one shining constant in my life. Elise, my wife, is in PR. She is tall and poised, with auburn hair that is still just as straight and as perfect as when I first touched it. Elise got one over on me when we first met in New York in 1998, and generally speaking she has had the whip hand ever since. Despite all we've been through together, we have come to realise that we would rather be with each other than be apart.

It was a Sunday afternoon. We'd brought along the traditional housewarming gifts: salt and bread and that king of the reds, a bottle of Chateau Musar.

Elise was taken on a guided tour and was doubtless making the appropriate comments. The girls were let off the leash and joined the other children in the basement.

I helped myself to a beer and went outside. It was a dull grey day and the barbeque was only just stuttering to life. Gerry, our host, was standing by in his pinny. I bantered with him, admiring the herbs that had been planted by the back door.

I saw some old friends and stood about chatting and laughing. I helped myself to a sausage, its skin thick and black and almost turned to charcoal; it was delicious. The party was taking off; children were pouring out of the house to be fed. I helped out at the barbeque. Gerry flipped the burgers and the sausages, while I stuffed them into rolls and passed them to the boys and girls; I was interested to see who thanked me and who did not. I didn't care either way, but children's manners always intrigue me.

When all the children had been fed and watered, it was time for the adults. I was reminded of my summer at the Knoll House. For everyone, there had to be a quip and a smile and a plate of food.

By now, there must have been sixty or seventy people milling around in the garden. I was looking down as I buttered some bread rolls.

'You're doing that very professionally.' A woman's voice, a deep hum that resonates.

'Years and years of training.' I looked up. Immediately a small fuse blew in my head. My face must have been registering a look of slight puzzlement. Haven't I seen you somewhere before? I thought.

The woman was wearing blue jeans and a blazer. She looked at me, smiled.

'What can I get you?' I asked. I flashed my tongs, and all the while, my brain was whirring, probing, trying to work out the connection. She was married, I could see that. Wedding ring and a large sapphire engagement ring.

'A burger please,' she said. 'That would be lovely.'

'One lovely burger coming right up.'

'Thank you.'

She took a spoonful of ketchup, smiled one last time, and joined the garden melee.

'What's her name?' I asked Gerry.

'Her?' he said. 'Fiona. She's Hooper's new wife. Only met her a couple of times. She's great.'

'She is.' I put the tongs down. 'Excuse me one moment.'

I followed her across the garden, easing my way through the guests. She was sitting alone on a bench. For a moment, I hovered. 'Do you mind if I sit here?'

She smiled at me, very warm. 'Be my guest.'

I sat next to her, a hissing trickle of memories suddenly turned into a thundering tsunami. It wasn't just her hair, which was near identical. It was the shape of her face, her beautiful cheekbones, her height and her buxom figure. But it was the smile that was the clincher. The smile was a total giveaway.

For a while, I just looked at her, taking it all in. I rubbed my hands together, palm to palm, as I wondered what it was that I wanted to say and how I was going to say it.

She was about to take a bite from her burger, but she must have seen something in my eye, for she returned the untouched burger to her plate.

'What is it?' she asked. No smile now, but rather a look of slight concern.

I looked at her, looked at my hands, and looked at her again. I could feel my thighs shaking against the wooden bench. 'I wondered,' I said, 'you remind me of a woman I once used to know. She lived in Dorset. Her name was Cally. She was an artist.'

Very, very slowly, Fiona nodded. She put her plate on the ground. 'Cally,' she said, and now she too studied her hands. Strong, capable fingers. 'She was my mother.'

My heart did a backflip. 'You're the very image of her,' I babbled, before I realised what she'd just said to me. 'Was?' I repeated. 'Was your mother?'

'I'm afraid she passed away,' she said. She had a paper napkin in her hands and she was screwing it into a tight ball. 'She died a long time ago.'

'Ah.' My brain convulsed. I felt as though I was on a speeding train heading full tilt for the buffers, but even so, politeness and good manners still kicked in. 'I'm very sorry to hear that.'

'So you knew her?' Fiona said. 'Was that in Dorset or in London?'

'In Dorset,' I said. 'I used to work in a hotel near where she lived—'

'The Knoll House,' she said. 'What year?'

'It was 1988.'

Fiona nodded, still disconsolate, even twenty years on, at the thought of her mother's death. 'The year she died.'

I gaped at her.

'What?'

Fiona nodded. 'I'm sorry,' she said. 'You didn't know. Was she far gone when you knew her?'

But I was still playing catch up. 'Far gone?' I said. 'What do you mean? I don't understand.'

'Cancer,' she said.

'Cancer?' I repeated, dazed.

'It started in her lungs,' she said. 'It ended in her heart. She fought it right to the end, Harley Street, everything that could be done, but in the end, there was nothing that could be done…'

I reeled, stunned at how casually she had delivered this news. 'But… But she always looked so healthy… And she was so strong. And her hair, and… There was nothing to be done?'

'You never knew?'

'No, she never told me. She never once mentioned it.'

'That was mum,' she said. 'She only told me in the summer, just a few weeks before she died.'

'But…' I was still struggling to make sense of it. 'When? When did she die?'

'September,' she said. 'September the second.'

'Jesus!' I said. I raked at my hair, staring at the sky, and then the tears come in a torrent. I leaned forward, head buried into my elbows. How could I have been so ignorant not to realise that all of Cally's trips to London had had nothing to do with her exhibition and everything to do with treating her cancer? Why hadn't I seen it? How could I not have spotted it? She must have died three weeks after we'd broken up. The thought of it all was so enormous that I could barely take it in.

'I'm sorry,' Fiona said. She stroked my neck, her fingers soft on my shoulders. 'I'm very sorry. You must have been very close to her?'

'I suppose I was.' I looked up at Fiona, wet, red-eyed, monstrous. 'Where did she die?'

'In her bed.'

'The four-poster?' I sniffed and smiled at the thought of that old black bed and all its history. 'She'd have liked that.'

'Forgive me,' she said. 'I don't know your name.'

I sniffed again and wiped the tears from my cheeks with my fingers. I shook myself, the shudder arching up my back as my heaving emotions were once again brought into check.

'I'm Kim,' I said.

'Kim?' she said, and now it was her turn to gape. '*You're* Kim?'

I nodded, trying to regain composure, aware that the other guests were now starting to look.

'Why?' I said. 'Did she ever mention me?'

'You're Kim!' she said and she clutched both my hands, now laughing, beaming with pleasure. 'You're Kim! I've only spent the last two decades searching for you!' She laughed and squeezed my fingers tight. 'It's funny, I always thought you'd be much older.'

'No,' I said. 'I was the toy boy.'

'And what a toy boy you must have been. She doted on you!' She tossed her hair. Even that small gesture was exactly like her mother's. 'Listen, I've got something for you. I've only been waiting twenty years to give it to you.'

'Really?'

'She said it was an atonement.'

'Atonement?' I asked. 'Cally showered me with nothing but love. What did she have to atone for?'

'Ah… well,' said Fiona. 'Thereby hangs a tale.'

As I write, I can hear the ever-same sound of the sea, rumbling as it sucks at the sand on the beach. Sometimes I spend so long here that the tide will come in and go out, and I will still be here at dusk when the tide turns back again.

Occasionally I sit out on the veranda with my chair and table set towards the sea, watching the endless sweep of the sand and waves. Like Cally, I take comfort from the knowledge that I am just a part of this chain: that we were watching these exact same waves for hundreds of thousands of years, and that we will be watching these waves for hundreds of thousands of years hence.

I prefer it when it is wet, as it is today, with the wind howling at the windows, the rain thundering onto the roof and the waves white and brutal, while I sit snug inside my beach hut with nothing but my words and my memories.

It has changed very little since I was last here with Cally. There are still a few of her books, but now mixed up with some of mine and I suppose a few of Fiona's. The hob is still here, the vast seascape painting is still here, Cally's vast double bed is also still here. Sometimes I think that I can still smell the turps and the linseed and the mulch musk of burnt umber and that irresistible tang of coconut oil. When the mood takes me, I spend the night and dream dreams of the love making these walls once witnessed.

The beach hut is Cally's gift to me, her atonement for a small wrong she had done me.

But I don't see it like that. Without that wrong, who knows where I would have ended up.

It turns out that being dispatched from Knoll House in disgrace had nothing to do with Darren or Greta. There was no conspiracy between them to set me up. In fact, I don't even think either of them ever told Cally about my tryst with Louise.

It had been Cally all along. Cally had wanted to break up with me because she didn't have much time left. She was dying and she wanted to save me from the hell of watching her die. So she ended it as quickly and as painlessly as she knew how, by planting the hotel's marked money underneath my mattress. I can almost picture it now: Cally sneaking into Anthony's office, stealing the cash and the dye that went with it, then planting them both in my room. It was as good a way as any of calling time on our relationship.

I like to think that if Cally had told me about her cancer, I would have stuck with her to the very end. I might even have taken something from the whole grim experience. She acted for my own good, but I hope I would have been capable of stepping up to the plate. Who knows?

On her last day, when Cally was doped up to the eyeballs on morphine and lapsing in and out of consciousness, she told Fiona about me. For a single summer, I had been this golden boy, a constant reminder of what joy it was to be alive. That's how she may have seen it, but funnily enough it had always seemed entirely the other way round to me. Right to the very last, it was always Cally who was showing me what it was to seize every moment. She grabbed every second of it.

The first time I returned to Studland, I went back to the Dancing Ledges. They were exactly as I remembered them, with the tide running high and the waves lapping up onto the ledges. I walk to the Dancing Ledges often, now that I have my beach hut by the sea; and they seem destined to for ever drip with her memory. When the wind howls and the rain is flecking at my face, I only have to close my eyes and I can see Cally sitting there, squatting by the fire as she draws her horses on the rock.

On that day, I clambered down the pathway and onto the flat ledges. They were slick and wet from the rain. In the indent where we had once sat kissing by the fire, there was a pool of brackish water. The rock was still there. It was virgin, not a mark to be seen.

It was from this spot that Cally had asked for her ashes to be scattered. Just as she would have insisted, I stood right at the very edge of the ledges. The waves were licking at my feet, and yet as I stood at the brink, I had never felt so absolutely rooted and secure, as if Cally's firm hand was even then holding me tight by the scruff of my neck.

In my mind's eye, I can see the top being eased from the urn and then with a full swing she is cast to the winds. I watch as she flies high and free, her ashes soaring into the air before they are swept over the waves and out to the open sea.

PREVIEW

The next romance in Kim's love life is The Woman Who Was The Desert Dream, *due to be published by Thames River Press in October 2013. The story is based on the events of the 2012 Marathon des Sables, which is widely held to be the toughest foot race on earth. This is the first chapter.*

CHAPTER 1

This is a story of love and desire and mid-life crises. And blisters and warm bottled water and dehydrated pap. Sandstorms, thunderstorms and hailstorms so vicious they left your skin bloody and bruised. It's the story of what it's like to run in the desert, as you trudge up mountains of stone and slip-slide down the dunes.

It is the story of heat.

You'll know all about thirty-degree heat. It is Centre Court at Wimbledon when the sun is blazing. It is the hottest day of the year in Cornwall when the ice creams are melting even before the first lick. It is a scorcher on the motorway, stuck on the hard shoulder as the radiator bubbles over.

Fifty-two degrees is different. When you're running at noon with the sun high overhead and the shadows small upon the ground. When you're running in the afternoon, as the sand and the rocks have started to fry. When there's a sixteen-kilo rucksack strapped to your back.

I will tell you the meaning of fifty-two-degree heat.

It's drinking eleven litres of water – and never once needing to stop for a pee. It's taking twenty salt tablets a day so that you don't start to cramp up. It's losing water as fast as you can pour it in.

On your face, the sweat dries instantly, leaving tidelines of white salt scum; on your back, your shirt is constantly saturated, and the sweat soaks through to the inside of your rucksack; and on your feet... yes, that is the big problem that faces all of the runners in the Marathon of the Sands. Until you've started the race, you have no idea how hard it's going to hit you.

Runners take all the precautions they can to prevent sand from getting into their shoes and their socks. They have their silk gaiters sewn into the soles of their running shoes and they tie the tops of their gaiters tight around their calves. But whatever you do, however snug the gaiters, you can never totally stop the fine sand from working its way into the shoes and into the socks and then next to the skin. And what happens next – not always, but sometimes – is that the sand mixes with the sweat in the socks and then it quickly turns into sand paper. If you are not taking care, and if your feet are already numb from all those Ibuprofen tablets that you have been chugging, the first you will know of it is when you get back to your tent. You tug off your shoes and your gaiters and from the burn of the sharp hot spots on your feet you know it's going to be bad. Like all the other runners, you are wearing the very latest Ininji socks, special toe gloves. They look faintly reptilian. You tug off the first starchy sock and all the plasters come of with it in a fine mist of sand and blood. It's only then that you realise that you are in for a whole world of pain. The sand has combined with the sweat in your sock, and the skin on the bottom of your foot has been sanded clean off. Your foot has been 'delaminated'. I was almost sick the first time I saw it.

On the second day, the heat was the least of my problems.

Like a lot of the other runners, I had contracted the most severe diarrhoea. It was a combination of the heat and the exercise and the disgusting dehydrated food and the salt and all the powdered electrolytes that I'd been cramming into myself to stay alive. Your body can't take it, and goes into immediate spasming revolt, as if to say 'get this muck out of me'.

And normally, if you were at home, you would take some Imodium and perhaps take the day off work. You would sip coffee, read the papers and lounge around near a lavatory as your stomach slowly sort itself out.

That isn't an option in the Marathon des Sables. It doesn't matter how bad your injuries, how severe your stomach cramps. For come 8.30 in the morning, there you have to be on the start line, ready for another twenty-four miles through the desert.

I felt like absolute hell. The daily starts to the Marathon des Sables overwhelm the senses. There is pounding rock music and the manic jabbering of the organiser Patrick Bauer. The sun is already blazing and you're crammed into this tight space with all the other runners – almost every one of whom is, like yourself, just that little bit stark-raving mad.

I was wondering how long I'd last before I needed to relieve myself behind some friendly bush.

The worst of it was that I was parched. There are a lot of things that can put you out of the race, but one of the most certain is dehydration. Over a dozen people had been knocked out on the very first day after messing up with their water.

On the Marathon des Sables, your water is severely rationed. Extra water is, of course, available. The first time you take an extra 1.5 litre bottle, it's thirty minutes added onto your race-time; second time it's an extra hour; and when you take a third bottle... well you don't take a third bottle, because if you take a third bottle, then you're out, and bang goes all your training, bang goes your £3,500 entry fee and bang goes your desert dream.

The previous night, I had watched, horrified, as the water had drained out of me, litre after litre of it; even with the pills, there was no stopping it. Sometimes I'd been so desperate that I couldn't even make it to the camp's makeshift latrines, and would squat in the middle of the desert, staring miserably at the moon. I took more pills and more pills, but nothing seemed to work.

And the next morning, I knew I was bone dry. I had already had my first extra bottle of water. But at that early stage in the race, I didn't dare take another.

We were assembled exactly where we'd finished the previous afternoon. Each day's finish line is the next day's start, and then you all charge straight through the bivouac, where the tents have all now been stacked onto the lorries and the site returned to what it once was.

Lawson was stretching, touching his toes, palms almost to the sand; his walking poles were forever falling to the ground. He would pick them up, balance them against his legs, stretch, and then the poles would drop back to the ground. He never tired of this routine.

He saw me watching him and grinned. 'May I offer you a wheelchair?'

'I didn't know you cared,' I said.

'Feeling good!' Lawson inspected his stubbled reflection in my sunglasses. 'Looking good!'

The two Irish medics earnestly talked to each other, as if you could ever have any sort of game plan for running twenty-four miles in the desert. 'I'm going hard,' Martin said.

'I'm going out slow, so I am,' said Carlo.

Simon, on his second Marathon des Sables, was edging his way towards the front of the pack, hoping to shave a few seconds off his time so that he could finally find redemption with that elusive top 100 finish.

Kurtz, an ex-Para, was the only one of us who really knew how to handle pain – and he was going to need it too.

I looked round for Kate, but I couldn't see her. I'd have liked to have seen her that morning, if only to wish her luck, for I wasn't at all sure that I was going to make it through the day. I had not seen her for half an hour. She was probably being interviewed by some TV station, or swooned over by a troupe of tanned athletes. I knew that and I was fine with it. Kate was a beauty and beauty is much in demand in the Marathon des Sables. The men are naturally drawn to it. Of the 853 runners on the first day's start line, I guess there were about 100 women. And of these 100 women, I can both subjectively and objectively tell you that Kate was a stand out.

But enough of that. I'd looked around and I still couldn't see her. It's difficult to spot a woman in white and red when you're in the thick of hundreds of bigger, burlier runners, all of whom are wearing near identical shirts and caps. Of all the other runners, I would have liked to have started the day with her; the sight of her damn cheery smile alone was a pick-me-up. But she wasn't there, so I'd just have to tough it out by myself. And I could do that. I wasn't looking forward to it. But I could do it.

At least I was going to give it my best shot.

A huge, craggy face, hewn from scowling stone, peered into my face. He was a few inches away from me, eyes hidden by wrap-around mirrored sunglasses.

'You look like shit,' he said.

'At least I'm ill. What's your excuse?'

Del's face continued to linger in front of mine. He was about the same height as me, and of much the same age, though with his wizened skin and receding grey crew-cut, he looked much older.

'It's not too late to pull out.'

'Don't you worry about me, Del,' I said. 'I'm not going for speed.'

'Like the sunglasses.'

'Thank you,' I said. 'They're my wife's.' They did indeed belong to Elise. I'd brought them out as a standby, though after a mix-up in the race shop I'd ended up having to wear them. They were Christian Dior, large, white, very expensive – and very inappropriate for a race like the Marathon des Sables.

'You haven't done the training. You haven't got the kit. And you've been up all up night with the runs.' Del smiled at me, yellowing gnarled teeth. 'You are so totally screwed.'

'I wish I could be like you, Del – you're a running machine.'

He took a swig from his water bottle. There was still a lot of water left in the bottle. He let the water cascade over his cheeks before pouring it down the back of his neck.

Nearby, Patrick Bauer was standing on top of a white Land Rover next to his pretty translator. A few years earlier, she had had a spat with Patrick and quit midway through the race, though he had charmed her back.

Patrick first started the race in 1986 as a way of introducing the world to the spiritual, cleansing heat of the desert. And even twenty-seven years later, and with some forty-eight nationalities now in the race, he hardly knew a single word of English.

He was a bluff bull of a man, tufty white hair on his tanned head. He loved the sound of his own voice. At the start of each day, as we all itched to get going, he would chunter on for a good quarter of an hour. But he also had passion and joy. He was living the dream: he had brought the desert to the world. I liked him.

We spared a few thoughts for the fifteen runners who'd given up the previous day. Some of them had been shipped back to their hotels in Ouarzazate, but a hardy few had decided to continue the week with their tent-mates. I don't know if I'd have been able to do that – still part of the Marathon des Sables, but no longer in it.

It was getting hotter and hotter. It wasn't even nine o'clock, and already we were way past a summer's day in England. I licked my sun-blocked lips and sipped some water from one of my water bottles. Almost all of the runners had two 750 ml water bottles attached to the shoulder straps of their rucksacks. Turn your head slightly and you could take a sip. In eight miles' time, at the first check point, we'd be given the next 1.5 litre bottle of warm water which would keep us going until the next checkpoint... and so it would continue for mile after mile and checkpoint after checkpoint until after 150 miles of it we were finally done.

My tent-mates looked the part. I did not feel a part of it. Maybe it was just my bowels making me feel so cheerless.

Ahead of us was a thin range of mountains, though in the shimmering heat it was impossible to tell how far away they were. Could have been five miles, could have been thirty. You can't tell distances in the desert. But you don't want to know distances in the desert. You don't want to know how far it is to the next checkpoint, or how many more hours you've got left. You're not thinking about that palm tree in the distance, or that hill that you might eventually reach by the end of the day. No, when you're stomach is gyppy and you're parched and you don't even know whether you'll make one mile let alone twenty-four, then the only thing is to be in the moment and to focus on that next step. And after that, you think about the next step, and you string all those thousands of steps together, and with luck you've made a checkpoint before you've been timed out; and with even more luck you've beaten the camels to the finish line, and congratulations, son, you are now allowed to do it all over again tomorrow, and the next day, and the next day, and the day after that too.

But it didn't do to think about the future, because all these preliminary stages were a just a mere taster before the main course. Though it wasn't so much a main course as an absolute monster: a double marathon, right through the day and into the night.

You always knew the monster was on the horizon. It was out there, waiting for you. But it was way, way off in the future. What was the point in fretting over a double marathon, when I might not even make the start line in two days' time?

Patrick was winding down and the music had started again. It was the birthday of two of the runners; a fully orchestrated version of 'Happy Birthday', very cheesy, was being pumped out through the speakers. The birthday boys waved to the French cameramen. The first time we'd heard it, we had crooned along. Not now though.

After all the pre-amble and all the hype, we were ready for the off, when the mad cacophony ended and we would be left only with the silent sound of the desert. Patrick gave a wave and we were surrounded by the blare of the Marathon des Sables signature tune: ACDC, 'Highway to Hell'. I've never particularly liked the song, but it has become such a part of the fabric of my life that, for better or for worse, it will have to number among my eight Desert Island discs.

Screaming, shouting, helicopters thundering overhead, blasting us with the downdraft. Runners waving for the cameras, Patrick bellowing out his countdown and ACDC drilling right through to the core of my brain.

And we're away and the mad ones tear off into the desert at a flat-out sprint, and the joggers amble out at a more sedate trot, and after them are the brisk walkers, striding along with their poles, and then, right at the back, are the walking wounded, the people like myself, who are wondering just what on earth possessed us to sign up for this insane race.

There are a lot of reasons why people enter the Marathon des Sables. We do it for the challenge and we do it avert our impending mid-life crisis and we do it because it's called the toughest foot race on earth. It's a rite of passage and a test of manhood, so that, in small part, we can have a taste of what our grandfathers went through in the wars.

As I ambled over the start line, with my poles glinting in the sun, it seemed like just about the most stupid thing I'd ever done in my life.

Trek 150 miles through the desert, with all my food and kit strapped to my back? What was the point? And it was such an arbitrary distance too. Why not 300 miles in a fortnight? Why not make us carry all our own water?

Any way I looked at it, the Marathon de Sables was just painfully ridiculous. And in the unlikely event that I ever did finish this nightmare, then I'd pick up the medal and get my kiss from Patrick and – so what? Would it make it me more of a man? Would I wear the medal in Hyde Park and watch as all the tourists fell at my feet? Would it give me bragging rights at the smart London dinner-parties, or...

It was ludicrous. I was plainly insane.

And the endless monologue of thoughts would continue to spin through my head, this cycle of daydreams, as one abstruse thought moved seamlessly and inconsequentially onto the next.

And I would take the next step and then the next step. That is the way of the Marathon des Sables. Even when you're delirious and on the very cusp of giving up, you still always have to take the next step.

The Sahara is not really the endless sand of most people's imaginings. There are rolling dunes, but much of it is dusty and hard and littered with stones that can tweak at your feet and burst your blisters.

The front-runners were already so far ahead that they were nothing but a sand-cloud. They'd probably finish the second stage in less than three hours.

I wondered if I'd make the eleven-hour cut-off. I might not. Whatever happened, I'd keep on walking.

At least my feet weren't hurting. After the first day, I'd only had three blisters. Compared to the others, that wasn't too bad at all. On the Marathon des Sables, it doesn't matter how awful your injuries are: there will always be somebody faring much, much worse than you. As in life.

I hadn't been paying much heed to the desert. I was heading northeast through stones and scrub and camel grass, the sun searing down and the drab sand crunching underfoot.

As you start out each day, you send out probes through your body, checking out how everything is holding up. My feet and legs were OK, but my guts were tremoring. It all just felt like incredibly hard work. My energy levels had fallen through the floor. If I'd been walking in London, I'd have stopped in a café, rested my weary feet and bought an ice-cold bottle of water.

Absorbed in the minutiae of my own little world, I had not been aware of the other competitors. But I gradually realised that somebody was walking right on my heels. They were about two yards behind me and walking at exactly the same dawdling pace as myself.

First time that day I actually smiled.

She divined my very thoughts.

'Pick it up at the back there,' she said.

I didn't bother to look round. 'What are you doing back here with the waifs and strays?'

With two smart steps, she was alongside me. 'Making sure you don't get caught by the camels.' She was giving me her very cheekiest smile, with just a coy glimpse of her tongue tucked into the side of her lower-lip. That was the thing about Kate – she didn't just look lovely; she *was* lovely. She threw her head back, gesturing behind her. 'They're only a hundred yards away!'

I thought she was joking. I looked back – only to find that, if anything, the camels were barely three cricket pitches behind me. The two camels were called, believe it or not, Charles and Camilla. They were led by a couple of Berbers and would trudge the Sahara at just above a leisurely two miles per hour. It was their job to pick up the stragglers. Once you had been overtaken by Charles and Camilla, then off came your tags and you were out of the game.

'They are a little close,' I said. 'So what have you been doing?'

'Looking for somewhere to pee,' she said. 'They'd taken down all the latrines. I had to find a dune. It was miles away. You know how I need my privacy.'

'Just so long as you weren't waiting around for me,' I said. 'You should be running now. I'm fine.'

'I like walking with you.'

'Thanks.'

'Who said this was a race, anyway?'

'Yeah – it's an ordeal. It's a rite of passage. It's a…'

'Despicable form of torture?'

'Yes, most definitely a form of torture, as well as being a challenge, and a bit of a schlepp. But a mere race? Well maybe for some people, but for the rank and file such as myself, then absolutely not.'

And I looked at Kate, and even though she was wearing mirrored sunglasses I could see that she was looking at me. She didn't have poles and was striding along, arms pumping, the very picture of blooming good health. Kate hadn't followed the dire MdS fashion of having her hair tied in tight, greasy cornrows. Instead, from the bottom of her white casquette – like the French Foreign Legion kepis – peeked the end of her ponytail. Taut, toned legs, with delicious tanned knees and thighs; skimpy shorts in the most brilliant crimson and a white shirt that, compared to my stained smock, was absolutely pristine. Even her gaiters looked good. My orange silk gaiters made me look like some bumpkin yokel who was out for a bit of rat catching; but somehow on Kate, they looked cool and sophisticated. From top to toe she looked the part; she was a woman who was ready to run the sands.

Now this might seem wrong for a middle-aged married man.

There were any number of reasons why I'd entered the Marathon des Sables. But I must also admit that one of the reasons was, pure and simple: I found this twenty-six-year-old woman quite intoxicatingly beautiful.

www.ingramcontent.com/pod-product-compliance
Lightning Source LLC
Jackson TN
JSHW020016141224
75386JS00025B/554